DRAWING FIRE

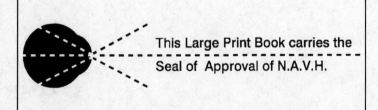

This Large Print Book carries the
Seal of Approval of N.A.V.H.

COLD CASE JUSTICE

DRAWING FIRE

JANICE CANTORE

THORNDIKE PRESS
A part of Gale, Cengage Learning

GALE
CENGAGE Learning·

Farmington Hills, Mich • San Francisco • New York • Waterville, Maine
Meriden, Conn • Mason, Ohio • Chicago

LIBRARY OF CONGRESS CATALOGING-IN-PUBLICATION DATA

Cantore, Janice.
    Drawing fire : cold case justice / Janice Cantore.
        pages cm. — (Thorndike Press large print Christian mystery) (Cold case justice ; 1)
    ISBN 978-1-4104-8154-2 (hardback) — ISBN 1-4104-8154-9 (hardcover)
    I. Title.
PS3603.A588D73 2015b
813'.6—dc23   2015022922

Published in 2015 by arrangement with Tyndale House Publishers, Inc.

Printed in Mexico
1 2 3 4 5 6 7 19 18 17 16 15

**DEDICATED TO
DORIS & JIM CANTORE,**
now in heaven.

Thanks for a safe home, many wonderful memories, and guidance that led me in the right direction. Miss you both; look forward to a blessed reunion.

ACKNOWLEDGMENTS

I'd like to acknowledge the help of Detective Stephen Jones (ret.) and Commander Lisa Lopez, the encouragement of Don Jacobson, my agent, and the overall support of Kitty Bucholtz, Marcy Weydemuller, Cathleen Armstrong, Kathleen Wright, Wendy Lawton, and Lauraine Snelling, my writing friends, for always being there to listen to the ideas as they bounce around — some good, some not so good — and to always tell the truth about what is what.

And thanks to Erin Smith, my awesome editor, and all the great people at Tyndale that I am blessed to be able to work with.

"Peace does not dwell in outward things, but in the heart prepared to wait trustfully and quietly on Him who has all things safely in His hands."

ELISABETH ELLIOT

CHAPTER 1

Two open cases, *two dead ends.*

Two faces stared back at Abby Hart as she studied the chart she'd made chronicling the progress in her open homicide investigations.

Or lack of progress.

I won't let them go cold.

Turning from the chart to her desk and swallowing a bitter taste in her mouth, she closed the Dan Jenkins murder book and placed it on top of Mavis Snyder's. She'd been working these homicides hard without any leads — or suspects, for that matter — shaking loose. Snyder had been on the board for a month, Jenkins two weeks.

What am I missing?

She stood and walked to the coffee counter and drained the last bit of the pot into her mug. The Long Beach homicide office was empty; day shift had ended two hours ago. Homicide didn't field a night

11

shift. Instead, there was always someone on call after hours. This week was Abby's turn in the "guaranteed to be awoken in the middle of the night" slot. A sip of the stale, acrid coffee finally convinced her she needed to surrender and go home as well.

After ditching the nasty dregs and rinsing her mug, she gathered her things and headed out, turning off the lights and locking the door behind her. Her thinking had been clouded lately, and it didn't help that she was exhausted. For the last two nights the same nightmare had sent her sleep screaming into the abyss, leaving her tired and sluggish. The dream was always about fire. Abby hated fire. Fire, and murder, had stolen her parents from her when she was only six, and the disturbing nightmare dredged up old, painful shadows of memories.

Abby calling for her daddy and getting no answer.

Smoke burning her eyes, her throat.

Blistered hands holding her, saving her, then melting away.

A treasured stuffed animal consumed by angry, red tongues of fire.

Worst of all, the dream reminded her of how frozen cold the case of her parents' murders was and threatened to remain. For twenty-seven years investigators had come up empty.

Abby's single-minded interest in solving the case had propelled her to homicide investigator status after eight years on the police force. But once there, other influences had kept her away from the very personal case. She vaguely wondered if the dream was telling her she should sit on the sidelines no longer.

No homicide case should go unsolved — not her parents', not any case currently on her desk.

Not on my watch, she vowed as she started her car and drove home.

"I don't need you to protect me by keeping the harsher aspects of your job from me." Ethan frowned and his displeasure vibrated across the miles as Abby rested her chin in her palm. They'd been chatting on Skype — Abby in her home in Long Beach, California, and her fiancé, Ethan Carver, in Western Africa on a mission trip.

"I'm not doing that. You've said you didn't care to hear the details of my cases."

"That doesn't mean you can't tell me what's wrong when you're having a bad day."

Abby rubbed her brow, hating this fine

line she suddenly had to walk with Ethan. She'd looked forward to a happy talk about their approaching wedding, the first discussion in two weeks, and he'd turned it into an argument.

Or was it something I said?

She didn't even know how this had started. "You think my job weighs on me — it doesn't. It's what I do. Chasing killers is as much my mission field as building homes in third world countries is yours."

"Stop. Don't compare the two. I bring hope. You deal with depravity. Your world is dark and dangerous, and I don't want it to destroy you, Abby."

His complete dismissal of her work left her speechless for a moment. This resistance to her career was new and growing: the closer their wedding date, the more he voiced his thoughts along those lines. Abby was sure she loved Ethan and just as sure she was not going to quit being a cop now or when they were married.

"Ethan, I —"

She could hear the music begin, the haunting strains of Cher's classic "Bang Bang," the song that served as her ringtone for homicide callouts.

"I can't believe it," she said, chest tightening as she reached for the phone. It was

14

three thirty in the morning her time — the Skype session had been arranged for Ethan's schedule. Abby had prayed she'd be spared an early morning callout this once. Guess not.

Ethan's frown deepened and further increased Abby's discomfort. This uneasiness with her job assignment was burgeoning from a pimple to an abscess.

"I do bring hope to people," she said while Cher sang. "The hope of justice for their loved ones."

He shook his head. "I think it's more about you and one case that you let define you."

She bit her lower lip, not believing he went there when she couldn't respond. "I have to answer."

"I know." The frustration faded from his features, replaced by resignation. "Be safe. We'll finish this later."

Oh, good, Abby thought as she answered the call.

"We have another elderly victim. Similar to last month."

Wide-awake, Abby cleared her throat. The watch commander was on the line, and he'd called her himself; he hadn't left it to dispatch. She knew why: this was bad. A cat burglar had murdered octogenarian Mavis

15

Snyder. If this homicide showed the same MO, then they had a monster in the city on the prowl for defenseless old women. The definition of serial killer echoed in her mind — *"the unlawful killing of two or more victims by the same offender."*

"We could have a serial killer on the loose." He voiced her thoughts.

Abby had been trained not to jump to conclusions, but two similar killings a month apart was not a good sign.

"I'll have to take a look before saying for sure."

"Confirm as soon as you can."

Abby promised she would and sped to the address she'd been given, though the exigency was long past. She was struck by how close the address was to the west police substation as well as being close to the address of the Snyder murder. Her stomach tightened as the ticks began to mount up that this had been committed by the same offender — a very bold offender.

To the WC, it was an important line on his incident log. To Abby, it was a slap in the face, a taunt that she was not doing her job. The Snyder case had attracted the nickname the "granny murder" in the homicide office. A priority, it occupied the lightest murder book because up to now she had nothing to go on in the way of evidence.

Until tonight. The upside of this callout — if there was ever an upside to murder — was that the watch commander indicated there was a witness on scene who could provide the first lead.

She arrived at the small bungalow, thankful for the early morning hour and that the place was not crowded with press and curious neighbors.

Abby reclipped her hair to keep it out of her face and briefly checked her appearance in the rearview mirror before climbing out of the car. The department allowed casual dress for early morning callouts, which for Abby meant pressed black jeans, a belt with a holster for her Sig Sauer .45 auto and cuff case, a homicide polo shirt, and a dark-blue police Windbreaker. She stuffed her handheld radio into a back pocket and grabbed her kit. A tepid, early summer breeze rippled the Windbreaker as she closed the car door. An immediate observation set her on edge as she approached the first officer on the perimeter.

"Where's the witness?"

"He went to the hospital with Officer Woods. The woman with him got hurt when they tried to chase the suspect. Woody said he'd bring the wit back as soon as they know how bad the lady's injury is. I have his information here." He handed Abby a neatly filled-out field interview card.

Abby read the card, but any peace she might have felt at knowing that the witness would be back evaporated when she saw his name. Warning bells exploded in her head. "Seriously? This is my witness?"

The uniform grinned. "Yeah. Isn't it cool? He's like Chuck Norris or Jason Bourne."

Abby glared at him until the grin faded and he went back to his perimeter position. If arguing with Ethan hadn't left her tweaked, the name of this witness would have.

One bright spot shone in the predawn darkness: Woody had responded to this call. Robert Woods, or Westside Woody as he was affectionately known, was a legend on graveyard patrol and, to Abby, a mountain of stability and police wisdom. Not only was she certain he'd bring the witness back, he'd help her put things into perspective. Right now she needed a strong focus.

The victim was hers now, a responsibility Abby took as seriously as a mother caring for a toddler. Justice for the dead, closure and assurance for the family that their loved one was not just a number on a crime log — these were goals Abby tenaciously clung to, earning her the nickname Superglue.

Closing out all but the scene she was preparing to enter, Abby took a deep breath and got her head into the investigation. She began with the outside. The victim's residence was a small, probably two-bedroom home neatly kept in a neighborhood of shabby homes with barred windows. She surveyed the exterior of the house and walked around to the alley, noting by the screen carelessly tossed on the ground that the point of entry was an unbarred window there. At this she frowned. Even if homeowners didn't like barred windows, they usually had the sense to bar the windows on the alley side. But it was a moot point; Abby couldn't ask the resident now.

Returning to the front door, she observed the other houses close by. Abby knew from Woody that before her time, this westside Long Beach neighborhood had been solidly middle class and Mayberry-like. But the freeway and the demise of the Navy base, coupled with an increase in shipping and truck traffic and the migration of a different demographic, had changed the vibe. Now, a diverse mix of street gangs dominated, and drug trade flourished, while decent, low-income folk hid behind the bars and tried to get by.

She walked up two steps, across the porch, and into the house. A narrow hallway led to the living room, and there she saw the body. A frail-looking old woman in a flowered nightgown lay on a frayed area rug. Like the previous victim, she'd been posed flat on her back, hands lying one on top of the other on her stomach, as if she were sleeping peacefully.

Except, of course, for the blood.

Abby's jaw tightened. Murder shattered more than just the victim. She knew that firsthand. Life would never be the same for family and friends, and she couldn't change that. But she was certain that giving the grieving the comfort of seeing someone arrested and prosecuted would allow for a modicum of closure. Many victims had told her as much, and it was that knowledge that pushed her hard to solve every case.

"One case that you let define you . . ."

Ethan, I do bring hope. Why can't you see that?

The small space was furnished with old-fashioned, ornate, and well-worn furniture. Abby pulled latex gloves from her kit and snapped them on as she began a methodical and careful inspection of the area, searching in an ever-widening circle without disturbing the body, leaving that for the coroner's investigator.

An eerie déjà vu gripped her. As with the other homicide, it appeared as though the burglar had woken the victim and then committed the murder by bludgeoning with something close at hand. Here, it was a brass-handled cane, tossed on the floor and already marked with an evidence tag.

Same MO. She shot off a text to the watch commander; he could enter serial killer on his log.

"What's your name, dear?" she asked absently, searching for information that would identify the victim. From what she could see, the woman lived alone but for a dog — obviously not a watchdog. Abby figured animal control had already responded.

Drawers were open and contents strewn around the house. In the previous murder, the suspect had taken small items — coins and jewelry, easily concealed and carried away — which was typical if the suspect were a crackhead. But the murder made it atypical if this was a simple burglary for quick cash. The posing said something as well, as it was a rarity with serial killers and usually done to shock, not to lessen the blow. Ultimately, the old women were no threat, so why kill them? Abby chewed on this question as she continued her survey.

On the bureau in the bedroom she found a California ID card and put a name to her unfortunate victim. Cora Murray smiled in the picture on the card, and Abby noted by the birth date that she was three months shy of her ninety-fifth birthday.

On the nightstand Abby spied an open Bible. She picked up the well-worn book, open to the fourth chapter of Hebrews. Goose bumps rippled down her forearms. Abby's favorite work verse was in this New Testament chapter, verse 13. She read it in the King James: *"Neither is there any creature that is not manifest in his sight: but all things are naked and opened unto the eyes of him with whom we have to do."*

She liked to say the verse was a holy version of her homicide motto: *You can run, but you can't hide.* What a coincidence. Her eyes perused a bit more of the chapter. Much was underlined, and neat handwritten notes covered most of the space around the text.

Abby paused as a bittersweet memory interrupted her train of thought. The only personal effect she had from her mother was an old Bible. It was the Bible her mother had been given upon her baptism at age ten.

Patricia had used it all through her high school years, up until she married Abby's dad and apparently walked away from God. Aunt Dede found the book in their mother's things after Patricia was gone, and Dede eventually gave it to Abby. She cherished the small brown Bible because it was filled with notes and insights — much like this one belonging to Cora — and it was all she knew about her mother's thoughts and dreams. She prayed that this Bible would be as important to someone in Cora's family.

"Why the frown?"

Abby looked up and set the Bible down. Woody was back; she hadn't heard him come in. A tall, lanky patrol officer with a full head of steel-gray hair, Officer Robert Woods studied her with an expressionless cop face. Woody had thirty-four years in harness, almost all in graveyard patrol, and as far as Abby knew, he had no intention of retiring anytime soon. It always tickled her to know that he pinned on the badge the same year she was born.

"I hate this," Abby said, not surprised she'd been frowning. "Why kill an old woman?"

He hiked a shoulder and rubbed the gray stubble on his chin. Then Abby saw the pain in his face, and it brought her up short.

"You knew her?"

He grimaced. "Been here a few times on calls — 415 music complaints, prowlers, you know. Sometimes she'd make me a cup of coffee. Tried to talk her into bars on the windows, but she refused to live in a prison. Poor lady had a hard time adjusting as this neighborhood went from quiet and genteel to —"

"Noisy and slummy?"

Weariness settled over his craggy face. "I'll fill you in later. Your wit is back. I left him on the porch. I know you'll want to hear what he has to say." His body language told Abby he had more to say and that this murder affected him more than he would ever let on.

She rubbed her nose with the back of her gloved hand. She'd finished enough of the scene survey to draw a diagram, and the lab tech had arrived to process and collect the evidence. And now the witness was here to be interviewed. That was a whole different problem.

Abby had one more question for Woody before dealing with the witness.

"Can you tell what's missing? Were you in here often enough to notice?"

He looked around. "Not really, but I'll take another look."

24

"Thanks." Abby turned and, shedding the latex gloves, stepped out of the living room and through the doorway to talk to the man who'd called in the crime: Luke P. Murphy, private investigator.

CHAPTER 2

Arrogant show-off.

That was how Abby mentally classified Luke Murphy. PIs often interacted with police, so it was no surprise she knew the name. But this guy did more than interact with the police. He was a local media celebrity. Two months ago he'd confronted a man believed to be trafficking in young runaway girls, forcing them into prostitution, and become a national sensation when a home video of the incident went viral on the Internet. Murphy claimed he had nothing to do with the filming — that he was only concerned about the girls, and missing and runaway teens were his investigative specialty.

Abby had seen the YouTube video of the altercation when she was at the academy for some training updates. Surprisingly enough, it was shown as part of an information piece on human trafficking in the city. The thug and his two bodyguards were seen advancing on Murphy in a threatening manner. Murphy incapacitated the two bodyguards without any trouble. The ringleader responded by pulling a handgun from his pocket. Murphy's masterful gun takeaway move earned him applause from a roomful of cops. As for the rest of the smackdown . . . well, Murphy was obviously proficient at martial arts.

The video showed the PI had acted in self-defense, and it rocketed him to cult hero status because of the way he'd handled himself in the face of three attackers, one of them armed. The suspect and his bodyguards were eventually arrested and charged with sex trafficking and a host of other crimes.

All the interviews Murphy had given afterward Abby interpreted as the worst kind of showboating. She wasn't about to let him turn her homicide into a media piece to publicize his business.

Murphy stood on the porch, facing the street. He was tall — at least a few inches taller than her five-ten — trim and fit, wearing tan cargo pants and a dark-blue Nike T-shirt. Well-defined biceps strained the short shirtsleeves.

She cleared her throat and he turned. His

eyes made a bigger impression on her than the biceps. They were a kind of hazel brown with gold flecks in them, and in spite of the early hour they were sharp and alert. The video image of a braggadocio's vigilante vanished as she took in the military posture and poise of a man who looked adept, ready for anything, and dangerous if you were on the wrong side.

Abby doubted Murphy missed much, and it surprised her that a spark of visceral attraction flared. She doused it quickly, conjuring up an image of Ethan and struggling not to feel guilty. The last thing Abby expected was to be attracted to another man, and that it was this man made it all the more disturbing.

"I'm Detective Hart. Thank you for coming back, Mr. Murphy." Something flickered in his eyes when she said her name — recognition, maybe. She didn't know him, but just as she'd read about him in the paper, he'd probably read about her.

His handshake was firm, his hand rough and calloused. "Sorry I called too late to help the resident." He reached into his pocket and pulled out a business card. "I know you have my contact information, but here's my card."

Abby glanced at the card. It read, *On the*

Mark Investigations, Luke Murphy, Private Investigator. It was masculine in design with bold colors and surprised her with the word *shamus* embossed at the bottom. She knew of no one besides herself who ever used that term. It was near and dear to her because of the old detective novels she loved. Mickey Spillane, Rex Stout, and Raymond Chandler had immortalized the term. She squashed the curiosity that begged her to ask about it.

The murder, Abby thought as she looked into those sharp, clear eyes. *Back to the murder.*

"Tell me what you saw."

He blew out a breath. "I'm actually looking for someone." He handed Abby a sheet of paper, a standard "Have you seen" flyer with a picture of a smiling blonde girl and text explaining why she was considered missing.

"I got a tip my runaway was seen in the neighborhood. I've walked the area for the last two nights, hoping to see her or get more info. I think people down here are starting to see me as a regular."

He pointed to the alley side of the small bungalow. "I saw a kid come out that window, and it looked wrong. I yelled; he ran. I started after him, but my partner tripped and went down. Turns out she broke her ankle. I had to stop and call medics." He paused, rubbing his hands together, and Abby indicated he could continue.

"Medics took her to Memorial. It was a bad break."

"If I need to, I'll contact her later. What happened next?"

"While the medics were on the way, I knocked —" he pointed to the victim's doorway — "and no one answered. Neighbors on either side don't speak English, so I called 911 again. Officers arrived quickly, and they tried to pick up the kid's trail with no luck. Officer Woods said he knew the lady who lives here and that something was wrong because she didn't answer the door. He forced entry into the house and . . . well, you know the rest."

Those eyes of his washed over her, and Abby saw pity, compassion, and a warmth that rattled her for a moment. For something to do, she brought a casual hand up to brush away a strand of hair that had escaped the clip.

"Did you get a good look at the kid? You think he was young?"

Murphy nodded. "His build made me think he was young. With the shadow on the side of the house, I'm afraid I didn't see much of his face. But he was small. I work with teens, and by his size I would judge him to be about fifteen or sixteen."

"Sure it's a he?"

"Yeah, the way he cut and run — I've never seen a girl who could move that fast." He gestured toward the telephone pole at the mouth of the alley. "Leslie tripped over the guide wire there and went down hard. I couldn't leave her and keep running."

Abby considered this for a moment, ignoring the rise she felt with his words. *I know girls who can move quite fast.*

"How close were you to the individual?"

Murphy took a few steps toward the corner of the porch and pointed to the sidewalk. "Leslie and I were about there." He indicated a distance of about thirty feet. "I started running toward him and was in the alley gaining when Leslie went down."

"Did he have anything in his hands?"

"I saw a backpack in his left hand. And I think he had a glove on." Murphy closed his eyes and frowned as if trying to remember. "It happened so fast, but the movement of the pack made me look at his hand, and I think he had a black glove on."

"Would you recognize him if you saw him again?"

Hunching his shoulders, he said, "I might.

31

He looked my way when I yelled but then turned away quickly. I thought at the least he was another runaway, and at worst he was a burglar. I never considered someone had been murdered."

"No, that's not a consideration anyone would make," Abby said evenly. "By the way, who gave you the tip?"

"Excuse me?"

"The tip about your runaway."

"Oh, a kid I know from martial arts. He works the night shift at the twenty-four-hour food mart in the truck stop." Murphy pointed back toward Pacific Coast Highway. "He was pretty sure he saw her but couldn't follow her to be certain."

Abby handed him her card. "Thank you, Mr. Murphy, for calling this in. Call me if you remember anything else, and if I need to talk to you, is this the best number to reach you, the one on your card?" *The card that says* shamus.

"Yes, ma'am, my cell phone is my work number, but I also added my home number to the back."

Normally *ma'am* bugged her because it could be patronizing, but when the term slid off Murphy's lips, it was charged with respect. Abby's opinion of the man began to soften. "Thanks. Do you want this flyer back?"

He shook his head. "Keep it. If you come across her, I'd appreciate a call. Her mother is worried sick." He reached the bottom porch step, stopped, and looked back. "I'm making a guest appearance on *Good Morning Long Beach* in a few hours. Do you want me to tell this story and ask for help finding the burglar?"

"What?" Abby stared, as exactly what he'd said sank in. "Absolutely not. This is a police investigation, not a platform to build your business."

"That's not what I meant." He shoved his hands into his pockets. "Some publicity might —"

"I don't want that kind of publicity," Abby said through clenched teeth. "Next of kin has not yet been notified. Would you like them to find out about the death of a loved one through you, on TV?"

For his part, Murphy stepped back. Abby hoped he was suitably shamed. *I hate show-offs.*

"Sorry; didn't quite think that through." He gave a cavalier tip of his head. "Thank you, Detective Hart. Don't hesitate to call me if you need my help."

He stepped down and walked across the

yard to the sidewalk, then made his way to a pickup truck parked down the street.

At the shock of his parting statement, Abby felt her jaw drop. *His help?* Not likely. His strong, sure stride across the yard brought one word to Abby's mind: *cocky. He probably would have caught the killer if someone were filming.*

When she realized her thoughts were dwelling on the man, she considered what he'd said and seen that concerned her victim. She needed to find next of kin and make notification, the only part of her job she disliked. Blood and guts didn't shake her, but naked grief often did.

CHAPTER 3

"No matter what, he's a good wit," Woody said when she turned to go back inside. He leaned in the doorway, a grin tugging at his mouth.

"He's a show-off," she said, and Woody laughed. He'd been her first training officer and was a good friend, a valuable resource. Even with the teasing, Abby was glad he was there.

"But what he saw is helpful — gold, I think," she continued as she reached the doorway and he stepped aside to let her in. "Let's forget Luke P. Murphy right now. What do you know about my victim?"

Woody followed her back into the house. "Cora Murray was old Long Beach money. You know that Victorian place — the big one near Cherry Park they just made a bed-and-breakfast?"

Abby nodded.

"Her dad built that, and a bunch of

these." He knocked on the yellowed lath-and-plaster wall. "Little two-bedroom bungalows in working-class neighborhoods." He paused, thumbs hooked in his Sam Browne.

They were back in the living room. The lab tech was still processing evidence.

"And . . ." Woody reached out and put a hand on her shoulder, his voice lowered to a whisper. "She's related to Lowell Rollins. She was his aunt, I think."

"The governor?" Abby's head jerked around. Forget left field, this news was out of the realm of consideration.

Woody held her gaze. He was one of only a few other people in her life who knew of her connection with Governor Lowell Rollins. The room seemed to shift and Abby had to sit. She stepped into the kitchen and sat at the small table, looking toward the tech but not really seeing her.

"His chief of staff will probably handle this," Woody said, taking the chair across from Abby. She forced herself to look at him, praying her face stayed blank. Worry now creased his brow.

Abby didn't say anything. Only a handful of people knew of her struggle with this issue. Ethan was the only person not connected in some way who knew who she was and what drew her back to Long Beach. The draw was so strong Aunt Dede had warned her the day she was promoted to homicide.

"Be careful, Abby. Obsession is never a good thing," Aunt Dede had said. *"It clouds your mind and steals your perspective, telling you that you can do things in your own strength when in truth you need to trust God."*

One case defines you. . . .

Abby took a deep breath now and decided to ignore what was screaming in her ear. *I do trust God.* This was no obsession; it was a tragic murder case with an unimaginable connection.

"I need to be prepared for anything," she told Woody.

His expression was one of understanding. "You might not have to deal with him." Woody's tone told her that this was what he hoped.

But even as she agreed with him, Abby knew that was not what she wanted.

For a minute she let her gaze travel over the room, and neither spoke. Woody's leather gear squeaked when he moved, and outside, faint daylight began to brighten the windows. *Focus,* she told herself. *Cora deserves my focus.*

When Abby spoke again, she was certain her cop face was solid.

"Was he . . . ? Was Rollins —" she cocked an eyebrow — "ever involved in her life? Is this going to be hugely political?" Skirting the hard issue, she felt her balance return.

Woody made a face. "News guys will jump on it no matter what. As for his involvement with Cora . . . well, *she* didn't care much for Rollins or any politician. When she had a car, there was a bumper sticker on it that said, 'Don't act stupid. We have politicians for that.' "

Abby smiled and tilted her head toward Woody, who rolled his eyes and went on. He'd never press past her comfort zone; she knew that.

"I liked the old lady; she had a lot of spunk. Cora never married and I think she did the best she could with a dwindling trust fund. Plus, she treasured her independence."

They both gazed at the body for a minute.

Woody cursed. "A killer knocking off old ladies."

"And the victim radius is not that big. I figure our guy has to be someone local, maybe a parolee. The burglary part is snatch and grab, so he's close. He's cruising alleys." Her investigator's legs were back, and she stood.

"Of course you'd figure that. I trained

you, didn't I? Murphy thinks it's a kid."

She brought her hands together, interlacing her fingers. "He saw what he thinks was a kid climb out the window. But a kid doing this doesn't wash for me. Plus, the staging is odd." She shook her head. "I'm thinking small man."

"Probably a safe bet."

"I don't pay much attention to politics. Is the governor in town or in Sacramento?" Abby asked, her tone now casual, unconcerned. The governor and his wife had a beautiful house on the peninsula, in the upscale Naples area of the city, but as far as she knew, he was rarely there.

"He's probably in Sacramento. He seldom stays here in town anymore. But if he is here, and you're pegged to do the notification, I'll help."

"Thanks. Notification duty will have to be bounced off the watch commander. I'll have time for breakfast before a decision, I bet. Join me? My treat."

"Deal."

CHAPTER 4

It was close to five thirty in the morning when Luke parked in his driveway, wanting a shower and bed. All he had time for was a shower and a quick breakfast. *Good Morning Long Beach* began taping at seven. He yawned, the early morning events playing over and over in his mind as he locked his truck, picked up the newspaper, and headed for his door.

As soon as he had seen the kid jump out the window, Luke's first instinct was to chase him. *I could have caught him, but there was no way I would have left Leslie.* When Officer Woods had told him a single elderly woman lived inside, he prayed. But then the officer came back with a look that told Luke the prayer was too late. This was a homicide.

He pondered whether the person he'd seen had really been a kid. Everything happened so fast. At first he was certain he'd seen a teen, but the more the incident rolled over in his mind, the more he doubted the person was young. Could have been a small man. He debated calling Detective Hart and telling her that new insight. *No,* he decided, *I'm not going to throw doubts into the mix after the fact. She's good; if what I told her was helpful, she'll run with it.*

Meeting Detective Hart had unnerved him almost as much as knowing that he'd nearly chased down a murderer. He'd seen her before, actually been as close to her then as he had been this morning, but there was no reason for her to remember. He just had never forgotten. About ten years ago, Officer Hart assisted with weaponless defense training for his police academy class. She'd been on the force for only two years back then and already was a rising star. Several academy physical training records bore her name.

She'd irritated and fascinated him at the same time. Luke leaned against the door, holding his key but not putting it in the lock, remembering how rigid and by the book she was. She'd knocked his grade on a takedown because he wasn't as exact in his technique as she was. *I got the job done, but Hart wanted perfection.*

At the crime scene today, he was certain Hart still wanted perfection, and memories

41

from his short stint at the academy came rushing back. But the vibe he felt toward her now wasn't irritation. Up close years later he observed more than a picky, driven weaponless defense instructor. He saw a competent woman . . . and he wanted to know more.

His stupid question about *Good Morning Long Beach* was a knee-jerk response to the strong attraction he'd felt. It wasn't that Hart was drop-dead gorgeous — no, he wouldn't even say beautiful. She wore no makeup and her face was set in seriousness. But she was pretty, her green eyes were alert and alive, and she had a presence, a charisma that hit him like the kick from a .40-caliber handgun.

I want to see her again.

He couldn't help but wonder about the road not taken, if he'd completed the academy and become a cop. Shaking his head at the notion, he unlocked the door and went inside. He'd dropped out of the academy after a couple of months, not because of Hart but because he was a single father and the regimented schedule and the shift work he knew awaited after the academy took too much time away from his then-infant daughter, Madison. Now it was to her room he headed.

She'd grown so fast. She shouldn't be up just yet, and since she was constantly in motion when she was awake, he loved the chance to steal a look at her peacefully sleeping ten-year-old face. He opened the door to her room and was not disappointed. A smile played on his lips to see her still breathing easily and resting quietly.

The smell of coffee brewing caused him to close the door softly and head to the front of the house. He and Madison lived in the back of his parents' house. His stepfather, a contractor, had added on the space especially for the two of them. When Luke decided he'd start his own business from home in order to be there for Maddie, James designed the addition so they'd have their privacy but Maddie would also have built-in babysitters when Luke had to go out.

A short walk down the hallway brought him to the main house and the kitchen, where his mother sat with a cup of coffee and an open Bible. Grace Murphy helped Luke's investigation business part-time by filing and taking phone calls, which had increased exponentially after that video went viral on YouTube. She knew his caseload and knew he'd been out looking for a runaway. But Nadine was more than

43

just another runaway case to Grace. The girl's mother, Glynnis, was a member of Grace's Bible study group.

"You're up early." Luke leaned down and kissed his mom on the cheek, then grabbed a cup and poured coffee for himself.

"I can tell from your face you didn't find her."

Luke sat and gulped some coffee. He rolled his head on his shoulders to loosen the kinks in his neck and finished half a cup of coffee before he told his mother what had happened.

"Murder?" Grace arched her eyebrows. "Leslie broke her ankle?"

"Yeah. Martin called me as I pulled in the driveway. He was at the hospital with her and she was heading for surgery. They have to put a pin in her ankle. Guess I'm short a partner again."

Leslie recently mustered out of the Army and was trying to decide what to do with her life. Luke had hired her part-time, and she'd been doing a great job as his partner.

"You'll be okay until she's back on the job. I'm glad her injury can be fixed. I'm still troubled about Nadine being out in that area."

"Kwan was never 100 percent on the sighting. Yet, runaways are attracted to the scene there." He sighed and started to say more but stopped.

"But?"

"This has never felt like an average runaway. Nadine was a happy kid, a good kid. I just . . ." He shrugged.

Grace smiled sadly. "I agree with you. I wish there was more the police could go on."

Luke said nothing. He'd talked to juvenile investigators about Nadine. She was listed as a missing person, but there was no evidence of foul play. She'd texted her mother, saying she'd be home when she was ready. With that information, she was not a priority. They'd detain her if they ran across her, long enough to call her mother, but that was it.

Grace stood. "I'm going to start breakfast. Are you hungry?"

"Starved, without much time. Can you get Maddie to the church this morning? The homeschool group is working there today. I have to hurry and get to the college for *Good Morning Long Beach.* I should be able to pick her up."

The local cable program was produced and filmed at Long Beach State University, five minutes away.

"Of course. And I'll pick her up. I have

some errands to run down by the church."

Just then Maddie burst into the kitchen and gave Luke a hug, crinkling her nose at the stubble on his chin. He hugged her tight anyway, considering Nadine and the thousands of other young girls out there in the big bad world and vowing that would never be Maddie.

As normal morning activity swilled around him, Luke kept reliving the events of the morning and his conversation with Detective Hart. His best friend, Bill Roper, was a narcotics detective for the PD and hoped to move to homicide. Coincidentally, a slot opened up because of the retirement of Hart's partner, so if Bill were selected, he'd told Luke that he would be Abby Hart's new partner. Bill hadn't asked Luke's opinion; he'd just raved about the prospect of working with Hart. "She's so focused when she gets a case, her nickname in the office is Superglue. She sticks to something until she solves it. Everyone respects her work ethic."

At the time Luke had teased him, in his mind's eye seeing the picky perfectionist from the academy. "Do you think you could work with someone like that? There has to be a little bit of fun in the work you do, even if it's solving murders. All work and no play would make Bill a dull boy."

Bill waved him off, excited about the new assignment. "I'm sure there'll be some give in a partnership. She can't be on 100 percent of the time. And I would like the opportunity to find out. She's the best. I've seen her testify in court and she's ice, man. Defense attorneys can't shake her. And it's because she's built the best case possible. She's superglue relentless when she gets a body — no stone unturned, that kind of thing. I want that slot to be her partner."

He'd asked Luke to pray about it and expected to find out in a couple of days. The new assignment with much more responsibility and a heartbreaking workload would be what Luke and Bill liked to call a "hard blessing."

It was something they'd come up with during their service in Iraq. The hard blessing of being able to serve together and fight side by side, the hard blessing of surviving when some good men didn't. While Bill joined after 9/11, Luke had already been a member of the Army Special Forces and wanted a career there. But his wife's death and his daughter's injury stopped his reenlistment cold. It had been hard coming back to a baby daughter in the hospital being treated for burns from the fatal car crash, a little girl who would never know her mother. And a hard blessing to come back to the faith he'd walked away from while living a wild life in the service.

Luke still ached when he saw the scars on his daughter's legs. They'd faded with time and hopefully would eventually disappear completely. Becoming a single father had been a hard blessing. Now Maddie was a vibrant, happy child, the image of her beautiful mother and never troubled by the scars that faded a bit every year.

Yes, he understood a hard blessing.

His conversation with Bill had been two days ago. Luke knew he'd get a call when Bill found out whether or not he got the promotion. *I wonder what he'll think when I tell him about my encounter with her,* Luke mused.

After breakfast, Luke kissed his daughter before leaving her with Grandma and went to his room for a shower, shave, and fresh clothes for the taping. Abby Hart stayed on his mind. *Superglue.* He chuckled as he remembered the horrified look on her face when he suggested publicity.

He realized he'd spoken without thinking and only made the suggestion because he wanted to see her again. Keeping a connection to the investigation might mean just

48

that. She was more striking than he remembered, even at four in the morning, when it was obvious she'd been dragged out of bed to come to a homicide scene. She seemed to shine, and it was impossible to imagine that a woman so focused on justice for innocent victims wasn't warm and worthwhile to call friend.

Her emerald-green eyes, so vivid and alive, touched him most. Add the hair, a color he couldn't quite place — brown and blonde, an appealing mixture. It was long, and she'd had it pulled back and bunched into a clip. Luke bet it was soft and touchable. Sighing, he was embarrassed with where his thoughts were taking him. Even if they did connect again on the investigation, he'd never take a step closer to her on any level, so why fantasize?

The last thing in the world Luke wanted to do was let another woman down like he'd let his wife down.

Even when he was back in the car heading for the college, his mind was active with thoughts of Abby Hart and Nadine. He winced as he considered Nadine's mother, Glynnis Hoover. She'd been widowed two years ago. Like Luke's wife, her husband was killed in a traffic accident. Unlike Luke, who lived with the memory of having a horrible argument with his wife on the phone while she was driving and hearing the crash that killed her because the argument had distracted her, Glynnis's last memory of her husband was warm and loving.

Lately she'd been sending out signals she wanted more than friendship where Luke was concerned. They shared a connection she clearly thought was a God thing. But he didn't share the attraction and planned to be honest with her. And then Nadine ran away. Glynnis was devastated and clingy and scared to death she'd never see her daughter again. Luke did his best to handle the situation professionally, but Glynnis was leaning on him hard, and he prayed that the Lord would give him wisdom so he wouldn't hurt the woman.

He pulled the card Detective Hart had given him out of his pocket. *Detective A. Hart,* it read, on a standard Long Beach Police Department business card. He ran his thumb over her embossed name and couldn't help but wonder if he'd ever have the chance to help Superglue put some bad guys in jail.

CHAPTER 5

"Let the dead rest in peace."

"But someone is getting away with murder."

"I don't believe anyone gets away with anything forever."

Woody and Abby'd had that conversation fifteen years ago, three years before she started the police academy. And twelve years earlier, a coroner had zipped up the body bags containing the remains of her murdered parents.

"I've dreamed about finding my parents' killers for more years than I had with them," she'd told Woody back then. She was fresh out of high school, and providence had brought her back to Long Beach on an athletic scholarship to play volleyball for Long Beach State. The first thing she did was look up Officers Robert Woods and Asa Foster. She knew from newspaper articles that the pair had been the first on the scene of her parents' murders that day and had

saved her from the fire that consumed their restaurant, the Triple Seven.

But neither of them thought much of her desire to plunge in, demand the case be reactivated. They'd gladly met with her and encouraged her aspirations to join the PD when she turned twenty-one. The encouragement stopped there. Their attitude about catching her parents' killers took her by surprise. Why didn't they want the cold case solved?

"We're afraid you could still be in danger, as well as your aunt. Even after all these years. Not only was the restaurant burned down, but your parents' house burned to the ground that day as well. It was a personal crime, and someone with a grudge like that won't quit."

"But so much time has passed — how can there still be danger?"

"Trust us. Be patient; patience always pays off, and an opening will come."

Reluctantly, she'd taken their advice and started life in Long Beach anew, not telling a soul who she was or why it was so important to her to eventually become a homicide detective. Abigail Morgan had been pulled from the fire and she was now Abby Hart, having been adopted by her aunt, Deidre Hart, and raised, from age ten, miles away in Lake Creek, Oregon. When she did apply to the PD, she knew that Woody and Asa stepped in to protect her secret, convincing the chief and her background investigator to seal her file when she was hired.

Over the years Abby built a cold case file with what she could glean from public record. While in the academy, as she learned about police work and investigations, she'd spent her weekends in the library, filling notebooks with ideas and theories.

Dede was aghast. *"Abby, you're young; you should be out having fun, meeting people, not shut up in the library on weekends."* The word *obsession* surfaced then, with Dede afraid Abby's preoccupation with the cold case would drown her.

After that, she'd kept her search to herself, adding more official paperwork to the file as she moved on in the department. By the time her promotion to homicide came, she and Ethan had a casual relationship that soon blossomed. She'd known him forever. He lived near her aunt and was a big part of the youth group at the church there. Abby went from looking up to him as a big brother to cherishing his friendship. When she moved to Long Beach, they still talked from time to time on the phone. She'd been a cop for five years when he took a job at her church in Long Beach as the missions director. It wasn't long before they began to date. When things got serious with Ethan, for a time she could let go and put the case in the background.

Six months ago, when he'd asked her to marry him and she'd said yes, she thought she'd shut the door completely on the past in favor of not jeopardizing her future with him. When she'd confided in him who she was, he'd joined the chorus and agreed with Asa and Woody.

"These men have been officers longer than you have and they think it's dangerous, so you should follow their advice. The killers will not get away with it. You need to trust that God will deal with them. You can, can't you?"

"Yeah, I guess I can."

"Then put it behind you and us. Don't let that tragedy be what defines you."

Now, one name brought the twenty-seven-year-old cold case screaming to the forefront of her mind. As hard as she'd tried to ignore and push back every emotion bubbling up about her parents' unsolved murders, today the door had been kicked open by the mention of Lowell Rollins.

Governor Lowell Rollins was someone she'd wanted to speak to for a long time but never had a valid reason to approach.

Using a murdered relative as an excuse was not a move Abby would normally ever make, but this might be her only chance.

Her phone buzzed with a text. Sliding it off her belt, she read a not-unexpected response to a query she'd sent earlier.

Coroner will make notification.

Turned out the governor was in Sacramento, and he was too big a VIP for Abby to presume that it was up to her to arrange the notification. As she told Woody, Abby had bounced the ball to the watch commander's court and he'd made the call to wake up the head coroner.

Even as she slid her phone back onto her belt, agitation roiled about not being able to notify Rollins.

I have to speak to him somehow. I came back here on a mission. I thought I could pack it away because people I care about wanted me to, but I can't any longer. I won't.

I need to find my parents' killers.

The governor might come to LB because of this murder, and Abby knew that if an opportunity arose that would allow her to approach him about what they had in common, she'd take it. Even if he remembered nothing, he was someone who could get the cold case reactivated. Maybe he would at least do that for her. Woody, Asa, and her aunt would have to understand that she'd been patient long enough. And Ethan . . . well, she didn't know what she'd say to Ethan, and that was the hardest part.

She imagined Rollins would inquire into the investigation at some point, for a photo op if nothing else. Maybe that would be her chance.

Abby rubbed her forehead as her own cynicism surprised her. Cora Murray was the governor's great-aunt, a family member no matter how far removed. *Let's not assume he doesn't care,* she scolded herself.

The clang of the coroner's gurney banging the steps as he wheeled Cora out of the house brought Abby back to the here and now.

She scanned the yard and found Woody at the edge of the sidewalk. He'd hung around and chatted with the coroner and swapped stories with the remaining uniformed officers. Since Asa had retired, Woody was the most senior officer on the force, and that earned him quite a bit of cachet. He was hardworking and smart, and every cop Abby knew looked up to him.

"Still up for breakfast?" she asked.

"Yeah." He scratched the gray stubble on his chin. "River's End?"

Abby smiled wide, happy with the pick.

"Okay, I'll leave you to finish up while I log out and change. Meet you there in thirty."

She flashed a thumbs-up and returned to her crime scene as the doors of the coroner's van slammed shut. Even as she'd been looking through the house, chatting with Woody, talking to the other uniforms about their reports, and struggling with her own demons, names of known burglars had been floating in and out of her thoughts based on the description Murphy had given her. She'd made an extensive list of known cat burglars after the first murder. Several had already been cleared. But now, with Murphy's description, one name from the list popped out at her. He'd need to be checked out ASAP.

"Detective?"

"Yes?" Abby faced the last officer on scene, frowning when she saw that the cop had a little black-and-white dog with a flat face in her arms. Abby had no idea what kind of dog it was, but it was small, kinda cute, and obviously scared because its little body shivered.

"This was the victim's dog. I put him in our unit so he wouldn't be in the way during the investigation, thinking animal control would be here by now." She shrugged. "We're past end of watch. Animal control is short; they want us to drop it off."

Abby glanced at her watch. The officer was past EOW by twenty minutes. Her gaze fell on the dog and the eyes got her. They were victim's eyes; she'd seen them too many times. And worst of all, she'd seen them once or twice when she looked in the mirror.

"I'll take it," she said, holding her arms out and noting the relief in the officer's eyes. "They just want me to drop it off at the shelter?" She asked the question as the dog settled into the crook of her arm and immediately stopped shaking.

"Yes."

The officer put a blanket and a toy in Abby's car before she turned to leave. "The dog did his business a few minutes ago, so you're good there, but he might want some water. And he's good on the leash."

"Thanks," Abby said, looking at the small creature that smelled like an old woman's perfume. He had a tag and she nudged it with her index finger. *Bandit* was etched on the small blue dog bone. "Well, Bandit," she said, "I'm sorry for your loss."

The little guy looked up at her, yawned, and then settled his furry head back in the bend of her elbow and closed his eyes. For a reason she couldn't identify, Abby felt a lump form in her throat as she looked at the little fur ball. Swallowing, she raised her head in time to see that public service had arrived to secure the house so she could leave.

The shelter was out of her way. She should hurry if she was going to meet Woody at River's End. She set the little dog on the passenger seat and walked around to the driver's side.

Once in, she activated her computer and sent a message to the sergeant on the Career Criminal Apprehension Team. She asked him to look for the crook whose name came to mind. He went by the moniker Lil' Sporty. An ex-jockey, Lil' Sporty Davis was a crackhead known to frequent hotels and businesses on Pacific Coast Highway. PCH was three blocks from the victim's residence.

Davis had never been violent, but he'd been pinched for cat burg before and he certainly fit the description Murphy had given — small build and quick. If he could be found, CCAT would find him. She referenced the homicide case and knew they'd move quickly. With luck she'd have Lil' Sporty in an interview room before the day was over.

She copied the records section what she'd

sent to CCAT as a shorthand way of filing a follow-up to the homicide report the patrol officers would have submitted by now.

At some point during her computer work, Bandit crawled into her lap, and she let him stay there.

She started the car, but before putting it into gear, for reasons she couldn't fathom, she did a little research about the missing case Murphy was working. After a few minutes she'd read everything she could find about Nadine Hoover and had no idea what she'd do with the information.

Yawning, she looked down at Bandit. "I know I'm hungry; how about you?"

Abby left the west side of the city for the east side and animal control. She'd have just enough time to drop the dog off before breakfast with Woody. Though she was preoccupied with how she was going to tell Woody she'd decided to pursue her parents' case in spite of his warnings, it impressed her that the dog barely stirred. Abby had no trouble driving with him in her lap. She pulled up at the city shelter ten minutes later but sat in her car with the motor running.

An animal shelter was sort of like a foster home for dogs, she thought, frowning at the drab brick building. Even in her car she could hear the barking and yapping of the prisoners within.

"Prisoners," she said out loud. "Funny I should think of them as prisoners."

The dog stirred and looked at her with those big brown eyes. She didn't understand why they flooded her all of a sudden, but she couldn't stop the memories — all the foster homes she'd been shuffled through, the fear and anxiety she'd felt not knowing if this new house would be a good one or a bad one, a safe one or a hurtful one. Her throat constricted and tears burned in her eyes. Taking deep breaths, she backed out of the parking space, knowing she couldn't dump this warm little body the way she'd been dumped so many times after her parents were killed.

This feeling further reinforced her decision to plunge ahead and dive into investigating the murder case. After she was orphaned and because social services wanted to hide her, she'd been lost in the system and it took four years for them to connect her to Aunt Dede. The years had been hurtful and hard for Abby.

She phoned the coroner and let them know she had possession of the victim's dog. If the governor wanted the dog, she'd have to give him up. Looking down at the fur ball, she knew getting attached would be a mistake.

"I'll deal with it, Bandit. I'll deal with it," she said as she drove toward River's End.

When she got to the restaurant, her pulse had slowed and the burning in her throat had subsided. River's End Café was her favorite restaurant, and the familiar setting calmed her angst.

"You kept Bandit?" Woody asked as Abby joined him in front of the restaurant, dog in tow.

"I didn't have the heart to take him to animal control."

Woody looked down at Bandit, and Bandit looked up at Woody. "He's a cute enough little dog. He always behaved for Cora. If the governor doesn't want him, someone would likely adopt him soon."

"Don't they kill them if they aren't picked?"

"I guess." Woody studied the little dog. "What do you want to do, keep him?"

The question gave her pause. "I don't know. I always wanted my own pet dog. My aunt had a working dog, an Australian shepherd, to help with her animals. He was never a lapdog. You think the governor will want him?"

"Got me. Probably depends on the dog's party affiliation. Let's talk about it while we eat. I suppose we're sitting on the patio?"

"Of course." Abby gestured for him to go first, and they found a table where dogs were allowed. River's End was a small grill in Seal Beach. It sat next to a bike path that ran along the flood control channel, ending here where the water emptied into the Pacific Ocean. The channel was a dividing line in more ways than one. This side was Seal Beach, while the other side was Long Beach.

Twenty-seven years ago her parents' restaurant, the Triple Seven, sat by itself across the way on the edge of the ocean. Today the area was a large, grassy park. Abby had returned to Long Beach at age eighteen, but she'd never visited the park. She liked the view from River's End, imagining the place her parents built, loved, and died in. Somehow Abby believed that visiting the park would destroy the illusion fixed in her mind. River's End's outside seating area was the perfect vantage point for her to gaze and daydream about a time and place she barely remembered.

River's End was also a homey locals' place. Sometimes Abby found herself humming the tune to *Cheers* because it was a place where everyone knew your name. And even though she didn't live in Seal Beach, the locals accepted her as one of their own. Today the patio was almost full because it was a nice, cool summer morning.

Regulars like the retired teacher — alone today — would push two tables together on Saturdays, and the group of old guys would argue politics over coffee and newspapers. Then there were the blonde bombshells, a mother and daughter who met there often after their long morning walks, and Kai, the buff veteran lifeguard having breakfast before work. All said hello and commented on Bandit's cuteness and his manners. River's End felt like a sort of home for Abby, and the "family's" goodwill toward Bandit buoyed her.

Maybe I'm worried for no reason, she thought. *Maybe some nice family would adopt him.*

"A new addition?" Sandy, one half of the team who owned the place, asked when she came to take their order. Bob, her husband, did the cooking, and their adult daughter helped when she was home from school.

Abby tilted her head. "He belonged to a victim. Not certain what will happen to him."

"Ooo." Sandy's brows scrunched together.

"If he needs a home, let me know. He's too cute. Now, what can I get you?"

"I'll have the usual," Abby said. For her that was a Belgian waffle with a side of bacon and two poached eggs.

Woody always got a Denver omelet with a side of River's End's hottest sauce.

"You guys are too easy," Sandy said as she poured them coffee.

"If by that you mean boring," Woody said with a shrug, "I can live with that."

Sandy smiled and left to put their order in.

Bandit settled down quietly at Abby's feet. "So you've got dogs," she said. "Will this be hard, taking care of the little guy?"

"One that small would be a Scooby Snack for my two." Woody chuckled. "Dogs can be great companions."

"Can be?"

Woody cocked an eyebrow. "Well, they take training. If you train 'em, get them to do their business where they're supposed to and not where you don't want them to, then they're good companions."

"I'm sure there's a book out there to tell me what to do if I keep him."

At that, Woody laughed as Abby knew he would. Books were sacred and respected to Abby. They had been the one constant in her life after the loss of her parents when she found herself shuffled from group home to foster home and back again. Even the bleakest group home she landed in had books.

"That's right; I know about you and books. Keep the dog. Your house will be the best place for him after you read your book."

Their meal came, and for a few minutes both of them concentrated on eating. After plowing halfway through her eggs and a portion of the waffle, she told Woody about her hunch, that Lil' Sporty was their crook.

Woody gave her a thumbs-up. "Good guess. You put CCAT on him?"

She drained her coffee and looked to Sandy for more. Once the cup was full and she had worked up the courage to tell Woody she planned to pursue her parents' murders, he surprised her with a question before she got the words out.

"You had a chance to talk with Murphy. What do you think of him?"

Abby choked on her coffee. "As a witness?"

"Yeah, he's an observant guy."

She wiped her mouth with a napkin. "He gave me a great lead — I have to thank him for that. Don't tell me you're a fan of that WWE video of him?"

Woody chuckled. "That was something, wasn't it? I like the guy. You know he almost became a cop."

"No, I didn't know that." Abby sat back in her chair. "Almost?"

"He quit the academy. When he told me about it, I remembered because a buddy of mine was the sergeant out there then. A lot of guys tried to talk him out of it. They thought he'd be a great cop."

Abby crinkled her nose. "Probably couldn't take the fact that real police work is not a TV cop show."

Woody shook his head. "He was top of his class when he quit."

Abby sipped her coffee, wondering why Woody wanted to talk about Murphy. But she let him talk, hoping to soften him up, prepping to broach a subject sensitive for her mentor.

"He's got a solid rep as a PI, WWE video notwithstanding."

"I will give him credit for getting that predator off the street. He'd been a problem for a long time."

Woody agreed and took a sip of his coffee.

It was time to ask the question she really wanted answered.

"You know," Abby began as she pushed

her plate away and switched the subject back to Cora Murray, "I don't like the idea of Governor Rollins having a connection to my homicide, but this might be my chance."

Woody's coffee cup stopped just short of his mouth. "What, your chance to talk to him about the Triple Seven?"

"I've wanted to for a long time. You know that."

He set the cup down, looked away for a minute, and didn't speak until he turned back. "I thought you decided to let it lie. What will you tell Ethan?"

Abby winced. Woody knew where to jab.

"I don't know. I, uh . . . I can't help it. To finally be able to speak to the governor —" she spread her arms — "this could open doors, jog a memory. It's time to tell people who I am."

"Once you do, who you are will never be a secret again."

"Does it really need to be? I mean, it's been almost thirty years. I never got to sit down with the original investigators. Now Ollie Cleaver is dead, and Zeke Russell has Alzheimer's. Maybe I need to come out, announce who I am, and reinvigorate the case." *Even if Ethan doesn't like it.*

Woody held her gaze with his steel one. "You want to smoke the killer out? Make yourself a target?"

"If he's still alive." She reached across the table and put her hand over his. "I'm a big girl now, and I even carry a gun. If the man or men who killed my parents are still alive, I hope they come after me. I want answers, and I can handle myself."

"Your dad thought he could handle himself." Woody spoke sharply, and she could tell by his expression he regretted the tone. He looked away again. When he turned back, the expression on his face was softer. "I guess old habits die hard. I've been looking out for you since the day that cook handed you to me through the fire. But you're not six years old anymore."

Abby smiled. "No, I'm not. I'm a big, bad homicide detective and I want more than anything to know who killed my parents and why. Rollins was my dad's partner back then. He knew my mom and dad. I remember him as Uncle Lobo. I need to talk to him."

Woody looked down and rubbed his cheek. Abby sensed he had something else to say and waited.

"It's hard to appreciate now how scary that crime was then." He took a deep breath. "The killers shot your parents point-blank and meant for you to burn to death.

69

Then they traveled a mile and a half and burned down your house. The entire city was frightened by the viciousness. Asa and I just wanted to protect you."

"I know, Woody." Abby had the case memorized. "I hope you'll lend a hand if I need one. You're my Yoda; you always give me the best advice."

Woody stayed silent, searching for words, Abby thought.

"That day changed my life," he said after a minute. "It changed my attitude about work. I'd seen death and destruction before, but it had never hit so close to home. I knew your parents. I liked them. The Triple Seven was more than just a pop stop."

Abby held her breath and waited for him to continue. She had heard often that her parents "popped" for cops, fed them for free. Many restaurants and businesses used to, acting on the belief that being a pop stop would encourage cops to hang around and discourage criminals. The practice was frowned on now; the PD brass discouraged businesses from giving anything away free to cops. They felt the businesses would expect something in return. In her parents' case, though cops loved them for being benefactors, it had not kept the criminals away in the end.

"I would have given anything that day to run down the pukes who killed them. Puff and Puff More worked that case hard." He used Russell and Cleaver's nicknames. Abby had been told they were both four-pack-a-day smokers. It was lung cancer that had killed Cleaver.

· "For all those reasons I need to talk to Rollins," she said. "I know he's been asked, but the question still burns inside me: who hated my parents enough to try to obliterate everything about them? Maybe he can force the case back to the top of the pile."

Woody smiled without pleasure. "Just remember, be careful what you wish for."

After breakfast as Abby walked to her car, Bandit in tow, she let the anger she felt about Cora Murray simmer and boil into renewed anger about her folks. Abby had settled back into the driver's seat when her phone rang.

It was Sergeant Page from CCAT. "We got a line on Sporty and we're getting ready to swoop. Wanna come?"

"You bet," Abby said as she started the engine.

Page gave her the address where CCAT was staging, and she pressed the gas pedal, thinking of Cora Murray and her mom and dad as her back tires squealed out of the lot.

CHAPTER 6

Luke turned off Atherton into the college parking lot and drove toward the building where the cable show was shot. For a college production, the show was extremely well run, professional, and watched by a large portion of the city. Luke had found the man he apprehended for human trafficking from a tip he received after an appearance on *Good Morning Long Beach,* and as a result three victimized young women were back home with their families. Today he planned to talk about Nadine and hopefully generate more tips, but before he even parked his truck, the activity in the lot surprised him. The kids who put the show together were out loading one of their mobile studio/film vans.

He got out of the truck and searched for the grad student who oversaw production. It was a minute before he saw the thin, knobby-kneed Arvli Harris, bouncing around on his tiptoes supervising.

"Hey, Arv, what's going on? Aren't we shooting today?"

"Yo, dude." Arvli slapped his forehead. "I meant to call you. No, man, we got a tip on some breaking news and we're gonna try and get our cameras in on it."

"You guys don't usually roll that way; it must be something big."

"You bet." Arvli nodded enthusiastically, Adam's apple bobbing. "Jay's got a girlfriend works at the coroner's office. The governor's aunt was murdered last night! Can you believe it? The best governor the state's ever had and his aunt gets whacked here in our city and we got the news first."

"What?" Luke froze as Arvli turned away to bark instructions to his crew.

"We got the inside on this, dude. I'll call and reschedule you when I can," Arvli promised as he hurried to get into a truck that was backing out.

Luke stepped out of the way so as not to be run over by the rapidly accelerating van and pulled out his phone.

It couldn't be, he thought as he punched his news feed app. There was nothing. Frustrated, he hit Refresh. What were the odds two women were murdered last night? Long Beach could be wild, but generally not that wild. Still nothing came up, and he realized that Arvli could indeed have the inside track on the murder of the governor's aunt.

A towering figure in California politics, Lowell Rollins was the odds-on favorite to be the next US senator from California. He was especially big in Long Beach, since this was where he kept a private residence and where he'd started his political career.

If that poor old woman was his aunt, Luke knew that the governor would be headed to Long Beach. And he also knew, even with everything else on his plate, he had to find a way to try to talk to the big man.

He was about to hit Refresh on the news feed again when his phone buzzed with an incoming call. The extension was Bill's narcotics line, but this was early for him to already be at his desk.

"Luke, you're talking to the newest member of Long Beach homicide."

"Hey, congratulations! Is that why you're at work so early?"

"Yep. Yesterday Lieutenant Jacoby gave me my two weeks' notice and then Deputy Chief Cox called early this morning to say I could start immediately because of a big case. I'm pumped. I want to get myself up to speed right away, so I'm here cleaning out my desk in narcotics."

Bill's voice vibrated with excitement as he continued. "It's fine with me to start now; this is my dream job. I've been looking over files, and I saw your name on her callout last night. Fill me in; what happened?"

"I planned to tell you about it, just didn't expect to be talking to a new homicide detective so soon. I was looking for Nadine and saw something else instead." Luke told him about what he'd witnessed in the early morning hours.

"You nearly caught a murderer — a serial killer, at that. That's the big case that got me fast-tracked."

"Serial killer?"

"Yep, same MO as another murder. What'd you think of Hart?"

Luke struggled to get his mind off of *serial killer* and back to Abby Hart. "Professional." *Fascinating.* "Definitely on top of things." *Can't stop thinking about her.*

"That murder case is her priority case — ours now. I'm just waiting for the LT to tell her I made the cut before I go down there."

"Bill, can I ask the victim's name?"

"Uh, official notification hasn't been made yet. Why do you want to know?"

"Was she Rollins's aunt?"

Silence. Then, "How did you know that?"

76

"Long story. You think he'll come home from the capital for this?"

"For the murder of his aunt? Probably. He's a politician, and he wants to be a senator. He'll get sympathy for sure."

"Maybe this is my chance to talk to him. You know, God opening a door."

"Whoa. Cart, horse. Let me review the official file. I'm in homicide now and I'm sure I'll be able to go through the old, unsolved stuff. With luck, I'll be able to answer your questions and you won't have to bother the big man."

"I appreciate that, but you know I want to look him in the eye."

"At least wait until things calm down a bit. He doesn't even know yet. Like I said — cart, horse. Be patient."

Luke said he'd try to wait before he did anything, but it was a halfhearted promise. He wanted to ask Governor Rollins about an unsolved homicide case, and he didn't think he'd find the answer he wanted in the file. He needed to be face-to-face with the man and hear the answers for himself.

Luke left the college for the hospital to see how Leslie was doing. The breaking news story about the murder of the governor's aunt was on all the hospital televisions. Leslie even had it on in her room, and he had to chuckle when he saw Arvli and the crew jockeying for position in front of the police station.

"Hey, boss." Leslie smiled when she saw him and pointed at the screen. "Am I right in extrapolating that the killer was the guy we saw last night?"

"Sure looks like it."

"I'm so sorry I slowed you down. You would have caught him."

"Hey, don't sweat it. Detective Hart is smart and good at what she does; she'll catch him."

"I just feel bad. And weak."

Luke shook his head. "Don't. You're a big help to me and I'll miss you while you recuperate. Stuff happens. It wasn't your fault."

"Thanks."

"How long will you be here?"

"They're letting me go today, but I think I'll have a lot of PT to get through before I'm back 100 percent. They put three screws in my ankle."

"Well, you concentrate on getting better. Your job will be waiting for you when you're ready."

"Thanks, Luke. Thanks."

■ ■ ■ ■

Back home, Luke pulled up a story about the homicide on the computer. He read what was probably an official PD press release that gave only bare facts. After a few minutes he set the fresh homicide story aside and turned toward the large whiteboard he kept in his office filled with the salient facts about the twenty-seven-year-old unsolved murder of his uncle and namesake Luke Goddard. He'd been eight years old when his uncle was killed and back then barely understood what had happened.

Now thirty-five, after six years in the Army and several more as a seasoned private investigator, he understood all too well the evil that a person could do.

Uncle Luke's murder was another incident that fell into the hard blessing column in Luke's life. Before that day, his mother had been a free spirit, a hippie. She never married Luke's dad and floated from man to man, in and out of relationships, not all of them healthy. Vaguely he remembered a procession of fake "uncles." His real uncle Luke had been a devout Christian, involved with a large church. So when he was murdered and the helpful, loving people

79

from his church circled around the family, Grace found a place she wanted to be grounded to. She accepted Christ and began attending the church, and that was where she met James Murphy, the man Luke now called Dad. Sure, Luke would rather have his uncle, but he was eternally grateful for the change in his mom and for James.

By the time he'd earned his PI license, his family was resigned to the fact that they'd probably never know who killed Uncle Luke and why. So Luke started his own file, talking unofficially and on the down low to everyone who knew his uncle, the people his uncle worked for, and anyone else who could give him background. The official investigation had concluded that his uncle's employers were the targets, not his uncle, and Luke concurred. Trouble was, even as he built a file on them, he uncovered no hints about who was responsible for three deaths.

Lowell Rollins was a central figure, but Luke had never had the opportunity to speak to him. Rollins had been the other half of the team who employed his uncle at the time of his death. But the politician's career trajectory had taken him out of Luke's reach. Twice when the governor was in the city campaigning, Luke had tried to connect but always got stonewalled by the governor's campaign manager, Gavin Kent. "The governor is a busy man, and he doesn't live in the past" was the standard rebuff.

What a coincidence that he'd come so close to a murder with connections to the governor. The other odd coincidence today was Officer Robert Woods. Luke knew from the police report that Woods and his former partner were the ones to pull his uncle from the fire. They were on his talk-to list. In his sporadic attempts to work the cold case, Luke had concentrated on avenues he thought the investigators had missed — friends, neighbors, critics of the restaurant, etc. He'd never spoken to Woods or Asa Foster. He'd missed a big opportunity today because he was worried about Leslie. All he could do was pray he'd get another shot.

With a sigh, Luke put his uncle's file away and turned back to his current workload. Since that YouTube video of him had gone viral, he and his mother had fielded calls from all over the country and listened to many a tearful parent. His heart broke with all the pictures he'd received — young girls smiling, innocent, and nowhere to be found. Especially heartbreaking for Luke, because he understood the pain, were the cold cases, the cases that left family members with no closure. He wished with all his heart he could answer every plea and bring home every missing girl.

But he couldn't.

He had to concentrate on the local issues, and Nadine Hoover was his most pressing at the moment.

He'd called Glynnis Hoover to give her an update on Nadine just before he'd left for the college. The conversation had been difficult. The woman was worried sick about her daughter, and he had no new news to give her. Before he'd started walking the west side, he'd spent an hour with a juvenile detective brainstorming about where Nadine might be. It had been a helpful session, but he understood that in situations where kids Nadine's age left home with no indication of foul play, there wasn't a lot the police could do. They didn't have the manpower to chase every kid who ran away from home. Nadine had sent her mother a text message saying she had money, she was fine, but she just wasn't coming home.

The disappearance and the message were so out of character for Nadine, Luke felt it sounded like someone else had sent it. He'd tried to ping the GPS in the phone, but

Nadine had turned it off almost immediately after she sent the text.

As uneasy as everything about the situation made him, he still held out hope that the girl would suddenly appear at home — broke, dirty, but none the worse for wear. He and Leslie had been walking the west side because of Destination X and because there were cheap hotels down there. A lot of runaways turned up in the area. Destination X in particular seemed to be a magnet for the lost and searching. When a kid Luke had taught in his martial arts class thought he'd seen her at a twenty-four-hour truck stop on PCH, two blocks from Destination X, Luke hoped to find her. He didn't have the heart to tell Glynnis that where Nadine had been seen was a cesspool of drugs and vice. As it was, he'd told her he was still hopeful and he'd be going out again that night to look. They'd ended the call with him praying over her sobs.

As Luke printed out more flyers, he prayed some more for Nadine, that God would keep her safe and bring her home to a mother and brother who loved her.

CHAPTER 7

Abby met with Sergeant Page a block south of the Willow Street Blue Line station. Commuters still streamed toward the station, but this time of the morning marked the tail end of the exodus. Abby glanced at her watch. The next northbound train was due in ten minutes and its departure would lessen the crowd even more.

She pulled up opposite and adjacent to Page's plain car in the parking lot of a fast-food restaurant. "Sporty taking a trip?"

"One of my snitches told me Sporty sold him a watch, said he wanted to get out of town." Page held up a gold watch in a plastic evidence bag. "I looked at the list; this is partial loss from the first murder."

Abby felt anticipation snapping like the crack of a whip. "Good obs. You think he's headed for this station?"

"He's spooked, from what my snitch said, probably because he knows someone saw him hop out a window. We worked our way up from downtown; he couldn't have gotten any further on foot. Sheriff is in the loop; they're watching the platforms and the trains."

Abby bit her lip at this information. The Blue Line was the LA County Sheriff's jurisdiction. She had nothing against them; she just wanted everything concerning her serial murder case to stay as local as possible, considering the governor's connection.

Sergeant Page continued. "Your homicide just hit big with the media, so if he is your guy, I imagine Sporty wants to be anywhere but here."

"What media?"

"Don't you have your radio on? KNX just broadcast info about the murder and are standing by for a reaction from the governor."

Abby's pulse quickened. "How could they know already?" Before the words were out of her mouth, she knew. *Murphy.* Heat rose as anger at the audacity of the man spread through her veins like hot oil. Page brought her focus back to the task at hand: catch Lil' Sporty first and then deal with the PI.

"Davis has a bench warrant in the system, so it's no problem hooking him up and taking him to the station for that. I've got Nelson keeping an eye on the north end. Freeman is on the east. I'll hang here." He pointed with his radio. "Why don't you eyeball the west side? Sporty has to pop his head out of hiding if he's getting on. We're on channel six."

Abby struggled to get back in the right frame of mind. "I'm glad I wore my running shoes," she said as she switched her handheld radio to channel six. Her gaze rested on Bandit. He was curled up on the passenger seat, sound asleep. She gave him a pat and focused her thoughts on the little burglar.

She left the lot and turned west, driving a block to Twenty-Seventh Street and turning right. This was the back side of the stop and a likely direction for someone to head if they decided to try the next stop up the line on Wardlow.

Abby had a feeling Davis would come this way. She felt it in her bones as she pulled to the curb and turned off the engine, eyes roaming, watching everyone within her line of sight, searching for a tell that would give the man way.

Then she saw him.

A diminutive figure appeared from around the corner of a building, walking rapidly her way, hunched over from the weight of a large backpack. Abby tensed. Lil' Sporty Davis — there was no doubt about it. She undid her seat belt and turned the car off, then grabbed her handheld radio. She pulled the door handle but didn't push it all the way open. Davis looked behind him and then crossed the street almost directly in front of her car.

Abby held her breath. He turned her way, and panic flashed across his face like neon.

She rocketed out of the car. "Police! Davis, I just want to talk to you."

He jumped and fled right.

"I've got him, Twenty-Seventh east of Pacific heading east!" Abby breathed into her handheld as she raced after him.

He hit the first fence he came to and was up and over in a second. Abby followed, scaling the fence with ease and hoping the backpack would slow the little man down.

Train bells and the hum of an approaching engine factored into the chase. Abby's adrenaline surged.

She lunged for her suspect, but he cut right toward the tracks, accelerating fast. As she stumbled to adjust her own gait, Murphy's words came back to her: *"I've never seen a girl who could move that fast. . . ."*

The thought of showing up the sexist PI gave her a rush of energy, and she redoubled her effort to reach Sporty as he neared the tracks. Abby could hear the rumble of the Blue Line.

Her heart pounded as fear replaced the prey drive when she realized where Lil' Sporty was going. *He's going to try to cross the tracks before the train hits the platform.* The train would be slowing for the stop but could never stop on a dime to avoid someone on the tracks.

As the train's warning tone shattered the air, Abby ran faster. Far away she heard Page on the radio calling for an update, but pulling the radio from her back pocket would only slow her down.

Again the warning tone, and now it deafened her.

Sporty lurched for the tracks and tripped, sprawling headlong on the rails. Abby didn't dare look toward the screaming train as the ground vibrated with the approaching engine.

She leaped forward and grabbed the backpack in both hands. Her momentum jerked Davis off the tracks and into a tumble with her.

She closed her eyes and in one horrific second thought of Ethan and Murphy and what irony it would be to be smashed beneath the wheels of a train trying to save a man who was most likely a killer.

CHAPTER 8

When Abby opened her eyes, she saw the train wheels scant inches from her face. She heard screaming, but every noise sounded far away to her ringing ears. The smell of hot metal and oil burned her nostrils.

Lil' Sporty tried to jerk away, but she tightened her grip. In her periphery, the tan-and-green uniform of a deputy leaping off the platform and running to help gave her the impetus to pull herself up and straddle the crook, keeping him secure in her grasp.

"Let me go!" He struggled, but his protests seemed far away.

Two deputies appeared on either side of them, and she heard a mixture of voices blending together.

"*You okay?*"

"*— almost roadkill . . .*"

"*People filming . . .*"

Ears still ringing, Abby pulled her cuffs from their case and corralled Sporty's wrists, nearly slipping on blood. It took a second to realize it wasn't hers but his.

"I'm okay. He's under arrest."

Page arrived, huffing and puffing. "Abby, that was too close."

He and one deputy grabbed Sporty while the other helped Abby to her feet. She looked to her left and saw how close the big train car had come to smashing them both to nothing. Her thank-you to God came out in a whisper.

Page handed her a bottle of water as she sat on the train platform and willed her breathing and heart rate to settle down. The ringing had stopped and voices were clearer now. She almost didn't take the water, fearing her hand would shake too badly. *I'm in control. I'm fine.*

"That was close," Page repeated, shaking his head in disbelief. "I thought you both were flat cats. You sure you don't want to get looked at? That train almost had you. That is not the kind of injury paperwork I would ever want to file." The normally unflappable Page seemed shaken, and that gave Abby pause.

"Sorry, Sarge. I just reacted."

"We have to take Davis to the ER." He pointed as he continued. "A cut opened up pretty deep on his forearm. Might need stitches."

"I saw that," Abby said after steadying herself with a sip of water. She looked down at her own hands and splashed water to rinse off Sporty's blood.

"But I'm okay." She rolled her shoulders and ignored the scream of pain. In the middle of an important investigation, the last thing she wanted was injury time off. Next to her, her scraped and twisted handheld radio had not fared so well and would need to be replaced. She hadn't rolled on her gun side, so the Sig was fine.

"Has he said anything?" she asked.

"Nah, we got the wrong guy; he didn't do nothing." Page imitated the appeal in a falsetto voice and the deputies laughed. Abby could have kissed him for the mood lightener.

"I told him he's under arrest for a bench warrant," Page said. "I'll call you as soon as we hit the station with him."

Abby walked back to her car slowly, ascertaining the extent of her injuries. Like the radio, her Windbreaker was history. Knowing that there would be lots of scrapes and bruises under her shirt, she decided she'd be fine after a hot bath and a couple of Advil. Her heart caught in her throat with surprise when she saw Bandit standing on his hind legs at the half-open window, tail wagging furiously.

Grinning, Abby pulled the little guy up and out of the window, holding him close.

"Ah, you missed me?" She got licks and more wagging and stood holding him with all aches and pains forgotten.

Her phone rang. She noticed four voice mails from the same extension.

Deputy Chief Kelsey Cox, acting chief of police since Chief Augusta was on vacation, wanted to talk to Abby in a big way. Probably something to do with the media Page had told her about. Switching Bandit to one arm, Abby tensed for the onslaught.

"Hart, where are you? Why aren't you answering your phone?"

"I was out with CCAT arresting a suspect." Abby frowned, wondering why Cox hadn't gotten that information from someone on her staff.

"The station is crawling with reporters, and you have not even filed a preliminary report. How did they find out about the governor's connection so quickly?"

Abby bit her tongue. Kelsey Cox had almost as many years with the PD as Woody. She had been one of the first female patrol officers allowed to work the field in a black-

93

and-white, and now she was the department's first female deputy chief. But she and Abby had a history of butting heads.

It started when Abby promoted to homicide. Cox was jealous and it showed. Then a lieutenant in patrol, Cox was vocal about not believing Abby deserved to move to homicide.

"You haven't paid your dues," she'd hissed to Abby one night.

"What dues are those?" Abby asked.

"You should have twenty years under your belt before you have any business thinking you can solve homicides. You'll fall on your face and victimize people all over again."

Abby never doubted she'd be a good homicide detective. She'd used practically every bit of free time studying investigations with one goal in mind: to eventually solve her parents' murders. When she ignored Cox, she incurred the woman's wrath. It wasn't just Abby who had a problem with Cox. Other women on the force complained that she was disposed to being cold and calculating with female officers. *"Hates competition,"* one had complained. Since Abby already had reason to believe that, she did her best not to antagonize.

Fortunately, as Cox promoted, she'd been assigned to other areas: patrol, then community relations. But two months ago she was promoted to deputy chief of the investigations division. Abby thought the bad blood was behind them.

Apparently not.

"Chief, I did file a preliminary about an hour and a half ago."

"How did the press find out about this homicide? Why did they know that it involves the governor before I did?"

Abby had no answer. She'd done her job and she was not about to whine about Murphy, who she guessed was the leak. And if she did say something about Murphy, Cox would overreact. She might even have Murphy arrested for some nonexistent penal code section.

Would serve him right was the peevish thought that crossed Abby's mind. But then she realized that Murphy didn't know about the governor's connection when he was on scene, so if he did talk to reporters, it was only about the homicide.

All she said was "I haven't had time to speak to the press."

"Well, you need to handle it." She disconnected.

Abby sighed. They were bound to cross paths eventually, but why did it have to be now? She called her lieutenant, who had a calm, level head and was adult enough to deal with Cox without making the incident a subject of gossip.

"I read your preliminary. I'm not sure why Cox didn't," Jacoby said. "Whatever, I'll take care of it. Just update me when you get in."

Abby thanked him and tried to relax in the car, but her shoulder burned. She needed a hot shower and a change of clothes.

She sat in the driver's seat for a minute, Bandit in her lap, feeling no urgency to get to the station. She needed time to decompress, get rid of the jitters resulting from almost getting squished by a train. The last thing she wanted to do was deal with the press while she waited to interview her suspect.

The press brought Murphy to mind. Anger that he'd rush to some reporter to talk about her homicide bubbled up.

After I told him no, what kind of ego he must have to head right out and call them.

Shaking her head, Abby set Bandit on the passenger seat. When she did, her eyes glanced across the flyer. Murphy's missing girl. A Woody phrase came to mind, and in spite of everything, Abby smiled.

"Just mud in the tires."

The press would have found out about the governor's great-aunt eventually. Murphy was a jerk, but he didn't create the press problem. And he was also a jerk who cared about runaway girls. Her gut told her he was genuine about that. She'd set Murphy's card on the dash and now picked it up, thinking not about him but about the girl he was looking for.

Abby had wanted to run away from a couple of group homes. She'd been so angry about losing everything that meant anything to her that she acted out a lot, and foster homes never felt warm or comforting. But fear was always stronger than anger. Fear of where she'd run to had always stopped her.

She decided to cut the PI some slack for the girl's sake, and only the girl. She put the car in gear and headed back to the station, yawning as her jacked-up adrenaline waned and the fact that she'd been up since three in the morning began to take its toll. She stopped at the locker room to clean up. Because she was called out so often in the early morning, she kept a couple changes of clothing at the station. While she didn't rush, knowing Page would not be back yet, she had no time for a shower because she'd want to stay under the water forever. So she settled for a new polo shirt and some clean slacks. Her shoulder didn't look as bad as it felt, and even after her nasty slide, the skin hadn't broken. But she knew she wouldn't be wearing a tank top anytime soon. Bruises weren't attractive.

By the time she stopped at property and exchanged her mangled radio for a new one, it was a little after noon. Lunchtime emptied out the homicide office, so Abby strolled into a quiet work area. They were already down two bodies. Detectives O'Reilly and Carney were away at an FBI school and had been gone for two weeks. They'd be back next week. That left three teams and Abby, currently without a partner. Long Beach averaged about sixty homicides a year, but homicide also handled kidnappings, critical missing persons, and officer-involved shootings, so everyone stayed busy.

Homicide shared one large room. Abby's desk and the empty desk that would serve her next partner were in the best spot — the back corner next to the window. It was as quiet and as semiprivate as could be in an open room and was Abby's because her first and only partner in homicide, Asa Foster, had had the most seniority in the detail. Abby's clearance rate assured she'd keep the space.

I do my job well. Why can't Cox just admit

she was wrong and move on?

She set Bandit down on the visitor chair next to her desk and then stepped to the coffee station. Making a face at what smelled like burnt and stale coffee, she emptied the carafe and put together a fresh pot. Just as she pushed the Start button, she heard the sound of footsteps.

"Good job, Abby. I got a text from Page. He's 10-15 from Community." Her boss, Lieutenant Jacoby, strode her direction, using the ten code for "in custody" so Abby knew Page was finished at the hospital with Sporty. "The press is still driving us crazy," the LT continued, "but press relations is on top of things."

"Sorry about that." Abby faced him and folded her arms.

Jacoby shook his head. "Not your fault; it goes with the job. And I've spoken to Chief Cox. I wish she wouldn't micromanage and would just let people do the jobs assigned to them. But then I also wish I'd win the lottery. She's busy now preparing for a big press conference."

"I haven't interviewed the suspect yet."

"No worries. It won't go off until tomorrow. Cox decided the best course of action was to coordinate with the governor's press relations so it won't be rushed from our end. Apparently Rollins wants to make a statement about his aunt. He made that decision as soon as he heard the news. If your knucklehead turns out to be our guy, it will just be icing. The governor and his staff are preparing to fly down as we speak. Now tell me about this suspect."

Abby leaned against her desk, trying to ignore the jolt that coursed through her with the knowledge that Rollins would be here soon, on her turf.

"The witness, Murphy, gave me a description of the suspect that matched a known burglar who made the list I'd put together after the first murder."

"I remember that list. A couple of the most obvious choices alibied out."

"Yep. Lil' Sporty wasn't picked up at the time because he wasn't an obvious choice. But today he had items in his possession listed as loss from the first murder and he was trying to flee the city. Maybe he was afraid Murphy could ID him. I have a good feeling he's our guy, but I need to talk to him."

Jacoby smiled broadly. "Outstanding. Great to hear it. And —" the smile faded and he shoved his hands into his pockets — "I have news . . ."

Bandit shifted in the chair Abby had put

him in and emitted a yawn that sounded like a yodel.

The lieutenant arched his eyebrows and stepped forward to look down at the little dog, bemusement on his face. "You put in a card to go to K-9 detail?"

"Ha-ha." She rolled her eyes at the joke. "He belonged to my victim from this morning. I didn't have the heart to leave him at the shelter."

Jacoby frowned. "Just when I think I can't be surprised. Anyway, I wanted to tell you who your new partner is."

Abby sighed and forced her shoulders to relax, working to keep her face neutral. She didn't want a partner, but she'd been down that road with Jacoby already. So she'd hear the name he'd give her and do her best to deal with it.

"Who?"

"We went with Roper. He was the most squared away."

She nodded.

"He was going to wait the standard two weeks, but I pushed that forward and he'll be contacting you today. With a serial murderer in the city and one of the victims related to the governor of the state —" he held his hands out, palms up — "we are going to be up to our necks in press for a while. Gunther probably already called you. Let's hope Sporty is our guy. Call me as soon as you hear from Page."

"Yes, sir, but . . ."

Jacoby was halfway out the door. He turned back. "Yes?"

"I'll nail this guy because he needs to be stopped, not because of the press or the governor."

Her lieutenant gave her a salute and left.

Abby sat at her desk, looked across at the empty desk that would be empty no longer, and relished the last bit of privacy she'd have. She didn't have anything against Roper, or any of the officers who'd put in cards to come to homicide; she just discovered since Asa left that she liked working alone. He'd been gone four months now. The process to replace him had moved slowly and she'd grown accustomed to working solo.

Partnering with Foster the last two years had been like working alone. He'd been a great teacher the first two years, imparting a lifetime of wisdom to Abby. But for the last two years it was as if a switch had turned off. His wife died after a long battle with cancer. He began drinking, often coming to work half in the bag. He clashed with superiors over little things. She'd covered for him more than she worked with him. When he finally did retire, the rumor mill said it was because he was given an ultimatum: retire or be fired and lose your pension.

Abby tried not to listen to rumors. Because Asa was one of the two who'd rescued her when her parents were killed, her affection for him went deep. She'd ignored the drinking, chalking it up to his wife's death and a thirty-year career of seeing too much death and human debris. By the time he'd started drinking, he'd already taught her so much. He always said she was a sponge, the best trainee he'd ever had. Asa had been ready to retire when she transferred to homicide but stayed to train her.

Thinking of Asa brought Jacoby's comment about Gunther to mind. Walter Gunther was the local police beat reporter. He was old-school and a drinking buddy of Asa's. Gunther always reminded Abby of a character from one of Raymond Chandler's novels. She could picture him at an old-fashioned typewriter, chomping on a cigar and typing his story with two fingers.

A glance at her desk phone told her five messages were waiting, and she bet they were all from Gunther. She ignored them for the time being because she didn't have anything to tell him.

The phone rang and she saw it was Sergeant Page.

"We're coming in with Lil' Sporty. He got eight stitches in his forearm."

"Has he said anything?"

"Nope. Other than whining about his arm, he won't talk. Still hard to believe he may be good for two homicides. He's such a little weasel."

"He fits the description and he was nervous enough. Shoot me a text when he's in an interview room and I'll be right down."

"10-4."

Abby hung up on Page and then punched in the number for the lab to see if the tech had found anything useful.

"I was just about to call you," the tech said before Abby even said hello. "Got nothing from the window but smudges. Guy must have been wearing gloves."

"Same as the other crime scenes. The wit did say he saw at least one glove."

"I haven't read your narrative yet, but that makes sense. These two crimes are as close to identical as they get. Serial killer."

"Can you give me anything? Shoe size maybe from the dirt on the floor? I do have a suspect on his way for an interview."

"I can estimate. Size seven or eight."

"Which fits with a person of small stature."

"Yeah. The guy coming in is a good suspect?"

"CCAT and I picked up a cat burglar who fits the physical the wit gave."

Something like a snort came through the phone. "You're the best. You'll get a confession, I'm certain."

"Crossing my fingers and unkinking the rubber hose. Thanks." Abby set the phone back in its cradle and looked at Bandit snoozing. "Gonna get justice for you soon, bucko."

Her phone buzzed with Page's text.

Abby called Lieutenant Jacoby to tell him Lil' Sporty was in interview.

"I'll be right down."

She found Davis's rap sheet and wondered if Bandit would be okay if she left him in the office while she went to talk to the burglar.

Since he was asleep, she decided she'd risk leaving him. She'd just finished committing the rap sheet to memory and grabbing her notebook and recorder to conduct the interview when the soft, muffled sounds of footsteps on the carpet alerted her to company. She recognized Bill Roper, formerly from narcotics.

"Detective Hart, you got a minute?" He smiled and she could see the nerves.

Biting back irritation, she kept her voice neutral. "I've got an interview to do, Detective Roper. My LT told me you're my new partner."

He flushed and Abby thought he'd better get over that.

"Yes, I am, and I'm ready to get to work. I hear we have something big."

Abby felt herself wince at the word *we*. Looking away from Roper as she struggled for the right words and prayed not to sound snarky, she saw Bandit stir.

"Look, if you don't mind hanging on to the dog —" she picked Bandit up — "you should probably come watch the interview. I'll fill you in on the elevator."

"This the suspect in the granny murder?"

"Yep."

"Great. I love dogs."

Abby handed him Bandit, and together they rode the elevator down to the interview room. She told him everything going on with their suspect and noticed that Bandit seemed to like him.

Maybe it won't be too bad having a partner,

she thought when the elevator doors opened.

Chapter 9

Woody couldn't sleep. He'd tried, but his breakfast hadn't settled right, and after raiding the Rolaids, he changed into his swim trunks, grabbed an iced tea, and sauntered out to the pool. His two dogs, Ralph and Ed — Labs almost as old as he was — heard the screen open, and they were up and out to the pool with him.

He lowered himself onto the first step and sat, sliding over so his legs would dangle in the water. Ed, the younger of his dogs, snuggled up behind him and licked his ear. Woody returned the affection with a hug, reminded one more time how happy he was that his last ex-wife left him the dogs. She'd not left much else, but then there wasn't much else that he cared about.

Abby was about the only person he counted as family now.

He'd never had any kids of his own. Abby was the closest he had to a daughter. The special connection he'd felt the day she'd been handed to him through the flames had lasted twenty-seven years. At least no ex-wife could ever take that away.

He'd brought his phone outside with him, and he opened it now, pressing one button for speed dial. He needed to talk to Asa. When it went right to voice mail, he simply said, "Call me."

He set the phone down and took a gulp of his tea. It was a warm afternoon and he considered a swim but just didn't have the energy. Yawning and rolling the tea bottle across his forehead, for the first time in his career he wondered if it was time to retire.

The phone chimed. Asa.

" 'Bout time," Woody said when he answered.

"Yeah?" His friend's boozy voice assaulted his ear. "What do you want?"

"She's gonna investigate it."

Silence.

Finally, "Can't you stop her?"

Woody sighed, closed his eyes, and rubbed his forehead. "Tried. I've run out of good reasons and she's too smart for bad ones."

Asa cursed.

"Look, what's it matter anyway?" Woody asked, never understanding his friend's wish to keep the case closed. "You're safe up there in Idaho. Just stay put. Why do you think this will bite you in the butt?"

"You don't understand."

"I know I don't. You've never told me everything. But I do know she'll find out. Once she starts digging, she'll find out."

"That's what I'm afraid of."

CHAPTER 10

Abby watched Lil' Sporty for a few minutes from behind two-way glass. Roper stood to her right and Lieutenant Jacoby and Sergeant Page were on her left. She felt a tingle in the back of her neck, a sensation that told her she was on the right track. Abby trusted her instincts, but instincts alone would not gain a conviction. And if Sporty was their man, the hard work of building a solid case was just beginning.

The ex-jockey could easily be mistaken for a teen from a distance. As she reviewed the window entries in her mind, she knew he would have had no problem climbing into the victims' residences. And the two victims were frail; the killer didn't have to be big and strong. But a nonviolent burglar making the leap to serial killer nagged. Lil' Sporty's last arrest had been eighteen months ago, on a charge of receiving stolen property, and he'd spent six months in jail.

Abby wondered if something had happened there to push the burglar to murder. She felt in her gut that the posing of the victims was the key. Almost as if he wanted to leave the women at peace.

As he fidgeted at the interview table, she noted his grimy hands and face. He'd definitely been living in the gutter for a time. By the way he sweated as he twitched in the chair, Abby guessed he needed a fix. His arrest record was long, and being interviewed was nothing new to Lil' Sporty, so Abby knew she'd have to tread lightly. They had little physical evidence, and if he shut up and called for a lawyer, they'd have no interview.

"Found a couple of interesting items in his bag," Page told Abby. He handed her an inventory sheet.

She immediately saw property from the first victim — gold coins. The victim's daughter had told her that her mother had collected them, and Sporty had ten.

"I know what you're thinking," Page said. "I asked about the coins. Sporty says a friend paid a debt with them."

"He name the friend?"

"Someone he just barely met." Page rolled his eyes. "I didn't want to press and have him scream, 'Lawyer.' You'd be madder at me than him."

Abby tilted her head in agreement, then looked at the other items: two rings and a couple of knickknacks. They might have belonged to Cora, but unless someone could tell them for sure . . .

"No gloves or burglar tools?" Bill asked Page.

"No, but he's been to this rodeo more than once. I'm sure he dumped anything and everything that could immediately connect him to actual burgling, especially if he thought someone saw him. Glad that PI came along when he did. We're still looking for where Sporty stayed. He says he's been on the streets, but . . ." Page shook his head.

"I'll see if I can get anything out of him. At least he hasn't lawyered up."

She stepped out to the hallway vending machine. Mountain Dew and a Snickers bar were the ticket. Coming to ground like he was, Sporty would need the caffeine and the sugar.

After petting Bandit once, noting he seemed content in Roper's arms, Abby headed into the interview room. Page held the door open for her, and she walked in to have a conversation with a murder suspect.

Davis looked up at her when she stepped into the room, a grimy finger in the corner

113

of his mouth. His gaze went directly to the food in her hand.

"How's the arm?" Abby nodded to the only clean patch on the man, the bandage covering his stitches.

He looked from her to the Snickers and back again, then sniffled.

"You hungry, Mr. Davis?" Abby asked as she sat across from the burglar.

He swallowed and she saw the Adam's apple in his throat work. "I could eat."

She slid the soda and the candy bar across the table, and he grabbed them, opening the can and drinking at least half before he ripped the wrapper from the candy bar and bit into it.

Abby waited a beat while she watched Lil' Sporty. He was used to telling lies and half-truths to evade in interviews, but if she could find a connection, something that would make him drop his guard, she might get the whole truth from him.

"Do you know why you're here, Mr. Davis?"

His cheek bulged with Snickers bar as he nodded. "You're mad I ran, so you're gonna try and blame me for something, I bet." Bits of chocolate spittle dotted his lower lip.

"I have questions for you." Abby pulled out a Miranda rights form and placed a mini recorder on the desk. She read Davis his rights and explained about the taped interview while he stuffed the rest of the candy bar into his mouth and drained the last bit of soda from the can.

"Yeah, I'll talk," he said after he swallowed. He picked up the pen Abby gave him and scrawled his name on the form, smudging the paper with chocolate and grime. "I didn't do nothing."

Abby arched an eyebrow, thinking about the particulars on his arrest record. It didn't surprise her that he'd quickly signed away his rights. Many career criminals thought easy cooperation would throw the investigators off the scent. They'd make up a plausible story about whatever was asked and outsmart the investigators.

Not me. Not today, Abby thought. "First off, I have easy questions for you. Where are you staying?"

"On the streets." He wiped his nose with a sleeve. "I told Sergeant Page that."

"Before that, an address for parole or government checks?"

He wouldn't meet her eyes. "No one wants to rent to an ex-con."

"You've stayed at the Pacific Hotel before; they don't care about your record."

"Streets are easier."

Abby folded her arms and decided to go a different direction. "What about family? Where does your mother live?"

Davis's head jerked her way, wariness in his eyes. "My mom? She's dead. Died when I was five."

Abby knew from his file his mother was deceased, but she hadn't known when she died. Now she had a connection.

"Sorry to hear that. I know how that goes. I lost my mom when I was six."

Davis ran one hand over the dark stubble on his shaved head before dropping it to the table and rolling the empty soda can back and forth, now watching Abby guardedly. She could see he was wondering where she was going with the line of questioning.

"I was bounced around in foster homes for a bit. Group homes, social services, you probably know the drill. Who raised you?"

Sporty sat up and sniffled. "Grandma. Grew up in Los Alamitos." He looked away.

"Did you learn to ride horses there at the track?"

"Yep. Because of my size I was good at it for a while."

"Is your grandma still in Los Al?"

He shook his head. "No, we moved to Shady Acres about three years ago."

Shady Acres was a trailer park on the west

side, on the other side of Santa Fe about five blocks from Cora Murray's home and within the radius where she expected the killer to live.

He continued to fidget with the empty pop can and appeared to have more to say, so Abby waited.

"She died when I was in jail last. Fell, broke her hip, and no one heard her calling for help. Took three days, but she died. She suffered."

Abby held her breath, watching Davis carefully.

"I hate to think of her suffering," he said in a whisper. "I should have been there. I would have heard her. I would have helped." A tear made a slow trail down his grimy cheek. "Old people shouldn't be left alone."

Abby exhaled, leaned forward, and asked in a quiet voice, "Is that why you killed the old women?"

Lil' Sporty nodded without looking at her. "I did them a favor. They won't suffer —" His head jerked up, and realization spread across his face like a curtain. "I want my lawyer."

Biting back frustration, Abby kept her face expressionless. She had to stop now, but she had enough. There was a foot in the door and she'd find enough evidence to force the door open. She told Davis he'd be booked, then left to confer with Page and Jacoby about getting a search warrant for the trailer Grandma had lived, and died, in.

CHAPTER 11

Relief.

Abby rubbed her neck and yawned. Her bruised shoulder screamed, but now she could finally let herself wind down. Page flashed a smile and a thumbs-up as he led Lil' Sporty away to be booked. Jacoby and Roper were equally congratulatory.

While the brief admission was not a full confession, it was a start. Grandma's address was listed on his last arrest report. They had probable cause to search the place and enough to hold Davis for a preliminary hearing while they worked to build a strong case. Abby felt confident that the serial killer was in custody and the killing would stop, and she knew she could do the work so that the rest would fall into place.

Roper left with Bandit to let Abby finish up some arrest paperwork, and she was glad to ride up in the elevator alone. Rollins should be overjoyed that there was already a suspect in custody.

Will I ever feel like that where my parents are concerned?

Stretching, she approached her office, needing coffee and a second wind to prepare the declaration for the search warrant. The only fly in the ointment was overtime. DC Cox was known for being stingy under normal circumstances. There was no exigency on a search with a suspect in custody, and Abby doubted hers would be approved in any event. Cox would send her new partner, she bet.

She stepped into the homicide office and stopped. Not only was most everyone back from lunch, but Deputy Chief Cox stood next to her desk conversing with Roper. Bandit was back in his place on her visitor's chair.

Lieutenant Jacoby was homicide's direct supervisor, but Cox commanded the entire detective division. She wore a sharp tailored black suit with a thigh-length skirt, a dark-red blouse under the jacket. She looked good and seemed calm and composed, so Abby guessed she'd gotten a handle on the press situation.

"Hart, I hear you have a solid suspect."

"Yes."

"I think you've done enough for today.

Roper can take it from here and call you if he encounters any problems."

Roper cleared his throat. "Uh, Chief, this is Detective Hart's baby. I think she deserves to be in on all of it."

Abby looked away, wishing she could have stopped Roper from pushing that button.

Cox straightened and looked down her nose at Roper, speaking as if she were talking to a four-year-old. "Are you responsible for addressing the city council when overtime runs over budget? I don't think so. Detective Hart has completed her shift with an arrest. You are more than capable of taking it from here and assisting CCAT with a search warrant."

She tapped a toe of her high heel shoe on the floor before turning to leave, but not before pausing to look directly at Abby. "The only dogs allowed in the station are working dogs."

Abby arched one eyebrow but said nothing as the chief continued her exit.

"Pick your battles," Woody would say.

Roper waited until the chief had disappeared. "Wow, I knew she was tough, but that's the first I've seen her like that."

Abby turned to Bandit, who stood in the chair, tail wagging furiously. Seeing the little dog made her smile and forget Cox.

"Don't worry about it," she said as she picked Bandit up. Irritation fled as she held the furry body and let him lick her hand. "I need to review all three crime reports carefully anyway, and I can do that at home. You surely served a lot of warrants in narcotics, so you'll know what to look for when you get in the grandmother's house."

"Thanks for having faith in me. You don't even know me and you trust me with this huge case."

"I trust you to do your job. We have time to build a court case. If you mess something up, then we will have issues. Right now your slate is clean." She closed her desk drawer for emphasis and gave Roper her best Asa look, a look he'd given her often when she was green. "See that it stays that way."

He smiled and for the first time she saw a competent, confident cop, not a nervous new guy. "You got it."

"Have you looked over the first granny murder?"

"Yep, it was the first on my list."

"Touch base with Page about the search warrant. He'll know about how long it will take to get it signed off. While he's doing that, put together a six-pack of photos and show it to our witness, Luke Murphy. I know he said he didn't see the suspect's face clearly, but give it a shot anyway."

Roper grinned. "I'll get right on it."

"Also put the Jenkins file next on your list." She pulled her yellow pad from under a stack of reports and tore off the top sheet. "This was my to-do list on Jenkins for today, but the callout canceled it for me. He was beaten to death at an unknown location and then left in his car in his driveway for his wife to find. But I can't find anything — no enemies, no arguments, nothing that would cause someone to want him dead. If you can make any of these calls today, great. I've hit dead ends for two weeks."

He took the paper from her. "Will do."

Grabbing her bag, she looked at her new partner. "I'm gone. If Murphy can help with the six-pack or if you find anything at Grandma's, call me; I don't care what time. Other than that, see that everything is cleaned up by tomorrow or we'll be starting off on a really bad foot."

Abby hated to admit she felt relieved about going home. The lack of sleep, the brush with the train, and this case that might bring her face-to-face with Lowell Rollins all conspired to throw her off-balance. She felt a little punch-drunk when she got back in her car. She'd decided to make a stop to pick up some dog food for Bandit when the missing flyer and the picture of the smiling young girl caught her attention again. She picked it up and studied it for a minute.

"Why are you running, Nadine?"

Sighing, Abby knew she had to make an additional stop before going home. It wasn't about Murphy; it was about a young girl, possibly in danger. There was a westside hangout called Destination X that had a reputation for attracting runaways and lost souls. It had been on the PD's radar for selling alcohol to minors in the past. That would be the place to ask pertinent questions.

A few minutes later she pulled into the parking lot. Luke Murphy, if he were good, would have been here already, but Abby still got out of the car and headed inside. She knew as she stepped through the door, smelling sweat and stale beer, that if someone had asked her why she was there, she would not have had an answer. She showed the flyer to the manager and received a surly grunt and shake of the head.

"Look —" Abby smacked the counter so the guy would look at her — "this kid is underage. Your license goes if I find out you're harboring an underage runaway. You've lost it before for a similar reason."

"I don't harbor anyone." His piggy little eyes narrowed. "I kick her out two days ago. She tried to sleep here. I kick her out."

Jaw tight, Abby pulled one of her business cards from her pocket and wrote on it, *Call me. I want to help.* She pushed it toward him.

He grunted and glared, clearly not wanting anything to do with her card.

"If she comes in again, just give her this."

Still facing reticence, Abby pulled a twenty out of her pocket. "Here." She handed the card and the twenty to the piggy-eyed man. "If you see her again, give her this card. If she calls me, there's another twenty in it for you."

The money and the card disappeared into his pocket as he pursed his lips.

Abby yawned on the way back to the car, thinking not only had she lost sleep over the runaway, she was out twenty bucks as well.

CHAPTER 12

While he waited for a callback from a client, Luke idly did a Google search for news articles about Abby. He knew he'd read about her over the years. She was a good cop and had been cited for bravery if he remembered right.

He quickly hit pay dirt. She'd been awarded the medal of valor. The heroic incident cited happened while she was still in uniform — a firefight where she risked her life to pull a wounded officer out of the line of gunfire. There was a brief synopsis of her career in bullet points for the article.

She'd never used deadly force and was given a meritorious service award for talking a man out of killing himself after he'd just killed his brother. She'd worked in patrol for five years and then moved on to an auto theft task force, which was her position when this article was written. He found a few more articles, but anytime she was interviewed, her statements were professional and frustratingly brief. The more he read, the more he was intrigued.

The phone rang, but it wasn't his client. It was Bill.

"Just met my new partner," Bill said, telling Luke about Abby Hart and his new assignment. "She asked me to follow up with you, show you a six-pack."

"A six-pack? She has a suspect already?"

"A cat burglar who all but confessed. She knows you didn't see his face clearly, but we're trying to build a case. You mind if I bring it by?"

"Can I meet you somewhere? I have a client to see in Bellflower — just waiting for a confirmation call. How about Tracy's? I hope I can help."

"That would be fine. I think I know why Hart's so good. She's not a glory hog. She had an idea on who the suspect might be, and instead of taking it all on herself, she tags Page and his team to bring him in. Now this gives CCAT a possible homicide collar and she's fine with that. She is in no way a hard person to work with, and what she's done with this case proves she's a team player."

"I'm glad to hear it."

As Luke hung up, he realized he envied

Bill. He'd love to spend eight hours a day with Abby Hart.

When his client finally called, Luke knew he couldn't devote any more time to studying up on the enigmatic detective. He had meetings scheduled that couldn't be postponed. His PI business paid the bills, but often it was feast or famine. In famine he would earn cash working with his stepdad. Now, as his plate filled with work, he didn't want to short anyone, so he switched gears and pulled out the client's file, amazed at how difficult it was to stop thinking about the green-eyed homicide investigator.

CHAPTER 13

Abby parked her car in the driveway but stopped before getting out. There was a large bouquet of flowers on the porch.

Hmm, she thought. *Not my birthday. Not a holiday. What then?*

She got out with Bandit in tow and stepped up to the flowers — her favorite, a mixture of red, white, and yellow roses — and plucked the note off.

Sorry about the argument. Hope your night wasn't too tough. Love, Ethan

She sighed and smiled. "That's why I'm marrying you. You are the most thoughtful man on the face of the earth." Ethan was always quick to apologize. Abby remembered that when they were kids, Ethan was always the peacemaker. He truly was even-tempered and easygoing. Abby wondered why they ever argued, and a twinge of guilt bit. *Is it me?* Too tired to go there, she pushed the thought from her mind and concentrated on simply enjoying Ethan's thoughtfulness.

Heart light, she brought the flowers inside and introduced Bandit to her backyard. He didn't seem particularly impressed. He sniffed the perimeter before scooting back to the door and yawning.

Granted, there wasn't much to be impressed with in her backyard. While Aunt Dede was the consummate gardener, turning two acres into something close to paradise in Oregon, Abby was content with a small lawn she paid someone else to mow for her. When Dede had visited, she'd been pleased with the front yard, which was populated with pretty plants that thrived despite Abby's lack of attention to them. But she'd called the backyard "sparse."

Smiling, Abby stepped aside as the dog pranced back into the house. "I'm right there with you, bucko." She opened the little bag of dog food she'd picked up on the way home and poured some into a cereal bowl.

Setting it down in front of Bandit with water in a matching bowl, she apologized. "Sorry I didn't get you a special food bowl. Maybe this weekend."

Bandit didn't seem to mind as he attacked

the food with gusto.

Abby's smile faded when she picked up the phone to make the last call she planned to make before bed. She studied the card Murphy had given her for a minute. As much as she wanted to dress him down for calling the press, this call wasn't about him; it was about the girl, Nadine. Taking a deep breath, she exhaled and dialed.

Just as she was expecting to leave a voice mail message, Murphy answered.

"Detective Hart." His breathless voice came on the line. "What can I help you with?"

Abby swallowed, mouth suddenly dry, irritated by the feeling of nervousness. "I have some information that may help you." She told him about Destination X and the piggy-eyed manager.

Murphy was silent for a moment. "Thank you. That's good information. Here you are in the middle of a homicide investigation, and you help me out."

Abby flushed, glad this was a phone call and he couldn't see. "It was just a quick stop on the way home, and it was for the girl. I hope you find her."

"Yeah, me too. Oh, uh, by the way, I heard you arrested a suspect in the murder this morning."

She frowned. "Did you find that out when you talked to the press about the homicide?"

"What? No, I haven't talked to the press. Bill Roper is my best friend. He just called to tell me he was bringing a six-pack of photos by. Was my information helpful?"

Bill Roper is his friend. That's why Murphy recognized me, Abby thought.

But if Murphy hadn't talked to the press, who had? There was nothing to be done about it now. *Mud in the tires.*

"Yes, your description brought to mind a person of interest. I had a hunch and my hunch appears to be correct."

"You make it sound as though you just got lucky. I think you know your stuff. You're a good and conscientious detective."

Abby squirmed, uncomfortable with his praise. "It's my job, Mr. Murphy. I take it seriously. Good luck finding your missing girl."

"Well, that's my job, and I take it seriously as well. Thanks again, Detective. I hope we speak again, and when we do, it's Luke."

Abby ended the call and wondered at the effect just hearing the man's voice had on her. She thought of Ethan and bent to smell the roses. Argument forgotten, the two weeks until his return would drag.

Yawning deeply, she walked into her bedroom, more than ready for a hot shower. Peeling off her clothes carefully, she inspected the bruise in the mirror. It was an ugly red-purple color now. She knew it would hurt more tomorrow and over the weekend. An image of the train bearing down on her threatened to bury her and she pushed it back. *I'm fine.*

"No volleyball this weekend," she said to Bandit as she tried to make an overhand serve, grimacing as she did so. She and a mixture of friends — some she'd played with in college, some she knew from church, and one or two from work — had a standing playdate for beach volleyball on the weekends.

Abby stepped into a hot shower, grateful for the soothing heat. She stood there for a long time, letting the frustrations and the aches of the day wash away. Once finished and wrapped in a robe, she stepped to the fridge to grab some milk for her Oreo cookies, her favorite wind-down snack.

Cookies in hand, she stopped at her desk and opened the book that was her personal investigative file into the Triple Seven homicides. The first page was a photocopy of the front page of the newspaper the day after the fire.

Suspicious, Horrific Fire Claims Popular Restaurant and Personable Owners

The murderous details came out later, but this page was Abby's curious favorite. The picture under the headline was of her, looking lost, held snugly in Woody's arms against a backdrop of smoke and emergency vehicles. The expression on Woody's face said he'd protect her to the death. Abby's tousled hair fell over one side of her face, and her right hand gripped his uniform collar. She often stared at the photo and tried to remember that day, tried to see back into that forlorn girl's mind, but she couldn't. The only memories she had came to her from what she had read — generalities about what it was like at her parents' restaurant back then. Her own memories were fragmented, and she didn't know what was real and what was imagined.

Everything changed for her that day. Like the victims she dealt with today, nothing could be put back the way it was. But something inside screamed that she be able to say that the killers had *paid. A part of me will always be that lost little girl until that day.*

She closed the book and settled into her reading chair, a big overstuffed leather chair with a large ottoman, exhausted but unable to shut down. It was early, only four thirty, but she was beat.

Munching Oreos dunked in milk and being in her home office calmed her and erased the bad parts of the day. Three walls were floor-to-ceiling bookcases, and the shelves were about 75 percent full. Against the only wall with a window was her desk. But it was the books that calmed her, entertained her, and kept her sane. When Dede had finally entered the picture and brought her home, adopted her, and became her family, the Bible became the most important book in the mix. It rested on the arm of her chair, and she put her milk down to pick it up and open it to the fourth chapter of Hebrews.

What was the last passage you read, Cora?

Abby's translation titled the chapter "The Promise of Rest." *I hope you entered God's rest, Cora,* she thought. Verses 12 and 13 were well known to Abby; they were memory verses. Verse 12 she'd learned in Sunday school: *"For the word of God is living and powerful, and sharper than any two-edged sword, piercing even to the division of soul and spirit, and of joints and marrow, and is a discerner of the thoughts and intents of the heart."*

And verse 13 she knew by heart. Both

Ethan and Dede used her love of the verse to convince her it was folly to get wrapped up in the twenty-seven-year-old cold case.

"Trust God with your parents' killers," Ethan had said. *"He knows where they are. They aren't getting away with anything."*

"Abby, I lost a sister I barely knew . . . and over what? I don't know. Don't put yourself in danger. Your motto is God's promise: they might run, but they can't hide."

Abby closed the Bible and set it on the arm of the chair again. She chewed on a thumbnail, feeling agitated all of a sudden.

I do trust God.

But I want the killers caught now.

Are the two things mutually exclusive?

Fifteen years ago, when she came back to Long Beach, she was ready to kick down doors. She let Woody and Asa convince her it was wiser to wait. But their *wait* turned into *never.*

I'm done waiting.

Bandit startled her when he jumped into her lap. Unperturbed by her momentary jitter, he curled up in a ball and closed his eyes. She finished the cookies, drained the milk, and ran her hand over the warm, hairy body. She found the feeling of his soft fur comforting.

Hate to say it, but I want to keep this dog.

136

With that thought, Abby closed her eyes and let exhaustion take over.

CHAPTER 14

"Sorry," Luke said with a shake of his head. "I didn't get a good enough look at his face."

He handed the six-pack of photos back to Bill. They sat in a booth at Tracy's, a cop bar and grill in East Long Beach.

Bill put the photos back in his briefcase. "Thanks for trying. I think Hart knew it was a long shot, but she wanted to give it a try anyway. She checks all the boxes." He glanced at his watch. "I've got to run. Serving a search warrant with CCAT."

"I guess you're off the hook for tonight."

"Sorry about that, but things look clear for the weekend. Nice of my partner to give you that lead."

"Sure was. When she took the flyer, I thought she was just being polite. I'd spoken with the night bartender and he said he hadn't seen Nadine. But if that day bartender did see her in Destination X, then she must be in the area, and tonight could be the night I find her and bring her home."

"I'll call you as soon as I'm sure of my schedule," Bill said. His phone buzzed with a text. He slid it off his belt to read it. "From Jacoby. Cox has scheduled a press conference about the granny murders for tomorrow afternoon. I'm to be front and center with Abby. Talk about big-time."

"Will the governor be there?"

Bill nodded.

Luke felt a jolt and chuckled. "The full dog and pony show for the big cheese, huh?"

"Whatever. I'm just glad to be in homicide." He rubbed his hands together.

"I'm happy for you. Now go break a leg."

Luke drove to Destination X as soon as he finished with Bill. The trip would make him late for his aikido workout, but he didn't care. Nadine had been *seen.*

"Oh, Lord, I pray that she'll surface for me, please." He breathed out the prayer as he drove, more hopeful than he had been in a week.

Destination X was filling up. Luke made his way inside and approached the bar. He recognized the squat, unpleasant-looking man as one of the managers. He held up his poster of Nadine.

"She was here?"

The little man gave half a nod and a wave of his hand. "Gone. You go or buy drink."

Luke spent a frustrating fifteen minutes trying to get more out of the man, but the workday had ended for a lot of the folks employed on the west side and the manager was busy.

Luke stepped outside, glad to be out of the beer-tainted air, and looked around. PCH was packed with traffic as daylight began to dim. The street vibrated with big rigs coming and going from the harbor, some on to LA. Voices chatted around pitchers, and he could smell food frying. It bit that he had to give up, had to admit defeat another night.

Nadine, where are you?

After meeting with clients and Bill, searching for Nadine, and missing his martial arts class completely, Luke returned home tired and frustrated. He sat at the computer to write up his client's report. But once he logged in, he saw the Google alert he'd set up for Lowell Rollins. It confirmed what Bill had said. Governor Rollins would be here in Long Beach for the press conference. The alert said he'd canceled some high-level meetings and rearranged a

140

crowded schedule for the appearance.

Luke studied the governor's photo, tapping on the desk with his fingers. The man wasn't a bad guy as far as politicians went. He was popular in the state because he kept a lot of the campaign promises he'd made. He had a reputation for having a big heart and for helping those who were hurting, and he managed to do it without appearing to be pandering for votes. Luke found him believable and had voted for him twice.

But even being a voter hadn't gotten Luke the audience he wanted. He hadn't been able to talk to Rollins about the Triple Seven murders. Two people in addition to his uncle had died in the fire that consumed the trendy restaurant. Buck and Patricia Morgan were part owners of the place with Lowell Rollins.

Now that the governor himself had lost family to murder, maybe he'd be more receptive to talking to Luke. Every day when he reviewed the twenty-seven-year-old murder, he knew that only new evidence would get the governor's attention.

New evidence in a twenty-seven-year-old unsolved murder was a tall order.

CHAPTER 15

The call woke Abby up after she'd just dozed off.

"Hey, you're not asleep, are you?" It was Megan, a teammate from college and her oldest friend in the city who was not a cop. They'd been roommates for five years until Megan got married.

"I had a callout," Abby said with a yawn.

"Is that why you're kissing Blue Line wheels all over the Internet?"

"Huh?" Abby stretched and struggled to clear her foggy brain.

"There's this video going around. Some tourist uploaded it to YouTube and it's going viral. You yanked someone off the tracks."

"That's on the Internet already?" Now fully awake, Abby wondered if this was good or bad. She wasn't beating anyone with her nightstick in the video, so she hoped it was a positive, not a negative.

Megan laughed. "The wonders of technology! Are you okay?" Megan was a physical therapist, so Abby knew the next question would be "Can I help?"

"I'm sore, that's all. The tourist knew my name?"

"I recognized you; the tourist just called you a hero. You up for some Chinese? Mitch is out of town and I hate to eat alone. Besides, I want to hear the train story. And help you out with your aches if I can."

Crumbs on the arm of her chair reminded Abby about her dinner of Oreos. "Yeah, I probably should eat some real food."

"Cool. I'll be over in a few. Any specific requests?"

"Surprise me." When she ended the call, Abby stretched again, causing Bandit to hop off her lap. After a few minutes she went to her room to dress, glad Megan had called. While she loved working alone, at home she liked having company. An empty house was not her favorite thing.

For some reason Abby's mood deteriorated after she climbed into a pair of sweats and a T-shirt.

"*Should* I have said yes to Megan?" she asked Bandit, who wagged his tail in response. She was tired and irritated. Ir-

143

ritated because she was tired.

"I won't be good company." She talked as she straightened up the dining room and kitchen. The little dog followed her from room to room, and she decided that he understood everything she said.

"Megan is on her way. I can't call and cancel now." She grabbed a Diet Coke from the fridge, hoping the caffeine would wash away the irritation. After the first sip she laughed out loud at how easy it was to talk to the dog.

"Maybe I'm crazy, Bandit. Maybe my job is making me certifiably wacko."

The dog just wagged his tail.

The doorbell rang. Abby opened it to see Megan and another friend, Jessica, at the door with a huge bag of Chinese food. Irritation fled at the sight of her smiling friends, and she waved them inside.

"I decided to bring a ride-along." Megan smiled; then her eyes got big. "Ooo, who's the little guy?"

Both Jessica and Megan went crazy over Bandit. Abby had met Jessica while at work. She'd been the victim of a domestic violence situation while Abby was still in uniform. Once freed from her abuser, Jessica embarked on a mission to become independent and physically fit and strong.

She and Abby became fast friends and sometimes gym partners. Jessica eventually became a part of the beach volleyball rotation, which was how she met Megan.

"He belonged to a victim from last night," Abby explained as she closed the door. The two women acted as if Bandit were the cutest thing ever. Abby didn't stop them because she agreed.

"I didn't have the heart to dump him off at animal control, so here we are."

"What's his name?" Jessica asked.

"Bandit. What are you doing here? I thought you were working parties all week."

"Tonight's got canceled. I ran into Megan at the Fortune Cookie and decided to invite myself over here."

"I'm glad," Abby said, and she meant it, irritation forgotten. "The more the merrier. Looks like you brought enough food for an army."

Megan held the bags up and headed for the dining room table. "Whatever is left over I'll take home for Mitch. Hope you're hungry." She saw the flowers. "Oh, gorgeous! From Ethan?"

"Yes, and yes to being hungry." Abby's stomach growled.

"Fill us in on the train," Megan said as she set the food down.

Jessica picked up Bandit and carried him to the table. "And maybe bring out your laptop. I haven't seen the video."

"Let's eat first."

Abby grabbed plates, silverware, and serving spoons from the kitchen, and her friends efficiently spread everything out and began serving.

"You pray," Abby said to Megan when they were ready to eat. "I'm still not awake."

"Sure thing. Lord, we thank you for the food and for protecting our crazy friend from her crazy impulses to save people. Bless it all . . ."

Megan and Jessica said a resounding *amen.*

"Aw," Abby protested. "Like anyone could just stand there and let someone get crushed by a train."

Jessica laughed. "We know you couldn't, which is one of the reasons we love you."

"So this poor little guy's owner got murdered last night?" Megan asked, pointing to Bandit.

"Umm, yeah, she did," Abby said with a mouth full of mu shu pork.

"You catch the bad guy?" Jessica asked.

Abby swallowed her food and a swig of Diet Coke. "I did. There'll be a big press conference about it tomorrow."

146

Jessica gave her two thumbs up.

"Oh, don't tell me the killer was the guy you saved from the train?" Megan dropped her chopsticks.

"Well, when I saved him from the train, I wasn't certain he was the killer. I am now." Abby told them about the granny murders, her witness, and Lil' Sporty.

"From time to time I wonder how you do it, how you deal with poor murdered people all the time," Megan said with a shake of her head.

"Sometimes it's rough." Abby dug into the chicken with snow peas, content. It was good to have friends.

"Yeah, but it's got to be satisfying when you put them away. I know the most satisfying day of my life was when the jury said guilty and Rory was out of my life for good." Jessica did a brief drumroll on the table.

"That, and knowing they won't ever hurt anyone else gives me satisfaction."

Jessica had unfolded like a flower once her ex was gone for good. The confident woman before her now bore little resemblance to the fearful woman Rory Brennan had beaten down. Justice put things right.

The governor invaded her thoughts and inevitably dragged them to her parents. The burning need to have her own life righted almost caused Abby to tell her friends her secret — about the hole in her life, her need for justice, and what drove her at a personal level. They'd understand, especially Jessica. But she hesitated.

" 'When justice is done, it brings joy to the righteous,' " she said after she swallowed. "That's in Proverbs somewhere. People who suffered the worst kind of wrong deserve a little joy."

They toasted, Abby with her Diet Coke and the others with water.

"So who was your witness?" Megan asked.

"What?"

"You said you had a witness who helped you decide on the jockey. Who helped?"

"A PI named Luke Murphy."

"Get out!" Jessica dropped her food back on her plate. "Mr. Hottie to the max?"

Abby grimaced but Megan chimed in.

"He is beyond hot! Oh, my goodness, if I weren't married . . ."

"Listen to you two. You sound like you're still in high school." Abby dished out some more noodles, irritation returning with the subject of Murphy.

"Come on, you're not married yet. And Ethan is hot in his own way, and he did send flowers," Jessica said with a shrug.

"Thanks." Abby looked down her nose at

them and they laughed.

"When does he get back?"

"Two weeks. I miss him; I'm ready for him to be home."

"You didn't say that with much conviction." Megan tilted her head. "Is he still having a hard time with your job?"

Abby sat back, full now and relaxed. "I do miss him. But yeah, we had another argument. He really doesn't like me working homicide."

"Ah, sweetie, has he asked you to quit?"

"Well, not bluntly, but he's moving that way."

"I thought he was proud of the work you did," Jessica said.

"He was, six months ago. We need to have a good talk, not a Skype talk."

Megan began closing food containers. "He's a reasonable guy. I know you two can work it out."

Abby nodded, wondering why the subject of Ethan brought Murphy to her mind. The rest of the conversation centered on Ethan and missions in general. She couldn't wait to see Ethan, but she kept thinking of Murphy.

CHAPTER 16

Friday morning the station buzzed with excitement over the — what was now plural — granny murders case and the impending visit by the governor. Abby received kudos from several coworkers as she walked in, and it served to lift her spirits.

"When justice is done, it brings joy to the righteous."

Bill was at his desk when she stepped into the office. He'd called her the night before, as she was climbing into bed after Megan and Jessica left, and gushed about the successful search warrant, giving her the high points.

"We found loss from the first burglary and black gloves like the type Luke thought he saw on the suspect. There are other items here that I wonder about; maybe they came from the second victim. This guy is toast!"

His excitement had actually made her smile. He'd reminded her of her first partner after she was off probation on graveyard patrol. A good-natured guy, Ty Wagner took a lot of ribbing because he had one of those forever-youthful faces; his nickname was Doogie. But he was a good partner and he made coming to work interesting.

Abby realized she'd been so stressed struggling with Asa at the end of their partnership, she'd forgotten what it was like to have a partner who pulled his weight.

"Good morning," she said as she set her bag down and headed for coffee.

He smiled and pointed to her desk. "I put a copy of the search warrant findings there for you."

"Thanks. I look forward to reading it."

Once she settled in with her coffee and read the entire report, she acknowledged Roper was right — the findings were great news. There were some expensive-looking items that couldn't be placed, but they could be from the Murray household.

She said to Roper, "I'd like to be able to show the governor these pictures and ask if he recognizes anything." The case didn't hinge on his identification of loss, but it would strengthen it and give her a chance for some face time.

"Ditto," Roper agreed.

The phone rang and Abby frowned; it was

a reporter from channel two. "They're starting early," she muttered.

Roper laughed. "It's been ringing since I
got here. I answered one and they told me
about a video of you making the rounds."

That got Abby's attention. "What? They're
calling about that?"

"Yep, they're wanting to know about the
guy you saved." He grinned.

"It wasn't that big a deal." She wished
she'd brought out her laptop and viewed
the thing last night.

"It was close, though."

She wondered if this was going to be more
trouble for her than she'd thought.

"Heads up." Lieutenant Jacoby strode into
the office. "Press conference is set for 1 p.m.
Rollins arrived last night and will give a
statement."

"Can I be at lunch for the conference but
still have a request for the governor?" Abby
said it jokingly, but the LT didn't crack a
smile.

"Nope, and from what I've seen, you like
the cameras."

It was worse than she thought. Abby
groaned. "Am I in trouble for that?"

"You could have been killed."

"I could be killed on the 405 freeway any
day." She held her hands out, palms up.

Jacoby glared. "You're lucky the video is being shown with the caption 'Hero cop.' But Cox has seen it and I don't think she's happy you took such a risk."

"I couldn't have stopped short and watched him get smashed. I wouldn't have been able to live with myself."

The lieutenant scowled. "I know. That's why you're so good at what you do. You stuck to him like superglue. But please be careful. I have no idea if Cox will weigh in on it or not." His phone beeped, and as he took it off his belt to read the text, he left the office.

I'm not going to worry about Cox, Abby thought. *There's too much to do.* She pulled out the contact list for the relatives of the previous victim. They all deserved to know the status of the investigation and not to hear it at a press conference.

CHAPTER 17

Where is Nadine?

Luke was stuck, so he went back to the beginning, poring over everything he knew about the girl. Nadine left home, telling her mother she was going to work to pick up her pay and then catch a ride with her best friend.

Luke's first stop had been the recycling yard where Nadine worked. But her boss, George Sanders, had been no help at all. He'd even been noncommittal about Nadine being at work that day. Sanders should have been the last person to see her at Crunchers, but he claimed that he had not.

"Her money is gone, so she picked it up." He tapped his fists together. "That's all I know. I didn't see her. We were busy."

When Luke pressed, Sanders got angry. "She's just a wild kid. She'll come home when she's good and ready. Her mother is wasting money by hiring you." He'd slammed the door in Luke's face.

Crunchers was not far from Destination X. If Nadine had swung by Crunchers, picked up her pay, and run away, Destination X was not out of the realm of possibility as a stopping point. But running away to the west side of Long Beach from the east side, where Nadine lived, made no sense, unless drugs were involved. Luke was certain drugs were not Nadine's problem. She didn't have a boyfriend, and Luke had spoken to anyone and everyone who considered her a friend.

Crunchers — and Sanders — always seemed to be under criminal investigation for something or other. Nadine only worked there because Janey Sanders was her best friend and the two were always there together. The day Nadine disappeared, Janey had arrived late, and she was no more help than her father, but she was a lot more concerned. She cried and tried to help, but her stepdad forbade Luke from dragging her into the investigation. Sanders was a gruff, blunt businessman Luke would never trust.

"He's shady." Tears had spilled down Glynnis Hoover's face the last time they spoke. "I never should have let her work there."

"Hindsight is twenty-twenty. Don't blame yourself, Glyn. It wastes energy that we need to use to find her," he told her.

When he went back to the beginning, Crunchers smacked him between the eyes. Something happened there; something made her run. If Nadine hadn't texted her mother that she was fine and she'd call after a while, the police would have been all over the recycling yard.

Luke felt like banging his head against the wall. Right now it would be as productive as anything else. He rubbed his tired eyes, then checked his watch. Madison would be through with her morning lessons. Every time he talked with Glynnis and endured her grief, he felt an overwhelming desire to see, touch, and talk to his daughter. He had time to take Maddie out to Serenity Park for some lunch. There was a hot dog vendor there that they both loved. They could spend an hour or so out there, and he'd get back in plenty of time for her afternoon session. Today was Friday, so she'd be working with the homeschool group at church in the afternoon.

At home Madison jumped for joy at the break in routine. While she changed her clothes, Luke closed his files. He didn't want work to overshadow time with his daughter.

Serenity Park was a beautiful, grass-covered portion of a jetty. To Luke, it was also a memorial park.

Luke picked up a picture of the old restaurant he kept at his desk, a picture of his uncle Luke with Buck and Patricia Morgan and Lowell Rollins. Back then Grace was a single mother and Uncle Luke was the only father figure in Luke's life. His mother had snapped the photo a couple of weeks before the fire. Uncle Luke had just received a top cooking award, and the group was all smiles with a gorgeous blue ocean spreading out behind them.

The restaurant was in the background off to the right, and it was a very stylish place in its day. The fire was believed to have been set to cover up a robbery/homicide. Lowell Rollins, who'd been in Sacramento at the time of the tragedy, became the sole owner. When the smoke settled and the police released the scene to be cleaned up, Rollins didn't want the parcel of land redeveloped, so for a few years the lot stood barren. Rollins became a city councilman and began a campaign to turn the area into a park. Eventually he was successful.

Five years after the tragic fire, the entire area — parking lot and all — was graded and seeded, and now a beautiful park spread out to the edge of the jetty with the appearance of an infinity lawn. A small plaque commemorated the three people who'd died in the fire.

Buck and Patricia were killed by gunfire before the flames charred their remains, while Luke's uncle died of smoke inhalation later in the hospital.

Any evidence was long gone, but Luke often found his jogging path took him to Serenity Park, or he and Madison would be out there flying kites on Saturdays. He prayed out there, for Big Luke and the Morgans, that someday he'd find justice for them all. His uncle's loss still cut deep, and the name Lowell Rollins reminded him how badly he wanted the case solved.

But today he and his daughter would eat hot dogs and enjoy the park. Today his prayers would be for Nadine, that soon he'd find her and bring her home.

CHAPTER 18

Walter Gunther was leaning against a parking structure pylon when Abby pulled into a space after lunch. She realized he was waiting for her when he gave her a mock salute. A cigarette hung from his mouth, and he looked rumpled and irritated.

That's what I get for being predictable about where I park, she thought.

"This could be construed as stalking," Abby said as she grabbed her bag and shut the car door.

"Wouldn't have to hang around in the shadows if you'd return my phone calls."

Abby stopped. She should have checked her voice mail and called him back. Gunther had never done her a wrong turn.

"Sorry; it's been hectic." She waved a hand toward the gathering crowd of press and onlookers in front of the podium outside the station's front door. "Not much I can tell you; you'll have to watch the flea circus."

Gunther dropped the cigarette and ground it out with the toe of his shoe. "I plan to. But that's not what I wanted to talk to you about. I had a question about the Dan Jenkins murder."

Abby arched her eyebrows. "Jenkins?"

Gunther nodded. "I liked him; he was a good guy. Have you made any headway on his case? I live in what would have been his council district. His loss is huge to my neighborhood."

Abby pursed her lips and considered his question. Jenkins had just filed papers to run for city council. She'd stayed awake for forty-eight hours straight trying to find a suspect and a motive or to ascertain where he'd been killed — all to no avail.

"Sorry, Gunther. I've hit a dead end. But I did send some evidence we got off his clothing to the feds. We don't have the technology to process it, but they may be able to tell us something. It's a priority for me, but you know they have their own timetable. I've got a new partner now, and that case will be back at the top of my list ASAP. I promise we'll get right back on it."

Gunther pulled out another cigarette and put it in his mouth but didn't light it. "Dan and his wife are good people. I know you won't let it go cold."

"No, I won't."

The reporter smiled. "I might have some information that can help. When you have a minute, call me."

"I will. But right now I have to get to —"

"The circus. Yep, I have to go find my spot too. Though I'm too big to ever be mistaken for a flea." He gave her another mock salute and lumbered for the crush of press.

Abby followed him out of the garage but then veered off in a different direction, looking for familiar faces. She'd talked to all the granny murder relatives and apprised them of the situation with Sporty. The daughter of the first victim had indicated she would be at the press conference. Abby picked Marion Snyder out right away.

Taking a detour, she approached Marion. "Miss Snyder?"

The woman turned slowly. Suffering from rheumatoid arthritis, she was bent over from the waist and had difficulty moving her head. The joints of her hands looked more gnarled than the last time Abby had seen her.

"Detective Hart, do you have any more to tell me?"

Abby bent down to hold the woman's gaze, not wanting to force her into an uncomfortable position. There were tears in her eyes.

"I'm certain we have the right man. But the court process may grind slowly."

"No matter. This is an answer to prayer." She grasped Abby's hand in her bent and twisted fingers. "Thank you so much. I've forgiven the man in my heart, but he still must face justice. Perhaps that will save his soul."

Abby acknowledged the woman's words and scanned the crowd before continuing on to the podium. They were waiting on the governor, and a couple of the governor's security staff checked her credentials as she headed to her place. She found Roper and stood next to him and half listened as he told her about security procedures because of the governor's presence.

The words Marion Snyder had said stuck in her mind like a warp on a CD. *"I've forgiven the man in my heart."* Abby'd had the forgiveness discussion with her aunt Dede many times. Abby always *said* she could forgive her parents' killers but never felt it at her core, in her heart. It struck her then that Marion obviously *felt* the forgiveness.

Will I ever be at that point? she wondered.

When she saw the governor, she knew that

no, she wouldn't. He was her father's age, and he'd had a productive twenty-seven years. What might her father have done if he'd not been stopped by a killer's bullet? *No,* she thought, *I won't be able to feel the forgiveness. Not as long as the killers evade justice.*

How do you forgive a monster?

Especially when the monster has never paid for his crime.

Content to stay in the background during the press conference, Abby studied the principals while Bill fidgeted next to her. She wished he'd relax. But she knew that most cops would rather face a carload of hostile gang members than a bunch of clamoring reporters, so she cut him some slack.

Cox wanted the spotlight and Abby was more than happy to let her have it. She focused on Governor Rollins, his wife, and the entourage around them. One person in particular caught her attention. Gavin Kent was the governor's chief of staff, and she found his body language intriguing. Though there was plenty of security everywhere — they were in front of a police station for pete's sake — Abby got the feeling Kent, a short, thickly built man, was tensed to body-block anyone he perceived as a threat to Rollins. He was very imposing with a hard stare and ramrod-straight posture, packing in a shoulder holster, she could tell. That surprised her as well. She'd have thought a glorified personal secretary would leave the firearms to security professionals.

Rollins was average in height and thin. His features reminded Abby of a gaunt distance runner. He'd been a marathon runner in the past, but she'd read that a knee injury ended that hobby. His gray hair was neatly styled and his suit looked well-tailored and expensive. Obviously in his element, he appeared relaxed and unaffected by grief at the moment. Alyssa Rollins probably qualified as a trophy wife. A tad taller than her husband, dark-red hair set perfectly, she seemed to glow. But her face wore a fake, frozen smile. Abby bet she really didn't want to be here.

When Rollins stepped to the podium, he was brief, to the point, and eloquent, almost the exact opposite of Chief Cox. Rollins's tone was charismatic, bordering on mesmerizing, and Abby guessed that was one reason he was so successful at winning votes. When he spoke, she heard grief in his voice.

"My aunt Cora was a precious lady, dignified and independent. She lived a long, productive life, and it breaks our hearts to see it end this way. I have every confidence in the Long Beach Police Department to successfully prosecute the individual responsible."

Abby tuned him out as he started to list the people he thanked for handling the homicide proficiently. She wanted five minutes with him but wasn't certain she'd get them. She'd noticed over the years that when high-powered people were involved with the police, they didn't want to deal with peons; they wanted the top dog. Since the chief was out of the country at the moment, the top dog was Cox, and she knew Cox would never give up any of her face time with Rollins, especially for Abby.

The governor yielded the podium to Cox for an update on the investigation. While Cox droned on, obviously not even going to let the district attorney speak, Abby reviewed the search warrant findings in her head. She'd spoken with the DA briefly before the conference and knew that she had no trouble with the circumstantial case they had right now and would proceed to file charges.

She heard Cox call for the last question and tuned back in, not wanting to miss a minute with Rollins if she had the chance.

To her surprise, Kent approached her.

"Detective Hart, the governor would like a word with you, please." He gestured toward the front door of the station and all but ignored Roper. A security agent moved to push the door open.

Abby looked into Kent's focused, unreadable gaze. "Certainly. My partner as well?"

Annoyance flashed in his eyes and a muscle in his jaw jumped, but he nodded to Bill.

Abby turned and headed into the station, Bill on her heels and Kent behind him.

CHAPTER 19

Luke listened to the press conference on the radio as he and Madison drove home from the park. Neither Hart nor Bill spoke; it was all Deputy Chief Cox and Governor Rollins.

Hot air, Luke thought. The gritty details of the investigation wouldn't be made public; he knew that. Cox sounded as if she were preening for the cameras and was probably bucking for an appointment somewhere. She and the governor said a lot without saying a lot.

When it ended and the station resumed its regularly scheduled programming, he wondered if he'd have any chance to get to Rollins before the governor returned to Sacramento.

"Earth to Papa, earth to Papa."

"Uh, sorry. What?" Luke glanced at his daughter in the backseat.

"I thought we were getting smoothies. You

missed the turn."

"I did, didn't I? I guess my mind was elsewhere," Luke said sheepishly as he pulled into the left turn lane to make a U-turn.

Madison gave him a silly grin, and he realized he needed to concentrate on what was most important now. Sighing, he prayed he'd get the chance to talk to Rollins but also reminded himself that Maddie came first, followed by his work and most pressing case, and that was finding Nadine. Madison loved smoothies, and while Luke would rather have a triple shot espresso, he loved spending this kind of time with his daughter. He settled for a Caribbean blast and listened as she told him about her day.

Bill called while he and Madison were enjoying their smoothies.

"Got some good news for you, buddy."

"You talked to the governor."

Bill chuckled. "Not quite. But the governor had his chief of staff deliver an odd request for you and my partner."

"Both of us? Don't leave me in suspense. What was it?"

"He wants Hart to meet him at his aunt's house and let him do a walk-through."

"That doesn't sound so odd. What does it have to do with me?"

"I'll explain tomorrow night. Got to go."

Luke protested to dead air.

Throwing his hands up, he made a face in the rearview mirror at Madison, who giggled.

"I'm getting my chance." Abby heard breathing, but Woody said nothing for a long moment.

"I saw the press conference," he said finally. "He's gonna talk to you about the Triple Seven?"

"Not yet, but he wants to meet me at Cora's house for a walk-through."

"One-on-one?" He let out a long, low whistle. "You lucked out. Just be careful once who you are gets out."

"Of course. You trained me; how can you not trust me to take care of myself?"

"It's not that. It's just . . ." He paused. "I guess sometimes in my mind's eye you're still that little girl wrapped in a wet towel. Even after all these years I can't get my mind around the fact that someone wanted you to burn to death."

"It's past time they paid."

He sighed — with resignation, Abby thought.

"Be ready for the attention. You'll be a story for a bit."

"I've been ready, Woody, since the day I pinned on the badge."

Abby worked to quell her rising excitement as she ended the call. Rollins had been interviewed three times by Puff and Puff More right after the murders. She'd memorized every word of every interview. He knew nothing, was shocked that such a horrific crime could happen. The two Puffs believed his shock and grief to be genuine.

Her burning question had also been asked by the Puffs, but she needed to ask it again. *Who hated my parents so much that they would murder them and then incinerate everything about them?*

When she'd promoted to homicide, she tried to talk Asa into reactivating the investigation. He told her they'd need something big.

"Be patient," he'd growled, killing her optimism.

As her optimism resurrected, she could see a light, a reason to believe her patience had paid off. It didn't even bother her that she'd have to call Murphy.

It had amused her to see Cox's face change colors when Rollins specifically requested her and *a civilian* for the walk-through. But Abby didn't like that someone else was calling the shots in her investigation. And it bugged her that all the requests were made by Kent as if the governor himself were speaking. Maybe it was protocol, but to Abby, it was weird.

CHAPTER 20

At midnight, Luke was back in the westside neighborhood near Destination X. He spent most of the early morning hours in or around the place looking, asking questions when people would allow it. He came up empty and called it a night about 3 a.m.

In spite of the big case and putting in a lot of his own time learning his new assignment, Bill joined him to search on Saturday night. Luke anticipated something important from his buddy. He was not prepared for the magnitude of Bill's announcement.

"I'll answer all your questions now," Bill said as he hopped into Luke's truck.

"I oughta smack you for making me guess for twenty-four hours. You can't imagine what's been going through my mind. What's up?"

"Kent would like you to be there when Rollins does a walk-through of his aunt's house with Hart."

"Me?" Luke pointed at his chest with his thumb, certain the astonishment showed.

"Yep, it's a royal flush, dude. Kent had a lot of conditions for the meeting at Murray's home. You were one of them." Bill shook his head. "Am I jealous. He wants to thank you for making the 911 call. Says the governor realizes his aunt may have stayed undiscovered for a while if you hadn't made that call. I also got the vibe that he feels a bit guilty about not keeping in touch with his aunt."

"Considering how rich he is and how she lived . . . from what I saw, maybe a little guilt is justified."

"Maybe. Anyway, he claims he wants to be certain the meeting is well out of the spotlight because it's a private matter."

"I don't know what to say. This is beyond what I expected."

"Count your blessings. It's happening tomorrow and has to be at the drop of a hat. Kent will call Hart, she'll call you, and you both have to be ready in like twenty minutes to meet him at the scene."

Luke frowned. "That's for security reasons?"

"That's what he said, but that guy is a tad paranoid. Maybe it goes with the territory.

You can always say no."

"Not likely."

Bill grunted. "Don't I know it. I'd love to be there. Regarding your uncle's murder, this may be the break you've been waiting for."

"A divine appointment?" Luke smiled and thought for a moment. "He give any indication when he might call tomorrow? Early? Late?"

"No. Last I spoke to Hart, she said she was hoping to get it out of the way early."

"I was out late last night and plan the same tonight. I sure hope when I get the call, I'm awake."

Luke remembered the promise he'd made to himself to concentrate on Nadine, so he changed the subject back to her as they drove to the truck stop on PCH, where he parked. They talked about what she was last seen wearing and just where a kid from the east side of Long Beach was likely to hide in the roughest part of the west side.

After an hour or two of talking to people and searching, Luke began to feel hopeless.

"It's like she's disappeared off the face of the planet," he said to Bill. It was around one, early Sunday morning, and he had to be at church by eight. "It's been over a week. Where is she sleeping? What is she

174

eating? How is she living?"

Bill clamped a hand on his shoulder. "Buddy, you've done all you can do for one weekend. For all we know she's watching us from the shadows and hiding every time we get close. You need to get some sleep. You have other kids depending on you."

Luke knew he was right. As youth pastor, he had thirty youngsters expecting him to be bright and chipper at church in the morning. Losing this one just hurt so much. He turned to Bill, but it was the man behind Bill on the other side of the parking lot that caught his eye. The man was watching them.

"What?" Bill asked.

"Don't turn around. There's a guy in the parking lot watching us."

Bill chuckled. "Probably a drug dealer who made me for a cop."

"No, I've seen him before. He was at Crunchers."

"Nadine worked there, right?"

"Yeah. I went there to talk to Sanders. I know that guy was in the yard, watching me then. He looks like a bouncer. Remember that big kid we met in Iraq? He watched the market for his father?"

"He's that big? Could it be a coincidence?"

"I doubt it. Let's take a walk and see if he

175

follows."

They left Destination X and crossed the street to Hotel Pacific, a seedy hotel Luke had watched the night before. Prostitutes went in and out of rooms all night. He and Bill strolled down Pacific Coast Highway, continuing to look left and right. The highway rumbled with truck traffic even this late. The twenty-four-hour truck stop was busy.

Luke could see that the big guy stayed on the other side of the street but was still following them. "He's still there, sticking with us."

"I see him. Boy, that's a BUG if I ever saw one," Bill said with a tilt of his head.

Luke smiled at the reference and agreed. He'd been in the academy long enough to know that BUG was an acronym from riot training for "big ugly guy," the guy you wanted in front in a skirmish line when you faced a riotous crowd.

Bill rubbed his hands together. "All right, let's be proactive. We'll cross back and confront him. I'll badge him and find out what his major malfunction is."

They started to do just that, but the tall man ducked into an alley and disappeared. Luke picked up his pace until he heard a car door slam. He and Bill reached the alley in time to see the red taillights of a vehicle disappear around a corner and out of sight at the other end.

"So much for that," Luke said, feeling exhaustion in every fiber of his soul. "I hate this to sound like it's a last resort, but I guess I just have to leave Nadine to God."

Bill smiled grimly. "Yeah, I guess you do. Let's pray."

They bowed their heads and prayed for Nadine and for any other lost teen in need.

Glad she could wait until Sunday for the call, Abby spent Saturday morning sipping coffee and reading up on the care of dogs. She downloaded a few books to her Kindle and skimmed through them.

By noon she was reasonably certain she could be a good dog owner. And while she knew this was way over the top, that there was at least a fifty-fifty chance the governor would want the dog, she visited a local pet store and bought a couple of cute ceramic bowls and a dog bed for Bandit, found a vet nearby, and made an appointment for a checkup. Her brain told her the money might be wasted, but her heart — knowing that the dog had lost his owner, his home, and everything familiar — drove Abby to make him feel comfortable and safe for the time he was in her care.

After she put his new stuff out, she hooked on his leash and they took a walk around the block, which seemed to be enough work for Bandit. Since his owner had been so advanced in years, Abby figured the little guy didn't get much exercise, so she wasn't going to push it.

The only annoyance of the day was the fact that, intertwined with her thoughts about Rollins, thoughts of Murphy kept invading.

What is it about him that sticks in my mind?

I love Ethan. Why does a showboat affect me this way?

Why didn't he finish the academy?

Why would a guy like him even appeal to me in the first place?

CHAPTER 21

After the second cup of coffee, Luke felt human. Not awake — four hours' sleep was not enough — but human. He arrived at church an hour before service time and alone. Madison would come with her grandparents in time for the service a little later. He doubted the governor's call would come before the service started.

"Pastor Luke."

The tiny voice startled him. He knew he wouldn't be the first in the sanctuary. The pastor was already here and so was the worship team. But he wasn't expecting the petite teenage girl he saw appear from the shadows to his left. It was Janey Sanders.

"Janey, I'm so glad to see you. Where have you been?" He grabbed her in a safe half hug and didn't miss the fact that her eyes were red from crying.

"My stepdad didn't want me to come to youth group. He thinks because Nadine ran away, I might run away too." She sniffled and rubbed her nose with a sleeve. "Why haven't you found her yet?"

The question pierced like a knife. Luke sighed and directed Janey to the back of the sanctuary, where they could sit and talk. The worship team was onstage, but they hadn't started playing yet.

"I've looked everywhere I can think to look. Is there anything else you can tell me? Are you sure Nadine didn't say something that might be a clue as to where she could've run away to?"

Janey shook her head. "The only weird thing that happened was something my stepdad told me not to mention."

Luke sat back in his chair, biting off a sharp "What was that?" A question that would ask Janey to disobey her father. Did he want to go there? Janey must have seen the struggle in his features.

"I have to tell you if it might help find Nadine."

"What happened?"

"These two guys came to Crunchers to talk to my stepdad. They creeped Nadine out and weren't very nice. She said she had to turn up her music because they were yelling and cussing."

"What were they upset about?"

"She didn't say. They were yelling at my stepdad, and she said they looked scary."

"Scary how?"

Janey looked down at her feet. "You can't tell my stepdad, but he has a security camera at Crunchers that he can access from home. No one else is supposed to touch it; he has it password protected. I was home and Nadine texted me, saying I had to look because one of the guys in my dad's office reminded her of André the Giant from *The Princess Bride.*"

"Were you able to do that? What about the password?"

Janey rolled her eyes. "Please. He picks the easiest ones. Anyway I only looked for a minute, but she was right; he was big like André and mean-looking. Later she texted that they had left and she felt like the place needed to be fumigated because of all the bad language that had been used."

Luke thought about the big man who'd shadowed him and Bill while they searched for Nadine. "Did these guys say something to Nadine to make her want to run away?" His phone buzzed, but he ignored it, letting it go to voice mail. He'd wanted to speak to Janey for a week and a half.

"I don't know. All I know is it's the only thing that happened out of the ordinary. I had to tell you. Maybe it means something. Anyway, the guys were mad at my stepdad about something."

"Do you know what made them mad?"

She shook her head and chewed a thumbnail. "I think Nadine said they wanted something and my dad didn't know where it was. Uh . . ."

"What? Is there something else?"

"I just realized — you know Nadine wants to be a police officer or an investigator like you someday."

"Yeah, she's told me as much."

"She might have . . . Well, she was curious about what the men wanted. Suppose she wanted to find out?"

Luke frowned. "How could she?"

She studied her bitten nails. "Promise you won't tell my stepdad?"

"I can't make that promise if I don't know what you're going to say."

She thought about that for a minute. "Okay, we know how to review the security tape. One time I thought my dad was meeting with another woman. We figured it out."

Luke knew this was important. He'd never seen cameras at Crunchers, but if they were there . . .

"The office is videotaped?"

Her head bobbed up and down. "The

whole place has cameras everywhere. My stepdad is paranoid about people stealing from him. He records everything."

Luke didn't say anything as he considered this new wrinkle.

"You think she saw something that got her in trouble?" Janey's voice was close to breaking, and Luke realized his expression probably scared her.

"No, no, I'm just thinking; that's all. Tell me what the second guy looked like."

"He was tall and skinny, but I didn't see his face."

A couple of smacks from the drummer signaled that the worship team was starting to warm up. Janey glanced toward the stage. "I missed practice, so I can't sing today. Do you mind if I go down and sit in on warm-ups? Worship helps me to pray for Nadine."

"No, go on. I'll catch up with you later."

Janey bounded down the aisle. Luke sighed and pulled the phone from his pocket to play the voice mail. When he heard Abby Hart's voice, he leaped up and ran to the office to tell someone he had to leave.

CHAPTER 22

Kent called around eight thirty Sunday morning.

"Detective Hart, the governor can meet you and Mr. Murphy at his aunt's house in twenty minutes."

Abby said she'd be there and hung up to call Murphy. The call went to voice mail, and she wondered if that meant he'd be a no-show. It bugged her that the prospect of his absence pinched her with disappoint-ment, so she concentrated instead on what she'd say to Rollins.

Help me dig up some new leads and find the killers.

Would he?

Expecting an early call, she'd already dressed in black slacks, a dark-blue homicide polo shirt, and black high-heeled boots. The boots added two inches to her height, and she hoped they made her more imposing. She didn't want Rollins dismissing her as a little girl. Pinning her hair back, she stepped to the sink and poured the rest of her coffee into a travel mug. Bandit lay curled up on the small dog bed in the corner of the kitchen, watching her.

For someone who'd never had a dog and who knew she shouldn't get attached, Abby felt more than a little pleased that the small guy had settled in so nicely. He'd slept on her bed, down at the foot; he'd done his business when she let him outside; and when she prepared his food, he pranced about in such a way that she couldn't help but smile.

What will I do if Rollins wants the dog?

Shaking the question from her mind, she picked up her coffee and her purse and headed out to meet the governor, wondering how on earth she'd be able to broach the subject of the Triple Seven.

She'd started her car and was almost out of the driveway when she realized she needed to pray. Abby blew out a breath and bowed her head. *Lord, you know I've wanted this moment for practically my whole life. I want to find my parents' killers. If Rollins knows anything, please help me get the information. Amen.*

There was only one black Cadillac Escalade parked in front of Cora Murray's home. Kent had asked her to phone in her duty log-on information, to stay off the radio, so she knew he wanted this visit to be quick and quiet, with no news agency involvement. Evidently he was certain the governor's visit would be under the radar if his instructions were followed. Enough under that the security detail was not needed.

It so impressed Abby that Rollins was not going to turn this into a campaign stop that she believed the governor really did feel the loss of his great-aunt.

She pulled her plain car into the alley and parked. Kent and another man got out of the Cadillac at the same time she climbed out of her car. She met them on the porch.

"Mr. Murphy?" Kent asked.

"I called him." Abby couldn't help but note that because of her boots she looked down on the man. But the way he carried himself didn't make him any less intimidating. He definitely had what cops called a "command presence."

Just then a four-door pickup pulled in behind her plain car. Abby didn't miss the fact that both Kent and the security man with him reached right hands into their jackets.

A flustered Murphy jumped out of the

truck and hurried to where she stood. She nodded to him and then looked back at Kent, who had relaxed.

"If you'll open the door, I'll get the governor," the chief of staff said.

"Sorry I'm late," Murphy whispered to her as he followed her to the door.

"Nothing's happened yet, so you're right on time." A thrill rippled through her at his closeness and the feel of his warm breath on her ear.

She opened the pocketknife on her key chain to cut the crime scene seal and nearly sliced her finger.

Get a grip, she told herself as she stuck her key in the lock public service had put on the door. When she turned, Kent and Governor and Mrs. Rollins were walking toward the house. Mrs. Rollins held her husband's arm and whispered in his ear as they walked. Abby watched the pair and wondered at their relationship. They were married a couple of years after the Triple Seven fire, so she was not mentioned in any of the old homicide reports. Abby really didn't understand women who were content to be in the background. *Maybe because I'm not married,* she thought. *What will it be like with Ethan?* He'd never said out loud that he wanted her to quit and follow him, but her intuition told her there would be no friction if she did just that.

Chiding herself for a wandering mind, Abby turned to Kent, someone she could understand. He was all about safety. Ramrod straight, his hard eyes roaming, danger humming around him like a bee . . . Yes, she got Kent. Lowell and Alyssa Rollins carried themselves like royalty — expensive clothes, dismissive gazes. They trusted Kent implicitly, she could tell.

She was aware of Murphy stiffening on her right. The governor looked at him first.

"Mr. Murphy, I presume. I'm glad you could make it. I wanted to personally thank you for notifying the police when my aunt was attacked." He held his hand out.

Murphy shook it. "No thanks necessary. I did what anyone would have done. Just wish I could have stopped what happened."

"You're modest." Alyssa Rollins smiled and gripped Murphy's hand in both of hers.

"Cora will be missed," Rollins said wistfully before turning to Abby.

"Detective Hart." He extended his hand. The smell of Old Spice hit Abby like a fragrant wave. Asa had used the same aftershave, and it was not unpleasant, even if a bit overdone.

"Governor Rollins." She shook the bony

hand and noted the firm grip, taking the opportunity to assess the governor, wondering if this visit would be emotional and difficult for him.

"I appreciate your meeting us here this morning," he said, appearing composed and steady.

"I second that." Alyssa Rollins gave Abby an appraising gaze but didn't extend her hand. Instead she held on to her husband's arm.

Abby concentrated on the governor. "If you can help determine what's missing from your aunt's belongings, you're doing the investigation a favor. And I had one question about the disposition of your aunt's dog."

"Cora had a dog?" Rollins raised an eyebrow.

"Yes, a small one. Do you want him or have an opinion on where he should go?"

"I'm allergic to dogs," Alyssa said. "Do what you think is best for the animal."

"I agree with Alyssa," Rollins said with a nod and motioned for Kent to enter the bungalow first.

A huge chunk of Abby's nervousness evaporated in a poof, and she knew she could focus completely on the other questions she needed to ask the governor.

Kent brushed past and flipped on the hall light as he strode toward the living room.

Rollins turned to Abby. "Do you mind if Mr. Murphy joins us? I've been told he's contacted my office several times. I'd like to give him the opportunity to ask his questions. Since I must hurry back to Sacramento, I thought it prudent to handle this before I leave."

Her curiosity was piqued and she was nonplussed. She thought Murphy was only here because he'd seen the suspect. What did he want to ask the governor?

Abby said, "It's your call. The crime scene has been thoroughly processed. The home will be released as soon as we know who to release it to."

"I believe lawyers are working on that as we speak."

"Okay, and I need to mention that nothing has been cleaned up." Abby looked from one Rollins to the other and then to Murphy, wondering if any of them would react.

All of them offered stoic expressions, so Abby turned to follow Kent, speaking to Governor Rollins as she walked. "I'll show you some photos of objects recovered from the suspect's possession and living area. I need to know if you recognize anything."

The governor and his wife followed Kent

and Abby while Murphy brought up the rear. The second security man stayed outside.

"Umm." Rollins mumbled something as the four of them crowded together in the small living room. The place smelled unpleasantly musty, and the evidence of fingerprint powder gave everything the tint of an old photograph. The alley window was boarded up, so very little natural light made it into the room.

For a few silent seconds Rollins looked around the room. "It's been years since I've been in this house." His tone was wistful and soft, not the commanding, authoritative voice from the press conference. Abby heard the vibration of underlying emotion but didn't think it indicated he'd break.

"The most vivid memory I have is of a Christmas we spent here." He waved his hand toward the corner of the room. "Aunt Cora had the tree there. She made the best cinnamon hot chocolate. I've never been able to duplicate it." There was a faraway look in his eyes, and he paused before continuing.

"I was about eight or nine and my brother, Louis, was nine or ten. Cora gave us hot chocolate and sat us in front of the tree after dinner while the adults drank coffee in the kitchen." He held his hands together in front of him and closed his eyes. "I think that was the best childhood Christmas I can remember. Later Christmases were never as fun or as peaceful."

Kent cleared his throat and Rollins took the cue. He turned toward Abby. "I apologize for the woolgathering. You have something you want me to look at?"

Abby stepped forward to hand the governor a folder of photos, items found in Davis's possession or at his grandmother's house.

"Can you identify any of these items? And please, walk around; tell me if anything stands out as missing."

He studied the photos and picked out one of a small gold music box and another of a porcelain ballerina. "These both belonged to my aunt. Louis got paddled for trying to play with the ballerina. It held great sentimental value for my aunt, but I'm not sure of its monetary value."

Abby felt the familiar zing of things falling into place, a case coming together. One thing remained — would she get the chance to ask Rollins about the Triple Seven? She took a breath to speak, but Rollins beat her to it.

"I know you speak to a lot of victims of

violence, Detective Hart, but have you ever lost someone close to you in a tragic fashion?"

Snapping the folder closed, Abby averted her gaze. This was her opening, and suddenly indecision roiled her insides like a bad meal.

Looking up, she seized the moment. "Yes, I have."

Everyone stared at her. Abby stepped through the open door.

"You don't remember me, Governor Rollins, but you worked with my parents, Buck and Patricia Morgan."

CHAPTER 23

"That's impossible." Kent spoke, voicing the words that stuck in Luke's throat.

How could Abby Hart be Abigail Morgan, the little girl his uncle died saving twenty-seven years ago? He knew her so well; he'd studied her parents and learned all there was to know about their life before they were murdered. *How did I miss this?*

For a minute Rollins just stared. When he did speak, the commanding, confident tone was gone.

"Uh . . . umm." He straightened his coat, glanced at his wife and then away. "Uh, I think what Gavin means is . . . Well, we'd been told you were placed out of state . . ." The governor's voice faded.

Luke's gaze bounced from Rollins to Abby to Mrs. Rollins to Kent. Shock seemed to suck the air out of the room. Only Hart appeared to have her footing.

"Eventually, yes. I went to live with my

aunt in Oregon."

"And came back," Mrs. Rollins murmured, and Luke saw something flit across her face, an indefinable emotion.

"My goodness, I don't know what to say." Rollins's voice was back. He held his hand out as if measuring the height of a child. "The last time I saw you, you were six years old. I — uh . . . They told me to stop asking about you, that I would endanger you. And now . . . well, I see your parents in you. Your mother's lovely eyes, your father's strong jaw and directness. I'm astonished. Astonished."

"You came back to solve the murders?" Luke found his voice. Everyone turned to stare at him — Luke could feel their eyes — but he kept his on Abby.

"That's one reason." She kept her eyes on Rollins. "And, Governor, if I could ask you some questions about what happened —"

"I don't know that I can help. I wasn't even in Long Beach the day of the fire. It was so long ago . . ." He started to say something else, but Kent interrupted.

"Sir, we're on a tight timetable here."

"Yes, Lowell." Alyssa Rollins tugged her husband's arm. "We need to be about the state's business." She faced Abby. "Are we finished here?"

"As far as Cora's murder, yes, but —"

"Then we thank you. And we'll be in touch when formal charges are filed against your suspect." Alyssa took the governor's arm and led him out of the house.

Kent addressed Abby. "I'm sorry, but that time period was the most traumatic of the governor's life. He not only lost his best friends and business partners, but two months later his brother, Louis, was killed in a hit-and-run accident." He gave a curt nod and hurried after his employer.

Luke felt his jaw slacken as the three people left with some alacrity. He watched Abby, whose face was a study in frustration. *What do you say to someone you've known on paper for more than twenty-five years?*

"I can't believe you're Abigail Morgan."

She faced him, a frown marring her features. "They sure left in a hurry."

"I feel as if I've known you my whole life." Luke felt something was odd about the hasty departure himself, but right now his needle stuck in the groove over Abby's news.

"What?" The frown turned to confusion.

"My uncle was the cook who pulled you from the fire." He stepped closer. "Luke Goddard was my uncle. Do you want to find your parents' killers as badly as I want to find my uncle's?"

CHAPTER 24

"Abigail Morgan? Are you sure?" Grace stared at Luke. He'd met the family at the door when they got back from church.

"Abigail Morgan. She and Detective Hart are one and the same."

"I can't believe it." His mother paled.

"Who's she?" Madison asked in the half-interested tone only a ten-year-old girl could manage. She walked by Luke, holding up a hand for a high five.

"Someone who hasn't been around for twenty-seven years," Grace said as she leaned against the doorjamb.

Maddie slapped her father's hand and continued on into the house, not the least bit interested.

Luke looked at his mother, certain her shock mirrored his own. When Abby had shared who she was, he'd been floored and wondered if he should have known, should have sensed who she was. But the picture in his mind of Abigail Morgan was that of a teary-eyed child who was all elbows and gangly limbs. For her part she seemed just as surprised at who he was.

"I've memorized the file," she'd said. *"There was no Murphy mentioned."*

"My mom married my stepdad about a year after my uncle's death. In your reports she'd be Grace Goddard. If I was mentioned at all, it was with that same last name."

Recognition had then dawned in her face. There was so much more he wanted to talk to her about, so much they had in common, but after Governor Rollins left the scene, she seemed intent on getting back to her own business.

Grace couldn't seem to get her mind around the news. "I can't believe I didn't recognize her."

"The last time you saw her she was what, five or six?"

Grace gave a slight head tilt. "Still, I spent a lot of time with her at the restaurant. She knew me and I helped them interview her. But they shuffled her off to protective custody quickly. I thought she moved out of state."

"She said she went to live with an aunt in Oregon."

The three of them went to the kitchen,

and over coffee Luke told them about the morning meeting with the governor.

Grace took it all in. "Years after the fire, I spoke to one of the detectives who told me that Abby was sent north, but he wouldn't be more specific. We spoke at length about it, but it was so long ago." She rubbed her forehead.

Luke's stepdad, James Murphy, gripped Grace's hand. "I remember you telling me that you wanted to adopt her. But at the time single moms didn't have a chance."

Grace pursed her lips. "I thought about it for a brief minute, but I had my hands full with Luke. And that crime scared the whole city. A lot of people were afraid for her safety. I was told she was fine in the hands of social services. Now she's an LBPD homicide investigator?"

"I couldn't believe it." Luke ran a hand down his chin, remembering the scene in the small house when Abby shared who she was. "It shocked Rollins as well. He left in a hurry without either of us being able to ask him anything about the Triple Seven."

Grace tsked. "I think you need to go easy on him. He just lost his aunt. I can understand him being shaken by anything, especially something related to the Triple Seven. You know they named it that because of their partnership. They were all born in July and considered that good luck, a happy omen."

"Maybe he's just shaken." Luke could still see Rollins's expression in his mind's eye. "But when I saw his face, something occurred to me. He looked scared. Maybe Buck Morgan wasn't the intended target all those years ago. Maybe Rollins was the target, and everyone missed it."

"From what I read," James offered, "it was Buck Morgan who had the wild reputation. That restaurant sure put Long Beach on the map. Remember when the Lakers won the championship?"

Grace smiled. "My brother was so proud when Buck hosted that party for them. Luke cooked his heart out. Magic Johnson signed his apron."

"As I recall, Rollins was more the designer and PR guy. Buck and Patricia were the faces of the restaurant." James rubbed his chin and frowned. "The police went over everything then, Luke. What do you hope to accomplish now after so much time has passed?"

"Maybe they did, Dad. I've read everything on the subject. But this morning Rollins was afraid, and Kent couldn't get him out of there fast enough. What does he have to be afraid of twenty-seven years later? Bottom line: I want to find out who killed my uncle."

Luke tried to focus on Maddie as they drove to the local elementary school. Sunday nights her book club met in the library there and, conveniently, the basketball league he and Bill were involved in played in the gymnasium. His daughter was excited about the book they were reading, a S.A.V.E. Squad book called *Dog Daze.*

"The kids in the book save animals," she said and went on to explain her favorite character. He only half listened, and when they arrived at school and she and Olivia darted off to the library, he felt guilty for not hearing everything she'd said.

Oh, well, he thought. *I'll make it up to her.* As soon as he got to the gym and found Bill, he told his friend about the events of the morning.

"What are you saying?" Bill gave Luke the same astonished expression that Grace had worn when he broke the news. "How is that possible? What was she, six when her parents were killed?"

"I didn't get a chance to talk to her at length about it, but the news about who she was sure sent Rollins spinning from the house."

"It could have just been emotional for the guy."

Luke's eyes narrowed. "I have a different theory. Suppose Rollins knows something but has stayed quiet out of fear? Suppose he was the real target twenty-seven years ago? Maybe keeping his mouth shut has kept him safe?"

Bill raised his hands, then let them drop. "Ah, my friend, you've been watching too many TV movies! The guy has never laid low, and he is a well-respected man. I can't believe it would have been missed if someone had a motive to kill him."

"Suppose he made a deal with the devil?"

"You mean he's known who did the killing all these years and his silence has bought his safety?"

Luke nodded, and Bill put his hand on Luke's shoulder. "I know it's important for you to find out who killed your uncle, but don't waste your time barking up the wrong tree."

Luke said nothing.

When the game started, he tried to lose himself in sweat and twenty-foot jumpers. He was thoroughly exhausted when Maddie skipped toward him an hour later and it was time to go home. But he couldn't get the idea out of his mind. The reaction he'd seen from Rollins that morning was one of a man hiding something.

CHAPTER 25

It was still dark Monday morning when Abby parked her car in the lot of a twenty-four-hour coffee shop to wait for Woody. Abby was agitated all day Sunday after the meeting with Rollins, and church that night hadn't helped. She hadn't been able to go to sleep, so she'd given up at 4 a.m. and called Woody. At 9 a.m. she and Roper had a meeting with the DA about Lil' Sporty, so she sipped coffee and laid her notes out on the trunk of her car to prepare while she waited for Woody's black-and-white to appear.

Luke Goddard . . . Luke Murphy.

Something in common.

Rollins was hiding something.

The scene from yesterday morning wreaked havoc with her concentration. She'd worked herself up to believing that finally meeting the man and telling him who she was would be a watershed moment and she'd learn some new insight or gain an ally to get the investigation reactivated. But in the end it was anti-climactic. Rollins, his wife, and Kent took off as if hearing who she was made the room smell.

"He not only lost his best friends and business partners, but two months later his brother, Louis, was killed in a hit-and-run accident."

They'd left Abby to lock up and to deal with Murphy. She was grateful she'd gotten in the question about Bandit. But she'd had no chance to ask about her parents' murders. And then there was Murphy. The PI had stared at her openmouthed. If the governor's reaction was odd, Murphy's was downright shocking.

"I feel as if I've known you my whole life," he'd said. *"Luke Goddard was my uncle."*

Abby still had trouble digesting that bit of information. She remembered his uncle — "Cookie," she'd called him — mostly from the police reports and the newspaper articles that hailed him as a hero. But now bits of her memory were conjuring up images of a warm, smiling man. And fire. Her nightmares slid into perspective. For whatever reason, the bad dreams she'd been having recently were of the day Luke Murphy's uncle saved her life. Now Murphy was a new variable in her investigation.

As far as the question of why the cook had been left to die, the two Puffs had documented their theory in the pages of the crime report.

The investigation concluded that the first two victims were shot and killed in the main dining room. Both bodies showed traces of accelerant. Evidence of acceler-ant usage was detected throughout the restaurant. Per arson, the fire was started in the dining room, adjacent to the first two victims. Further investigation determined the suspects fled through the kitchen and exited the rear door as the fire spread. As they exited, they blocked the rear door with a large trash bin. The only conclusion investigators could draw from this was that the suspects knew there were still living victims in the restaurant and the door was blocked to prevent their escape.

Investigators believed the murderer or murderers confronted the couple where their bodies were found. They were dead when the fire started.

The Puffs also believed that when the murders happened, Goddard had been in the kitchen freezer completing an inventory.

Abby had been in her parents' office napping, something she did often — so often her parents had the room soundproofed, other employees told the Puffs. Goddard wrapped her in wet towels and tried to get her out the back door. If Woody and Asa hadn't shown up when they did, rushing to the restaurant when they saw smoke, there would have been four victims in the restaurant instead of three.

Woody and Asa opened the back door when they heard Luke Goddard call for help. He handed them Abby. Goddard died two days later in the hospital from smoke inhalation without being able to make a statement.

Because there was no evidence that the killers knew Goddard was there, investigators concluded it was Abby who was intended to die in the inferno, and that resulted in her lost years in social services. For all her adult life the deaths of her parents had been two-dimensional: a collection of police reports, newspaper articles, the occasional regurgitation on a television program devoted to cold cases. Standing there face-to-face with Luke Murphy and hearing his connection suddenly brought everything into three dimensions, made it jump off the page, made the brutal murders of her parents painfully real.

"I feel as if I've known you my whole life."

She'd gone home and pulled out everything she could on the cook. There wasn't much. Goddard had been a clear-cut picture of collateral damage: in the wrong place at the wrong time. There'd been an investigation into his background to eliminate him as possibly the target. He wasn't even supposed to have been at the restaurant that day but had come in early so he could take the night off. She'd mentally closed the door on that dead end and concentrated on her mom and dad.

Could Murphy know more than I do?

Unsettled after her search, she'd tried to contact Asa. He'd retired to Idaho and didn't often answer his phone. Woody was the only other person she could talk to, and she needed to talk.

A black-and-white pulled into the coffee shop lot, and her friend stepped out, a worried look creasing his brow as he joined her. "What's wrong?"

Abby gulped the stale coffee she'd purchased and tried to keep her voice level, not completely understanding why she was so antsy.

Woody listened to what she had to say without interrupting.

"Murphy . . . That name was never part of the original investigation. There's no way you would have known he was related to the cook. I remember talking to the Goddard family at the hospital. Told them the cook died a hero." He leaned against her car. "Man, oh, man, this takes me back. Goddard barely got you out of the office. We'd just put him in the ambulance when the alarm went out about your house being on fire. After that, Asa and me and the Puffs just wanted to keep you safe."

Abby rubbed gooseflesh on her arm as the wisp of a memory surfaced. Fire. She hated fire.

"You okay?" Woody put a hand on her shoulder.

Abby realized she was breathing hard. "I don't know. I'm remembering. I remember coughing and calling for my dad. . . . It was smoky, it was dark, and it was scary. Cookie was the one who told me that God would protect me."

She jerked away from Woody, jammed her notes under her arm, and tossed her cup in the trash, pacing the lot, working to relax.

"I remember him picking me up and telling me not to be afraid, that I'd be okay." She put her hand over her mouth as her breathing returned to normal. Facing a worried Woody, she asked, "Why didn't I remember this before? Why now?"

"I don't know. Maybe meeting a guy like Murphy triggered something. Do you remember the shooting?"

She hugged herself. "Just heat."

They were quiet for a minute.

"I didn't even get to ask Rollins anything. Do you remember his brother getting killed sometime after the Triple Seven burned?"

Woody tapped a fist with his palm, frowning. "Traffic accident. I recollect a fatal involving his brother. I was off that night, but Asa told me about it. Louis Rollins was riding his bike somewhere in East Long Beach; I don't know where exactly. It was bad, a hit-and-run."

"They catch who did it?"

"No, but I was there when they found the car a few nights later at Marine Stadium. Driven into the water at the boat launch. Stolen."

Abby felt her world shift back into perspective. Woody's presence usually did that for her. Plus, she now had something else to take a look at — the unsolved hit-and-run traffic accident report.

"Wonder if it's worth looking up the report."

"You think it's related?" Woody frowned.

"On the surface, maybe not. But Rollins knows something. I'm convinced. The look on his face yesterday is frozen in my head."

"About the murders?" Woody frowned. "He was looked at hard and came back clean as a whistle. The Puffs were good. If they'd thought he was involved, he'd have gone to jail. He wasn't no governor then."

"I'm not mistrusting the Puffs, but I do trust my instincts — you know that. The Rollins I saw yesterday was afraid and maybe guilty."

"And he's a murderer?" He grunted, not convinced. "He's a saint in this state, done a lot of good over the years. Leopards don't change their spots. If he were a cold-blooded killer two decades ago, he'd still be one. How'd he hide all these years?"

Abby hiked one shoulder. "It's just a feeling, and it's all I've got right now. I wish I could talk to Asa."

"If you left a message, he'll call you back."

Woody's call sign came over the radio; he needed to answer.

"Thanks for everything." She held his gaze, glad to see he wasn't worried anymore.

"Just be careful. Whoever murdered your folks was as ruthless as they come. Like I said, leopards don't change."

He gave her a look that she recognized

before he headed back to his patrol car, and it tugged at her heart. It was his look when things got serious or dangerous, and it said he feared for her.

Abby stayed in the parking lot after he drove away. She knew that her parents were considered the main targets twenty-seven years ago. The idea that Rollins was the killer had been ruled out quickly and thoroughly. If there had been any shadow over him, he never would have won his first political contest. To find anything that would implicate him would truly be a new lead.

I need to talk to the governor now more than ever.

CHAPTER 26

What could Murphy know about the Triple Seven that I don't?

Abby bought a carton of milk from the doughnut shop and sat in her car munching Oreos while her thoughts dwelled on Luke Murphy. Yes, they had something in common, as he had observed — something big. But where could it possibly take them?

She finished her milk and cookies and had started the car when her phone rang. Fear jolted through her when she saw it was Ethan at this time of the morning, not yet 6 a.m. It was, of course, a normal hour where he was, but if he needed to call her now, something must be wrong.

"Abby, are you okay?"

"I'm fine. A little better now that I'm talking to you. Is everything okay on your end?"

"Yeah, yeah. But some kids on the team came across a YouTube video. I couldn't believe what I saw. What were you thinking?

You could have been smashed beneath that train!"

Abby frowned, ruminations of Rollins and Goddard and Murphy muffling her thoughts. Then she remembered Lil' Sporty and the tourist's video.

"Ethan, I'm fine. It wasn't really that close."

"Wasn't that close?" He made a strangled sound, and Abby imagined him running a hand through his hair in exasperation.

She closed her eyes, not certain how to respond and not wanting to have this discussion right now. "I couldn't stop and watch the man be crushed."

"The image is stuck in my mind. Abby, I could have lost you." The emotion in his voice bothered her for some reason, and she worked to squish the irritation. He didn't deserve that.

"I'm fine, really. I'm okay."

He was quiet, so she went on. "The upside is, I caught a serial killer, and he all but confessed."

Ethan sighed. "Your job is dangerous enough without you being reckless."

Anger flared, but Abby bit her tongue. This divide about her work had to be crossed, or she didn't know how they could be married.

"I didn't look at it as being reckless, and I'm sorry it bothered you." She paused, hesitant to tell him her other news, but knowing deep down that he deserved to hear the update.

"I am glad you called, though. I have something to tell you. It might not make you any happier than the train video, but you need to know." Bottom line, now that Luke Murphy knew who she was, everyone else would soon know. Abby didn't want Ethan to hear about it on the Internet.

"Promise me you'll be more careful first."

"I will, I promise." She told him about her encounter with Rollins.

The line went silent for a minute.

"I don't know about this," he said finally. "Opening this door doesn't seem smart."

"I just want the truth about my parents' murders — that's all I've ever wanted." Her voice faltered as emotion threatened to overwhelm her.

"I thought you — we — had decided to trust God and let this alone."

"I wish I could explain everything behind my reasoning, but this isn't a good time. I'm on my way to the station."

"We are going to talk about this soon."

Abby stifled a sigh and agreed before changing the subject. "Thank you for the roses. They made my day."

"Good. Please be more careful. And, Abby?"

"Yes?"

"Don't put work before you and me, and before God."

"I would never consciously do that."

"Don't let it happen subconsciously either."

Abby promised she wouldn't and ended the call as she parked at the station. She grabbed a Kleenex and blew her nose, then double-checked her eyes in the mirror. They were bloodshot, but there was nothing she could do about that.

Don't put work before God. That stung.

Until the conversation with Ethan, Abby had actually been more settled than she had been before talking with Woody. Now, among other things, she wished she had looked at the stupid train video when Megan brought it up.

The station was still graveyard sparse and quiet. Taking the stairs instead of the elevator, she quickly unlocked the door to the homicide office, entered, and flipped on the lights. On the way to her desk, she stopped in the records room and pulled the Triple Seven file from the drawer. The accordion file was wrinkled with age and use, bound in spots with tape. All of it had long since been transferred to a computer file, but today she felt the need to riffle through the originals.

Coffee was already set to brew, the job of the last person leaving for the night. Abby hit the Start button and waited. Once she had a full mug, she sat at her desk, powered up the computer, and logged on as soon as she was able. When the phone rang, she was going to ignore it, but she saw that it was Gunther.

"Hart," she said tersely as she answered the phone.

"Whoa, I expected your voice mail."

"Well, this is your lucky day. Maybe you should buy a lottery ticket."

"Ha. I always said you had more of a sense of humor than Asa. And a better poker face. What a secret you've been sitting on, Miss Morgan."

Abby's jaw hit the floor. "What? How did you hear that? There were only five people in that room and it wasn't even twenty-four hours ago." She expected people would eventually hear, but so soon?

"You're not my only law enforcement contact. And I can keep secrets too. Are you going to reopen the Triple Seven case?"

It took Abby a minute to collect her

thoughts. Finally she sighed. "I have plenty on my plate right now."

"Not an answer. I assume you stayed below the radar for so long because of fear for your safety. Not worried now?"

"I'd love to talk about this another time."

"Fair enough. Will you let me know if you reopen the Triple Seven? In case you've forgotten, I covered the story at the time."

"I haven't forgotten. And you'll be the first to know. By the way, what did you have on the Jenkins case?"

"Crunchers."

"What?" Abby knew the junkyard, but until this moment she'd never connected it to Jenkins.

"Yeah, I don't know what it is about that place, and I'm not certain about the connection, but that name keeps coming up. I'll let you know if I hear anything else. Later."

"Thanks, and later."

Abby hung up, still reeling from the progression of Ethan's phone call to Gunther already knowing what she'd told Rollins. It was almost too much to process, and she had a lot of work to do. She held her head in her hands and prayed for clarity, peace — both of which eluded her. Grunting in frustration, she turned her attention to the hard copy of the Triple Seven file, the report number faded on the well-handled cover.

My energy needs to go here for now. I'll deal with the other later.

Rereading what she knew by heart gave her a reasonable facsimile of peace. Puff and Puff More had been thorough and diligent. Would they really miss a suspect like Rollins right in front of their faces? They'd asked the hate question several times to Rollins and others: *Who hated the Morgans enough to murder them and attempt to murder their child?*

Why, no one. Everyone loved them.

Not everyone.

Frowning, she glanced at her computer screen. Since nothing new in the old case had jumped up and bitten her, she opened her e-mail. Her in-box was loaded with messages from news organizations. Scanning the list for anything urgent or from a friend, she saw one from Luke Murphy.

What could he want?

Sipping her coffee, she opened the e-mail.

Hi, hope it's okay to contact you at work. I'd really like to get together and talk about your parents and my uncle. I bet you want to solve this as much as I do.

She wanted to talk to him, yet she didn't. As much as she wanted to kick down the door to Rollins, she feared this door Murphy wanted to open. *Why?*

What are you keeping from me? Ethan's voice; she had said nothing about Luke Murphy.

There was no time to work it out, no time to smooth out the wrinkles in her life. The workday was starting. She and Roper were due in Jacoby's office at eight thirty. From there, everyone would walk across the parking lot to the court building for the 9 a.m. meeting with the DA.

Abby poured another cup of coffee and forced her concentration back to the granny murders. There was enough evidence to arraign Lil' Sporty Davis and enough for a trial. She didn't mind trials and testifying, but she bet Davis would cop a plea to avoid the death penalty. Placing the granny murder book on top of the Triple Seven file, Abby began a review. She was halfway through when Roper arrived.

"Good morning," he said with a grin. "I hear Rollins identified some loss."

"Yep, the case is getting stronger." She braced for a question about who she was, certain Murphy would have said something. But Roper didn't ask.

He sat and started going through paperwork on his desk.

She went back to her review, wondering if Murphy's friendship with Roper would make it easier or harder to have him as a partner. It didn't change the fact that she liked working alone with her own thoughts and hunches. Ideas and solutions came to her quickly if she wasn't slowed down by having to explain her thought process to someone else.

As if on cue, Roper interrupted her review. "I looked over the Jenkins file." He whistled. "That's a tough one."

Abby closed the Murray file, determined to think business, not personal preferences. Working the Jenkins case had become secondary to the granny murders, and she hated setting anything aside. Besides that, Gunther had offered another avenue of investigation. "It needs some legwork, time on the streets. I bet we can shake loose some information with a little effort. And I might have a lead. Walter Gunther said there might be a connection to Crunchers, which is the first I've heard."

"Wow, I wouldn't have seen that, but then that place is so grimy anything is likely to stick there."

"I agree."

"After we meet with the DA, we'll put some time in for Jenkins."

"Sounds good."

Abby formally put the Triple Seven file away and shifted to the present, going over aspects of the first granny murder she wanted to be certain Roper was familiar with. Technically, the Triple Seven was not closed and never had been. It was open-unsolved. People often thought of cold cases as closed, but that was inaccurate. Every open case, no matter how old, was assigned to an investigator as the contact person in the event new information came in. Asa had been the contact person for the Triple Seven as long as he'd been in homicide. No replacement contact had been assigned as of yet. Abby always assumed it would just be her next partner but now doubted that.

One day the Triple Seven would be moved to the open-current file officially, but not today.

Ethan, I'm trying.

Still, the door Murphy was opening beckoned. What was there to lose in just talking to him? He obviously did care about finding the Triple Seven killers. He could be an ally. She knew the idea would bother her until she did something about it. When she had a chance, she'd make a call, ask him to meet. It might go nowhere, but it would at least answer some of the questions she had. She hoped.

CHAPTER 27

Luke pulled up to a Laundromat in the city of Santa Ana. Or rather, it was a *lavandería.* Every business name on the weather-beaten strip mall was in Spanish. Santa Ana was an Orange County city squeezed in between Anaheim, Costa Mesa, and Buena Park. It housed a heavily Hispanic population and was plagued in areas with gangs and gang violence. This particular area was tired and poor, but not terribly dangerous. It was also not where the young girl he was looking for should be, but it was where she'd ended up after running away with her boyfriend.

Crystal Smith had run away from the San Fernando Valley to be with her boyfriend, Ricardo. Luke had done a lot of leg-work in the case; Crystal's family only had a general idea of where she might be. He'd discovered Crystal and Ricardo living in a cheap motel next door to this strip mall. They were surviving on what Ricardo scraped up by securing day work.

The Smiths asked Luke to confront the girl. *"We've pushed her away. We were so angry and hurt to hear that she was pregnant at seventeen."*

You're right; anger and unforgiveness won't solve the problem, and you don't want your daughter and grandchild destitute somewhere.

At the same time, they were afraid if they confronted her again, they'd push her further away. They'd asked Luke to contact her first. They didn't believe that they could force her to come home; rather, they hoped Luke could persuade her to return voluntarily.

Luke waited for Ricardo to leave for the day. Idly, he wondered what Abby or Bill would do in this situation. Crystal and Ricky were a gray area. Both seventeen, almost adults and old enough to be on their own. The police wouldn't force her to return home. Add to that she was four months pregnant and she willingly left with Ricardo — Luke knew it would be a tough sell on every front to get the girl to go home.

The only thing he could hope was that the contrast of where the girl was now against where she grew up would work to help convince her that going home to the valley was best for all involved. Luke prayed for wisdom as a battered pickup truck pulled into the hotel lot. Ricardo ran out, hopped in, and the truck pulled away.

Luke got out of his truck, intending to knock on the hotel room door, when it opened and Crystal stepped out, dragging a garbage bag behind her. In the other hand she had a bottle of laundry detergent, so Luke assumed she was on her way to the Laundromat.

He waited until she was inside the *lavandería* and packing clothes into a machine before he walked across the lot.

Crystal was the only person in the place, Luke noted. Which was good, he hoped. He didn't want to scare her.

"Crystal?"

She turned at her name, and the look on her face could only be described as deer in the headlights.

Luke held up both hands. "Hey, I'm not here to scare you. I just want to talk; that's all."

"Who are you?" She dropped the clothes in her hand and looked toward the door, wanting an escape route, Luke guessed. Crystal was a slight, pale girl, with only a hint of her pregnancy showing. It broke Luke's heart that she looked as though she should still be playing with dolls instead of preparing to be a mother.

"My name is Luke Murphy. I'm a private investigator. Your parents sent me."

"You touch me, I'll scream." She backed up.

"I'm not going to touch you. I just want to talk."

"What about? You found me, so now my parents know I'm here. Me and Ricky will have to move again."

"Yes, I found you and I told your parents. They've known you were here for a week."

"My parents hate me."

Luke shook his head. "They don't hate you. They said some things they regret, but they love you and they're worried about you and the baby."

She chewed on a thumbnail and seemed to digest that.

"I'm not going to lie — they're not thrilled with Ricardo, but they want you home, and they are willing to talk to you about the situation without all the horrible stuff that was said when you told them you were pregnant."

"I'm fine here with Ricky. What if I told you to go away?"

"I'll leave, and I won't bother you again. But would you speak to your mother? That won't hurt, will it? If, after you talk to her, you want to stay here, they won't force you to come home. They only want to know that you're okay and that you have all you need for the baby."

Two women entered, chatting in Spanish. They eyed Luke, and he nodded and smiled. They moved to the other side of the Laundromat and began doing their laundry, continuing the conversation as they did.

"Is my mom here?"

"No, but you can talk to her on my cell phone. She's waiting to hear, one way or another, how you're doing."

Crystal turned away from him and finished filling the machine. She poured in soap, added her coins, and started the cycle.

"Are you happy here, Crystal? I think that's all your mom wants to know. And if you need any help. She's ready to help. She only wants what's best for you."

Luke stepped closer and leaned against a machine, watching the girl. He prayed this scene was never repeated down the road with Maddie. Mrs. Smith had told him how Crystal had been a straight A student with plans for college until she met Ricardo. Now she'd dropped out of school and run away. Would Maddie meet a boy and run off the rails like this? It twisted his gut in a knot to think it was remotely possible.

"They know I'm here. . . . Have they been watching me?"

"No, they've been praying, wondering how best to help you."

"Praying?" She snorted. "They don't go to church anymore."

"They do now. Crystal, everyone in this situation has made a mistake. You got pregnant too young, your parents reacted badly, and then you and Ricky ran away. All your mom wants is a chance to make her part of it right. Will you just let her talk?"

She sniffled and wiped her nose with her sleeve, then looked at him, defiance in her eyes. "If I tell her to go away and stop bugging me, she will?"

"If that's what you want."

She nodded after a minute.

"Let's go outside so you can hear."

She followed him to the parking lot, and he took out his phone, punching in the Smiths' number. Mrs. Smith answered on the first ring.

"She's all right?"

"Yes," Luke said. "She looks fine and she's agreed to talk to you." Just before he handed the phone to Crystal, he thought he heard a sob from the phone.

The girl waited a moment, then took the phone. "Mom?"

Crystal spent twenty minutes crying on the phone with her mother. In the end, bridges were mended and the girl agreed to talk to Ricky about returning home, to be certain she received the medical care necessary for the course of her pregnancy. Her parents also agreed to speak to Ricardo and maybe help him find employment in the valley so that the two could be together and hopefully get married. Mrs. Smith had made it clear they didn't condone what had happened, but a child had been conceived and needed to be cared for, and hopefully with everyone communicating, other problems could be solved as well.

Luke left Santa Ana gratified. His first job as a PI had been with a seasoned investigator, a way to learn the ropes in order to get to the point where he could open his own business. The PI he'd worked for had retired from LAPD after thirty-two years in uniform, and Luke had learned a lot from the man and was eternally grateful for the experience he'd gained. He'd been assigned a lot of work for insurance companies and had taken classes in accident reconstruction. He participated in a lot of fraud investigations — once tracked down a treasurer who absconded with a church bank account to Mexico — and some bounty hunter work. He had also logged some unpleasant work conducting surveillance on cheating husbands and wives. But when he found his first runaway girl and reunited her with her family, he knew that would be what he wanted his business to concentrate on. Sure, there were some girls who fled abusive situations, and he'd been able to see that some stepfathers were charged, but a lot of girls were deceived into leaving home and then exploited, and those were the ones he felt compelled to work to save.

Even if there wasn't a lot of money in it, that didn't matter. And the Lord always seemed to provide.

After leaving Crystal, Luke returned home to catch up on e-mails and paperwork. An e-mail from an old friend piqued his interest.

Bullet, saw news blurb on a cold case in your neck of the woods. . . . Would love to chat about it and catch up on old times. I'll be calling.

Todd Orson, aka Ice Age, was someone Luke served with in the Army Special Forces. He used Luke's nickname, one he hadn't heard in quite a while, one that brought up mixed feelings.

Luke sat back in the chair and read the note over and over. His Army days were a source of pride and shame for Luke. He'd been true to his uniform and his oath of service but not to his marriage vows, leading a wild life overseas. He hadn't become a Christian until after his wife's death. The *if onlys* tormented him still. If only he hadn't argued with her over the phone when he knew she was driving. He'd wanted to reenlist; she'd wanted him home. The scream and the crash and the disconnected phone call would stay with him forever.

Ice Age reminded him of segments of a life he wished he could forget. His old friend worked for the FBI now, Luke had heard through the grapevine. He didn't know if Orson was as wild as he used to be. *He may have settled down like I have,* Luke thought.

In any event, Luke hoped Ice Age did call. He'd like to catch up and show him how his life had changed.

CHAPTER 28

District attorney Drew was thrilled with the case against Lil' Sporty. In spite of the fact there was no direct evidence and the confession was brief, she liked it and felt they had their man.

"He's been assigned a public defender and there is a chance he'll cop a plea," she told Abby, Roper, and Lieutenant Jacoby.

"I don't think anyone has a problem with a plea." Jacoby looked at Abby.

"I don't," she said. "He's off the street — that's what counts."

Bill nodded in agreement.

"Okay," Drew said. "I'll be in touch."

After the meeting, Abby had her plate full explaining to her coworkers why she'd never been forthcoming about her identity. How the news had traveled so fast, she'd never know. It could have been Murphy; it could have been someone from Rollins's staff. But the cat was out of the bag and running like a champ. Jacoby told her he'd heard from DC Cox. Abby could only guess who'd told her.

"All this time you've been here and kept quiet. I didn't think secrets were possible in the PD," Lieutenant Jacoby said.

"Woody and Asa convinced me it was for the best."

"Your parents' case is the biggest unsolved crime in the department's history. They still talk about it in the academy. Zeke Russell never got over not closing that case."

Everyone had questions for her and she answered them all. Coworkers were supportive and curious, and she was glad the Triple Seven case was now out of the dusty world of cold cases and in the open. As much as she didn't like talking about herself, she found it a relief that everyone knew her secret and she could be totally open about wanting the case solved. Even so, by the end of the day she felt all talked out.

Abby's hopes for a quiet evening with no more talking were dashed when her cell phone buzzed before she reached her car.

"It's my lucky day. Twice you've answered." Gunther's cigarette-coarsened voice assaulted her ear. "I'm calling in my favor."

"Which one is that?"

"Abigail Morgan."

Abby stopped at her car and leaned against the driver's door, thinking but not saying anything. She didn't want to go there again. She'd told Woody she was ready, but was she?

"This has become hot hot. I know you're still there. I've got to get a piece out about you. I think it's only fair you give me the first interview."

"Gunther, I am so busy right now."

"CliffsNotes so I can show my editor something."

"What do you want to know?"

"Where've you been? Why hide? Why tell the governor who you are now?"

Abby closed her eyes and told the story — again.

"Aunt. Is that Deidre?"

"Yeah."

"Hart must be her married name."

"It is. Her husband died about a year before my folks."

"Why did it take so long to find her?"

"She was in South America on a missions team —"

"I remember that. Your mom called her a Holy Roller. You lived with her until college?"

"Yes. When I graduated high school, I got an athletic scholarship to LB State."

"Volleyball. That I know. Did you come back always planning to solve your parents' murders?"

"That has always been my dream."

"Are you reopening the Triple Seven investigation?"

Abby waited a beat, wondering how to answer. "Technically it was never closed — no arrest, no suspect, it's open. But, Gunther, officially I can't go there right now."

"Did the governor inquire about the case at all?"

"Why would you ask that?"

"Because reporter equals curious, and when Rollins comes to town, your carefully hidden identity becomes hidden no more, etc., etc."

"I've had a long day and I'm on my way home."

"If you think this is going to go away quietly, you're delusional. Anything connected to Rollins will be big. He's all but officially filed to run for the senate. Every cable network in the country will probably visit you in the next couple of days. Did he quash the Triple Seven invest?"

That gave Abby pause. Could Rollins

close the case permanently? His reaction made her consider him a suspect. If he did quash the case, it would only increase her suspicion. She would never tell Gunther her suspicions. He would run with it and things would get beyond crazy. But then that was what she wanted, wasn't it? To surprise the killer and hopefully smoke him out. If the killer was Rollins, that would do it, wouldn't it?

"You still there, Hart?"

"To my knowledge Rollins has not interfered with any investigation. As far as the Triple Seven goes, I have a full caseload."

"You should run for office."

"Do you have what you need? I really have to get going."

"For now, but I hope we can talk again."

The connection ended, and Abby frowned. She'd probably catch it for speaking to Gunther, but so be it. Sighing, she got in the car, too tired at the moment to give it serious thought.

CHAPTER 29

There was not much rest to be had when she got home. There were messages on her home phone, and it was still ringing. While she didn't plan on calling back any news outlets, she knew there was one call she had to make, and that was to Dede. She also knew that she should call Ethan back, but she didn't have the energy. She'd probably wait until he called her.

Dede answered on the third ring. "Abby, what a nice surprise, but I hope there's nothing wrong."

Abby sighed, truly sorry that her aunt would think she only called when there was a problem. Dede didn't have cable service, so Abby knew it was likely she had not heard about Abby and the Triple Seven. She explained what had transpired with Governor Rollins.

Dede was quiet for a moment. Abby waited.

"Well," she finally said, "I knew it would come out sooner or later. Frankly, I'm amazed you were able to keep it a secret for this long. When you left here to go to college, I feared you would scream it from the rooftops that you wanted to find your parents' killers."

"You're not mad?"

"Mad? No, of course not. I just want you to be careful. Abby, don't let this investigation consume you. You were so angry when you came to me; do you remember?"

Abby pinched the bridge of her nose. She'd smashed a set of china at her last foster home when she saw a three-year anniversary article about the murders. "Yes, I do. But that was then. I'm an adult now."

"Maybe in most things, but not where your mom and dad are concerned. My fear has always been that unforgiveness and the need for revenge will eat you up. Please don't let that happen."

"It's not revenge I want; it's justice."

"There's a fine line between those two concepts. Those killers may have been free all these years, but they will not get away with anything in the long run."

"I believe that too, Dede. But I need to know why my parents died as well as who killed them."

"Those answers may never come. Please don't let the search consume you; don't let the quest for justice become your god."

After Abby hung up with Dede, she thought of her friends — mostly Megan and Jessica, the people at church, and her friends from volleyball. Would they understand her reasoning for keeping such a big secret?

Then there was Ethan. The earlier conversation with him played over in her mind. Part of her feared that he would never try to understand her need to solve the Triple Seven. *Forgive, move on* — those were phrases she could imagine him saying. He'd never suffered a traumatic loss. Well, that could be said about a lot of people.

But not Luke Murphy. Murphy understood completely.

Shaking that thought away, she turned her landline off and set her mobile to vibrate. There were so many e-mails that she gave up and powered down the computer. She and Bandit sat on the couch and watched Abby's two favorite escape movies, *Casablanca* and *The Thin Man*. While it was difficult for her to wind down, a good movie from the thirties or forties always did the trick. The black-and-white world of Nick and Nora Charles was so much simpler than Abby's colored world of present reality.

When the second one ended, she was ready for bed. Abby bit back the fear inside about what the morning might bring. She spent some time in the book of Psalms, concentrating on chapters 27 and 34, and fell into a peaceful sleep.

The next morning, after a shower, Abby braced herself for the front-page story about her and the Triple Seven murders. Gunther's lead featured a grainy picture of her at six years of age in the arms of Woody, side by side with a picture of her from a few years ago in uniform. She cautiously turned her cell phone back on as she read the story and sipped coffee.

Prominent Homicide Detective Lost Parents in Infamous Cold Case, read the headline. Before she had a chance to read it, her phone vibrated and she saw that the caller was Deputy Chief Cox. She answered.

"What do you mean by doing this?"

"Excuse me?"

"We're in the middle of maybe the biggest serial homicide case since Randy Kraft, and you decide to grab the headlines with a personal vendetta?"

"I didn't —"

Cox was furious and almost incoherent. Abby set the phone down and picked up

Bandit. Her phone beeped with another call, but she didn't interrupt Cox. Finally the DC took a breath and Abby listened to see if she had just hung up. No such luck.

"No interviews are approved. None. Do you understand that order?"

Abby answered, "Yes." The connection was broken. Almost immediately the phone buzzed again. It was Woody.

"Be careful what you wish for."

"Are they bugging you?"

"Yep. I'm the only cop still in uniform with any connection to that case. They say you aren't answering your phone, and they want to know if the Triple Seven invest is active. Is it?"

To Abby, it had never been cold. But with the deputy chief's voice ringing in her ears, she said, "No. I just had a call from Cox."

Woody snickered. "Bet this has twisted her panties in a big knot."

"You could say that. Bottom line, do I want to activate the case and charge after Rollins? You know better than anyone that I do. Can I figure out how to do that without getting fired? Not yet."

"You will. In the meantime, be careful. And turn on the television. Murphy is not beholden to Cox."

Abby startled Bandit by putting him down

and rushing to the living room. She found Murphy giving the last bit of an interview on *Good Morning Long Beach*.

"I've been working on this case for years. My uncle was a hero that day and he deserves justice."

"Do you plan to join forces with Detective Hart?"

"I feel as if I know her because I've studied her parents so carefully. I would love to be able to compare notes with her and have the investigation formally reactivated."

"I'm amazed no one figured out who she was by now. Were you surprised?"

"Shocked, actually. I'll always have the picture of that little six-year-old crying in the arms of Officer Woods in my mind."

"After all this time, over twenty-seven years, you have hope the murders can be solved?"

"There is always hope; criminals, especially murderers, can't hide forever. And yes, I believe this crime is solvable. We just have to open the right door."

Abby switched the TV off and folded her arms, staring at the blank screen and considering Murphy's words. She believed the crime was solvable as well, and now that she had a lead, she knew what door to open.

I'd love to see what Murphy has in his notes, she thought. *Maybe we do need to join forces.*

Even as the idea crossed her mind, chagrin rose up about Murphy and his showboating. Besides, she knew it would never be possible to investigate the case with DC Cox in charge. Jacoby might say yes, but Cox could override.

But like Woody said, Murphy was not beholden to Cox. She remembered the PI's e-mail, his offer of coffee. Maybe it was time to step out of her comfort zone. She'd pretended to sympathize with killers once or twice to gain their trust and a confession, and Murphy was not a criminal — just annoying.

"Anything to solve my parents' murders," she said as she fed Bandit and started her own breakfast.

Luke was grateful to Arvli and the crew for rescheduling his appearance on *Good Morning Long Beach* after the news about Abby leaked out. He was amazed the news about her traveled so fast. Arvli had learned from someone on the governor's staff, but he didn't tell Luke who.

"No such thing as a secret in politics, Luke," Arvli had told him. "Rollins's opposition for the senate is probably already trying to figure out how to tie the governor to the murders. Think that would knock him out of the senate race?"

"Probably."

The politics was the last thing Luke considered. For Luke, Abby's revelation brought the cold Triple Seven murders into present reality, and he appreciated any opportunity to talk about the case. He hoped it would gain some traction. And at the same time he wished he knew where Abby stood. Was she going to push to investigate? He prayed she'd respond to his e-mail soon. He itched to call Bill and maybe accidentally get ahold of Hart. But he had a lot of open cases of his own, not the least of which was Nadine.

After the interview, he drove to Crunchers again, wanting to be an annoying itch Sanders would eventually have to scratch. The eyesore recycling yard always gave him the creeps. He remembered visiting the place for car parts with his uncle when he was a kid. Back then he'd thought he'd seen monsters in the spaces between wrecked and rusting car bodies, and even now as an adult it made him nervous.

The junkyard trip was a disappointment. He was told Sanders was out of town and unavailable. The story was far from believable, but Luke had no leverage to press the issue. He got back into his truck and was intending to make his next stop Destination X when his cell phone rang. The number was unavailable and he almost didn't answer. Thinking it might be another reporter, he answered on the last ring.

"Mr. Murphy?"

Luke inhaled. "Detective Hart?"

"Yes. I'm responding to your e-mail. Are you available for coffee sometime today, say around 1 p.m.?"

"Uh, yeah, I am. This is a pleasant surprise." Luke felt excitement course through him.

"Java Shack on Second Street?" Her voice was all business.

"I'll be there."

CHAPTER 30

As Governor Mulls Senate Run, Decades-Old Cold Case Rears Its Head

Governor's Connection to 27-Year Unsolved Multiple Murder Surfaces

Both the *LA Times* and the local Long Beach paper had detailed stories on the Triple Seven, and both papers were waiting for Abby when she finally made it to her office.

"Who put these on my desk?" she asked Roper.

"Woody stopped by on his way home. He dropped them off."

Abby sat and scanned them. Reporters had stopped calling her. From news reports she gathered they really wanted a comment from the governor, but he hadn't issued one yet.

Abby had been summoned to the DC's office first thing that morning. It did her no good to explain to Cox that she had not revealed who she was to the press. Rollins or Murphy could have. Gunther certainly wasn't giving up his source. But as far as the DC was concerned, it was her fault. Surprisingly, it was the issue of the YouTube video that seemed to mollify the deputy chief. While Cox chastised her for taking such a dangerous leap, the video cast the department in a positive light, and that was a good thing for LBPD even if the Triple Seven still rankled.

"The last I checked, you have made no progress on the Jenkins murder; is that correct?"

"Yes, ma'am."

"How can you presume to work an old open-unsolved when you have current, fresh cases on your desk? Not that you would even be allowed to investigate the murders of your own parents, for heaven's sake!" She threw her hands up and paced. Abby stood in front of the DC's desk, doing her best to appear unmoved.

"All of this news coverage has caused the chief to cut his vacation short. He's on his way back as we speak."

"I admit I spoke to Gunther, but he was the original reporter —"

Cox waved her quiet, but Abby knew now the core reason for her anger: the chief was coming back, which meant Cox would no longer be acting chief of police.

Cox faced her, hands on hips. "The damage is done. All we can do is try to contain the blowback. But I want you to know that if for some reason the Triple Seven case is reactivated, it will be handled by Carney and O'Reilly, not Hart and Roper. Is that clear?"

"Yes, it is."

"Good. And I want you to give a brief statement to press relations about why and how you kept your identity quiet for so long in case the chief wishes to give an official comment on it."

With a wave of her hand, Abby was dismissed.

She visited community relations and gave a statement to the officer on duty. The woman was happy to have something to put in a press release, telling Abby the news channels were driving them crazy.

Abby was perplexed. "They stopped calling me. I knew this would be news, but I admit I never thought it'd be this big. Why am I such a big deal?"

"You're not," she said with a laugh. "But the connection to the governor is huge."

Woody had said as much, Abby thought as she walked back to her office. *Rollins makes all the difference. And I'll bet, in more ways than one.*

"Let's go work on Jenkins," she said, setting the newspapers aside.

She and Bill left the station and walked the neighborhood around the victim's business, talking to people without uncovering anything new. When they returned to the station, she gathered her purse to leave for her meeting with Luke.

"Anything wrong?" Bill asked. "You've been awfully quiet."

"Just annoyed by all the press." She opened her ancient Rolodex, something left to her by Asa. Since they were on the Jenkins case and Gunther had cryptically mentioned Crunchers, the reporter needed to be recontacted. But Abby didn't have the energy to field any of Gunther's inquiries about her past. One excellent perk of having a partner was being able to share.

"Do me a favor; call Walter Gunther." She gave him the card with Gunther's number. "He gave me the Crunchers lead on the Jenkins murder. See if he has any more to add."

Immediately interest sparked in his features, and as Abby turned to leave, Roper picked up the phone.

Wish everyone was that easy to please, she

thought.

All the way out to her car, she wondered at the wisdom of meeting Murphy. She almost called to cancel, but the phone rang before she could dial. It was DA Drew calling to say Lil' Sporty was indeed ready to cut a deal.

"That was fast," Abby said, surprised and a little relieved. Death penalty cases were often tough and drawn out.

"He's remorseful, according to his public defender. He's also on suicide watch."

"Probably more because he's in forced detox than anything else. Are you going to deal?"

"Only with the death penalty. We'll take that off the table. Nothing else."

"Thanks for letting me know." Abby hung up, certain Davis was her killer and knowing that without direct evidence, a jury trial could be a coin flip. The jury pool watched too many TV crime shows. They wanted to be wowed by DNA and super-secret crime lab techniques. Though Abby knew she'd give solid testimony, she wasn't an eyewitness and she couldn't show them a direct DNA match. She was too pragmatic not to appreciate that a sure conviction was a good thing.

Second Street was busy but not horrible

for afternoon. At noon the area was usually packed. Abby parked the plain car and sent dispatch a message saying she was code 7, out to lunch.

She saw Murphy as soon as she got out of the car. He stood on the sidewalk at the corner of Java Shack. He turned, and when she saw recognition in his expression, butterflies erupted in her stomach, a reaction she couldn't fathom. *I love Ethan,* she thought. *I don't even like this guy.*

Working to keep her face as blank as if she were going to interview a suspect, Abby walked up to him. "Thanks for meeting me." She extended her hand.

Murphy took it in a rough, strong grip. "Believe me, it's my pleasure. But why the frown? Do you have bad news?"

Mouth suddenly dry, Abby couldn't believe he'd read her so easily.

"Sorry; the press has been persistent to say the least."

He arched an eyebrow in understanding, then turned to open the door to the Shack. Abby entered first with Murphy right behind her. They both ordered coffee before finding an open table in the back.

"I was surprised by your call," Murphy said once they sat.

Not as surprised as I was that I made it,

Abby thought. But what she said was "It was a no-brainer. We both want the same thing. I saw you on TV and heard that you've been investigating the Triple Seven for a while. You've studied my parents?"

He nodded, and Abby sipped her coffee, nerves surfacing, wanting something familiar to settle them.

"When I put together a file, it was obvious that your folks were the targets, not my uncle. I tried to talk to the lead investigators but they were both retired. They were less than helpful, seemed to think I was criticizing their investigation." He tapped the table with two fingers. "I only wanted to help."

"Don't take it personal. It's a sore spot that the crime never was solved."

"Are you going to work the case?"

Abby shook her head. "I've memorized the investigation. Now that everyone knows who I am, I've been told that I'm too close. If the case is investigated, Carney and O'Reilly will be assigned."

"I know them; they're good guys. But that has to be rough. I mean, you tell Rollins who you are — I would imagine to get information to activate the case — but that ends up making it impossible for you to investigate the case."

Abby sat back, amazed he could see the whole picture so quickly. Her identity was the only thing she had to wager, and she'd staked everything on being able to elicit info from Rollins and lost.

Finally she sighed. "I hoped he'd talk to me. I also hoped he'd show some interest in finally resolving the case. It was a long shot."

"With you investigating?"

It felt like he had punched her. *"I feel as if I've known you my whole life."*

"Yeah, but he sure didn't seem to want to talk about it," she managed, hoping she didn't sound as jumbled as she felt.

"He did have a strange reaction. It's important for you to close this case, isn't it?"

Meeting his gaze and seeing the intensity there unnerved Abby for a minute. She played with her engagement ring and looked away before answering. "Of course. The murders of my parents changed my life. I drove myself to make it to homicide to find the killers." She stopped, feeling old anger and hatred boil up, emotions she thought she'd buried forever. Dede's words rang in her mind: *"Don't let the quest for justice become your god."*

"I get it," Murphy said simply, and Abby knew he did. His eyes calmed her and validated her anger all at the same time.

She sipped her coffee.

"I don't know how you stayed away from it for so long. I'd have been ramming my head against walls, shouting in the streets, probably gotten myself fired by now."

Abby smiled and studied the design on her coffee cup. "At first it wasn't easy. When I got hired, of course the background investigator knew but kept it confidential for Asa and Woody. Then during training, there was so much to learn about being a cop. When I finally did reach homicide, Asa was my partner and he really wanted me to leave well enough alone. And when my fiancé found out . . . he also wanted me to stay quiet."

"What's he say now?"

"He and my aunt both worry about my safety." She cleared her throat, not really wanting to talk about Ethan with Luke Murphy. "After working homicide for four years, I've seen how much an arrest and conviction can help the victim's friends and family. It can't put things back the way they were, but it does provide a measure of stability, I guess. Something they can lean back against and say, 'This bad thing happened, but there's justice in the end,' you know?"

"I do. I want my uncle's killer dealt with." His warm gaze regarded her, and the perusal made her shift in her seat. "You called me," he said. "I'm assuming it's because of this case. You want to talk to me about it?"

She wondered how to tell him what she wanted. He could refuse, and then how would she gracefully back out? But her parents' murders were too important for her not to try.

"I'd like to compare notes."

Murphy sat back and Abby relaxed. He was intrigued; he wasn't going to say no.

"How would you like to have dinner at my house tonight? Bring your files and we'll go over everything."

Abby stiffened. "It's not a date."

Murphy reddened and held his hands up. "Sorry; I didn't mean it that way. You just told me you're engaged. I live with my folks and my daughter. I just thought we'd be more comfortable going over everything in an informal environment."

Sipping her coffee, Abby struggled to keep her expression neutral. The invitation caught her off guard because she hadn't thought that far ahead. Did she want Murphy at her house? No.

"That might work," she said after a long

minute of awkward silence. "Would you mind if I brought my dog?"

CHAPTER 31

Abby pulled up in front of the East Long Beach house a little before six. She'd picked up her phone three times to call Murphy and cancel, scrolling through her contacts each time but stopping before dialing his number.

What am I thinking, going to his house?

In the end, the desire to learn what he knew overrode her discomfort. She scooped up Bandit and got out of her car, keeping an eye on two young girls playing basketball in the driveway. *Which one is Murphy's daughter?* she wondered.

As she walked toward the house, the taller of the two girls, with a long blonde ponytail bouncing, skipped toward the house.

"Dad, your friend's here!" She then turned toward Abby. "Can I pet your dog?"

"Sure," Abby said as the two girls charged her way. The taller girl was definitely Murphy's; the eyes confirmed it. Abby liked kids, worked in the nursery at church when she was able, and smiled as the girls got close.

"His name is Bandit," she said, anticipating their question.

"He's soooo cute!" both girls cooed at the same time the front door opened and Murphy stepped out onto the porch.

"Can I hold him?" Murphy's daughter asked.

Since Bandit seemed to be enjoying the attention, Abby said yes and handed her the little dog. His tail wagged ferociously, and when he began to lick their faces, the girls giggled.

"Detective Hart." Murphy stepped off the porch, a smile on his face. "Glad you could make it." He shoved his hands in his pockets as his daughter turned to him with Bandit next to her cheek.

"Look, Daddy, he's so cute. Can't we get a dog like this?"

Murphy grimaced. "We'll talk about it some other time. Right now you and Olivia need to wash up for dinner."

"But I want to hold Bandit."

"Later, I promise." Murphy's tone was firm, and Abby wondered if she'd made a mistake bringing the dog. She'd felt bad because she'd left him all day while she was at work. She didn't want to leave him all evening as well.

The girl made a face but handed the dog back to Abby and turned to go inside.

Murphy stopped her. "Just a minute." He gestured to Abby. "Detective Abby Hart, this is my daughter, Madison, and her friend Olivia."

"Pleased to meet you," Madison said, holding out her little hand.

"Likewise," Abby said. She shook two small hands, first Madison's, then Olivia's, then watched as the girls ran into the house.

"Sorry if bringing the dog created a problem for you," she said, facing Murphy.

He gave a dismissive wave of his hand. "Don't worry about it. Kids sometimes want everything they see. That's the dog from the other night, isn't it?"

"That's right. I forgot you would have seen Bandit then. I didn't have the heart to dump him off at animal control."

"Rollins did say that you could do what you thought best."

"I'm glad I got that out of him before he fled."

Murphy's mouth cocked into a lopsided smile. "He sure left in a hurry, didn't he? Makes me wonder about some things."

"Me too," Abby said. Her gaze shifted

when she saw movement over Murphy's shoulder. An older woman had stepped out of the front door.

"Luke, dinner is ready."

With those words Abby found herself following Luke Murphy into a house and a dinner with a family she would have avoided like the plague if it hadn't been for the Triple Seven investigation.

To solve the murders of her parents, Abby knew she'd step into any and every situation no matter how uncomfortable. Or dangerous, she realized, as Woody's fear and warnings echoed in her mind.

CHAPTER 32

"I'm sure you don't remember me, Detective Hart, but I knew you when you were six. I knew your parents as well." Grace Murphy spoke as everyone sat at the table.

Luke tried to watch Abby without staring. She had such a cop face, but he thought he saw an array of emotions briefly before she could shut down: discomfort, curiosity, maybe longing?

"I remember your name from the reports. I know your brother died getting me out of the fire. Please, call me Abby."

Grace took her seat. "That was my brother, always thinking of others. Luke was named after him. He loved working at that restaurant, loved your parents and Lowell."

"Cookie. I called him Cookie."

"Oh." Grace put a hand over her mouth. "You remember that? Your dad gave him that nickname. My brother made the best sugar-orange cookies. He made the best because he loved to eat them." She smiled and raised her hands, indicating it was time to bless the meal.

The girls stopped their chattering, clasped hands, and bowed their heads. Abby was on Luke's right, and it was a couple of seconds before she took his hand.

Luke's dad gave the blessing, ending by thanking God that Abby could join them for the meal. After the *amen,* the girls resumed their chatter, and Grace served everyone. While Luke had a million questions he wanted ask Abby, he let his mom start off.

"What a surprise when Luke told us who you were. My land, I'm amazed that you'd be back here. I admired your mom and dad; they were loving parents."

"I wish I remembered more of that period of time."

"You don't remember anything about the fire?" Luke asked.

Abby shook her head. "Not really. Only heat and Cookie telling me I'd be okay."

"Probably just as well," Grace said, her brow furrowed. Luke knew that meant time for a change of subject. "I don't recall your mother ever talking about a sister," she said. "And I was at the restaurant a lot. I adored my big brother."

"From what I know, my mother and her family were estranged. My grandparents let her stay here with friends to finish her senior year while they and Dede moved to Oregon. She never moved to rejoin them."

"I actually talked to the family your mother stayed with," Luke said. He wondered if Abby knew the family history he'd discovered during the course of his investigation. By the look on her face, he was betting no.

"You did? The Turners, right?"

"Yep. Betsy Turner was your mom's best friend. Your mom didn't want to be uprooted, and she was already dating your father."

She twirled her fork on her plate, and Luke hoped he wasn't upsetting her. But when she looked up, he saw only curiosity in her eyes.

"I know she married my father right after high school and before he joined the Army."

"Yeah, I don't know much about those years. I think your mom moved to where your father was stationed, and then they moved back to Long Beach after he got out. Most of the people I talked to remember her and your dad trying their hand at different businesses before they struck gold with the Triple Seven."

"That I remember," Grace said. "The first business was a flower shop — that was where my brother started working with them. He worked there while attending cooking school; then he went out of state for a while. When he got back, Lowell was in the picture with money, and they were talking about a restaurant."

"Yeah, Lowell had the money to get the restaurant started." Luke held Abby's gaze. "Your mom and dad did all the work; he just supplied the capital."

"The arrangement worked for them," Grace said. "I never remember seeing any friction. What about your grandparents, Abby?"

Grace took over and Luke listened. He'd seen the interest in Abby's eyes; they'd get back to Rollins soon enough.

"Something happened between my mom and my grandparents; I don't know what. From what Dede says, my mom cut them off. I certainly don't remember them at all. My dad's parents were deceased. My dad's brother, my only uncle, is in prison somewhere, so he was not an option. From the report I know police tried to notify my mom's parents, but by then my granddad was dead, and my grandmother was in a nursing home with dementia. Word didn't get to Dede about the murders for a couple of years. When she did hear and tried to find me, she spent a long time cutting red tape."

"All that to keep you safe?" Luke asked.

"That's what they told Dede. Social services was adamant that she keep quiet about who I was. As I got older, I wondered if they were more concerned that she might want to file a big, noisy lawsuit."

That comment brought chuckles, and Abby paused before continuing.

"In any event, my aunt was happy to take me away from the big city. When she adopted me, I took her married name, Hart."

"Is there still a threat for you?" Grace asked.

Abby grimaced. "Now? I don't know. People I trust tell me to be cautious."

"Which is wise," Grace said. "I remember that day, the day we found out what happened. It was such a horrific crime. Now you hear about such brutality on a daily basis, it seems like, but then it seemed a rarity."

"I can't imagine what it would have been like growing up, knowing your parents were murdered." Luke fought the urge to grip Abby's hand, knowing the gesture would be misinterpreted. "It was tough enough dealing with the loss of my uncle."

Abby held his gaze for a moment that Luke did not want to end.

Grace cleared her throat. "How about we move to a lighter subject. Do you attend a local church?" she asked.

Abby looked away. "Coast Christian Fellowship. My fiancé is the missions pastor there. He's in Africa right now on a mission trip."

"Ethan Carver is your fiancé?" Luke stared.

For her part, Abby looked surprised. "You know him?"

"I'm a part-time youth pastor at Central Community Church. I've heard Ethan give his testimony and talk about his trips."

"He's passionate about his work."

"He is." Luke didn't say more, but he thought about Ethan and wondered at the match. While he didn't know either Ethan or Abby very well, he didn't see them as a couple. Ethan was too serious, too dour. What did this vibrant, dedicated woman see in him?

"How did you meet Ethan?" Grace asked.

Luke looked down at his plate, sorry this subject had come up. Maddeningly, Abby didn't seem to mind.

Abby smiled. "I feel like I've always known him. My aunt Dede heads up the mission work for her church in Oregon. Ethan was a part of the group when I moved up there. He was just fifteen when I moved in with Dede. Over the years, we became good friends. Then after I moved down here, we reconnected when he came to church to speak about his work. About five years ago he accepted the job as head of the missions department here, and we started dating."

"When did you get engaged?"

Luke felt like sticking his fingers in his ears and saying, "La, la, la, la, la." He didn't want her to belong to someone else, but she did.

"About six months ago. When he gets back from this trip, we're going to set a date and start planning."

"How exciting." Grace beamed while Luke felt as though he were going to lose his dinner.

CHAPTER 33

Dinner took her by surprise.

"You have a nice family," Abby told Luke as she carried her Triple Seven book into his office.

Once she'd shifted the conversation away from her life and gotten Luke's parents to talk about their life, she was able to relax. Abby found she envied the warm, lively atmosphere around the table and in the household. It wasn't that Dede was cold — no, not at all. Abby loved her aunt and was thankful for how she had been raised. But it was usually only the two of them, and Abby remembered always wishing for what had been: an intact family with a mom and a dad.

"Thanks. I know that I'm blessed."

His office had obviously been converted from a garage. The space was masculine with a large desk, a couple of chairs and bookcases on one side, and assorted exercise equipment on the other. Abby noted the heavy bag, the weight set, and the elliptical machine and knew how Murphy stayed in such good shape.

"This is heavy," he said when he took the book from her and set it on his desk.

"I've been working on it for fifteen years."

"Seriously?"

"My aunt thinks I'm obsessed. I —" She stopped, realizing that the cozy family dinner had caused her to drop her guard.

But Luke simply smiled and pointed to a large bulletin board set up on one side of the room with the time lines for the Triple Seven murders and investigation along with quotes on Post-it notes from those he'd interviewed. "Maybe I'm obsessed as well."

Abby stepped to the board and studied it, realizing just how much investigative work Murphy had done.

"Do you think having this obsession means that we don't trust God?" she asked without looking away from the board. She was fascinated by his attention to detail.

"I think if the obsession causes us to sin or do things that are illegal or unethical, then it's time to worry."

She faced him. His no-nonsense expression gave her pause. He'd understand. Swallowing, she shared something she'd never even told Ethan. "When I was in foster care, I fantasized about finding the people who killed my parents and killing them."

"Sounds reasonable." Folding his arms, he sat on the edge of his desk. "You'd never do that. You'll settle for arrest and trial. I know that."

Abby smiled. "You don't really know me that well — you sure about that?"

"Anyone who'd dive in front of a train to save a serial killer is not the type of person who would take justice into her own hands. Even if it was personal."

"Uh, let's not talk about that train video."

He chuckled and watched her. His gaze had such warmth, Abby felt like she knew him, felt like he understood her in a way no one else ever had.

"Have you forgiven them — the people who killed your uncle?"

He rubbed his chin, and she knew what he was about to say came with effort. "I have to. I've been forgiven so much; I can't hold back my forgiveness for them. It would eat me alive. And you?"

"I try," Abby said, suddenly needing a change of subject. Forgiveness was essential, she knew, but she also knew at times it was as elusive as fragrance whisked away by a breeze.

She pointed to the upper left corner of his board. "You go all the way back to high school." The pictures looked as though they were cut from high school yearbooks. Her parents' youthful faces stared back at her.

If Murphy was troubled by the abrupt subject change, he didn't let on. He stood next to her. "I started with what I could get. Your mom, my mom, and my uncle graduated from Millikan High, while your dad and Rollins went to Jordan."

"I knew everyone was around the same age. Dede told me that my mom actually met Rollins first. He had money and a car, but she fell hard for my dad, who was his best friend. My dad was the reason my mom never moved to Oregon. I didn't consider going that far back to be germane to the investigation."

"Maybe it's not, but I was able to talk to a lot of people they went to high school with." He pointed to some sticky notes with writing on them. "Like Betsy Turner — she's in Arizona now."

"I see now why you feel like you've always known me. You know more about my parents than I do."

"I hope that's not creepy for you."

"Not sure how I feel about it yet. Let me digest this."

She soaked in the new information, not certain how long she stood there before Murphy spoke again.

"This is what I do in my spare time. Which lately hasn't been much."

She turned and saw a charming smile playing on his lips. "I imagine that video of you taking down a human trafficker lit your phone up."

"It did. It was worth it. He needed to go to jail. Though I could have done without the video."

"You didn't arrange that?" Abby wondered at how she'd read him so wrong. He seemed to have no trouble reading her.

"No! On the contrary." He shook his head. "I prefer doing my work quietly, using publicity only when I absolutely have to. The video was a double-edged sword. It brought me tips, but it also kept people from talking to me because —" he adopted a gangbanger pose and voice inflection — " 'Hey, you that private cop from YouTube.' "

Abby fought to keep from giggling and getting off track. "I guess I can see that. And I understand it somewhat."

"You're a YouTube star as well."

She threw her hands up.

"Yeah, I think you get my dilemma now."

"I guess I do."

She looked back to the board, uncomfortable in his gaze. There were also interviews with most of the people the police talked to. "Your board is amazing. I'd have to study it more to see if it provides any leads, but you've asked some important questions and gotten some fascinating answers."

"It's important to me to find out who killed my uncle." His expression turned hard and he focused on the board. "I idolized him when I was a kid. I was eight when he died, and it affected me."

"I understand where you're coming from."

He looked at her. "Of course you do."

Abby felt warmth flooding through her. For a second neither said anything, and Abby felt a connection that almost made her shiver. She looked away first.

"I'm especially interested in these comments from people who knew Rollins," she said, folding her arms. "You noticed his reaction the other day."

"I did. It made me think that maybe he was the target twenty-seven years ago and not your parents."

"What?"

"He was afraid. Maybe he fears your investigating the case will put him in danger."

"That wasn't my thought at all. I was thinking Rollins's reaction was one of a guilty man."

Murphy raised his eyebrows. "But he was cleared. His alibi was solid and never shaken."

"He profited in more ways than one from the deaths of my parents. He got the property; he got the notoriety that won him his first election."

"But the property and the insurance money he donated to the city for the park. And he's been an honest politician, at least as much as is possible in politics. Do you really think that someone who could callously murder three people could be such a good actor for twenty-seven years?"

"Woody said the same thing. I think that politicians are one step removed from actors. They learn to project an image — the best image, the one that will get them the most votes."

Murphy frowned and sat, motioning to Abby to do the same. She took a chair beside his desk.

"I like to think I have a sense about people."

"You mean you think you can read people?"

"It always served me well when I was in

the Army, and it has helped in the PI business. Rollins doesn't strike me as a killer."

"I've learned that killers are not always that easy to spot. I once handled a homicide where a seven-year-old killed his two-year-old brother. That's extreme, but my point is, Rollins appears good, but we don't know what's in his heart."

"I'll give you that. Only the Lord knows his heart." He picked up a paper clip and began to bend it back and forth. "Do you think that telling people you were Abigail Morgan put you in danger?"

"It does if the killer fears I'll uncover something. If the killer is Rollins, maybe he'll want to know exactly what I remember. Maybe he'll think I could point the finger at Uncle Lobo."

Luke leaned back. "Uncle Lobo — is that what you called him? I knew Lobo was his nickname, but 'uncle'?"

"He was always around. I remember that. But other things . . ." She bit her bottom lip in frustration. "No. I think I liked him, but I do remember that he and my father argued a lot. At least I think they did. It's all jumbled."

"If you remembered seeing him in the restaurant that day, that would be a big thing."

"I told you earlier what I think I remember of that day. But I'm not sure if it's because people have told me things, or I've read speculation. I'd been asleep." She opened her book, pulled out some pages. "I've added some notes, similar to what you have, based on things I learned after becoming a police officer. My father had a rep for being wild, but from what I've read, he and my mom worked hard to keep anything negative from affecting the restaurant. That place was their life."

She spread some papers out on the desk, and Luke leaned forward. Abby felt energized and relaxed at the same time. For so many years she'd been alone in the struggle to find her parents' killers; to be able to share and discuss the situation with someone as invested as she was acted like a stimulant. They bounced clues and theories back and forth for a while.

"There were three named suspects," she said. "Piper Shea, Ed Hendricks, and Tucker Jordon."

"Hendricks and Jordon were the robbery team."

Abby pulled out some photos. "They were good for several liquor store robberies. There are several interviews with them in the file."

"They always denied."

"And they had solid alibis. Plus, it was a stretch to think that after a botched robbery they'd burn everything down, especially my parents' house."

"What about Piper Shea?"

"He was never questioned, which bothered me for a long time. Their reasons for naming him had to do with his arrest at the restaurant selling drugs a few months earlier. My mom called the cops on him."

"Does it still bother you?"

"Yes and no. He was not violent like Hendricks and Jordon. And he never threatened my parents. Plus, what motive would he have to burn down our house? Your mother mentioned the viciousness of the crime. That strikes me as personal. Why would a two-bit drug dealer have such a personal grudge against my mom and dad?"

"I agree that the crime was intensely personal. The other day it looked as though Rollins might have been the target, but the more I thought about it, that idea really makes no sense. All the anger was directed at your parents. Why was Shea never interviewed?"

"From what I can tell, they never found him. In fact, a couple years ago I did a little search for Shea myself. No luck."

"You still can't find him?"

"He disappeared twenty-seven years ago. While I hate coincidences, I have to think that's all it is. The people we're looking for hated my mom and dad."

"And like me, you believe there was more than one person involved."

"Yeah, I do. There was too much destruction involved for one person."

For a minute there was silence as they studied the board and paperwork.

"Go back with me to high school. Though they went to different schools," Luke observed, "they all graduated the same year."

"Then they went different directions after graduation. Rollins to UC Berkeley, my dad to the Army."

"Even so, let me show you some yearbooks." He pointed to the bookcase. "My uncle also graduated from Millikan —"

There was a knock on the door, and they turned toward it at the same time. It was Madison with Bandit.

"It's my bedtime, Dad."

Abby and Luke both looked at the clock. It was 9:30.

Abby stood. "I had no idea it was so late." She held her arms out for Bandit, and Madison put him there.

"Grandma let me stay up a little later because she thought you'd finish, but now I have to go to bed."

Luke came around the desk and tousled the girl's hair. "Sorry about that, Maddie." He turned to Abby. "I'll be back in a few minutes."

"I should probably be going."

"Let's check out the yearbooks and then call it a night."

Abby agreed. She really didn't want to go. The connection she'd felt with Murphy while they pored over notes and interview transcripts was like nothing she had ever felt, and she didn't want it to end.

Madison said good night, and Luke left the room with his daughter.

Setting Bandit on her chair, Abby stepped to the bookcase and saw yearbooks from both Millikan and Jordan. Abby remembered Grace saying at dinner that she'd gone to school with her mother, though she was two years behind and had never interacted with her then.

Abby had few pictures of her parents. What hadn't burned in the restaurant had burned in their house. What she did have, she got from Dede and they were mostly of her mother growing up. But the images that stuck in Abby's mind when she thought of her parents were the photos from the old newspaper stories in the investigation files. The idea of seeing pictures she hadn't seen before was intriguing.

She found one of the proper years and opened it on the desk, turning to the *M*s. She found Buck Morgan and smiled when she saw his picture. Her dad had what Woody liked to call a "punch-me face": a face with a ready smirk. And apparently a personality to match, with a propensity to start trouble and get in fights. Since this yearbook was from her dad's junior year, there was also a picture of his older brother, her uncle Simon.

All Abby knew about Simon was what his police record told her. At age thirty-one, two years before she was born, he'd been involved in a bar fight with a bouncer who tried to throw him out. The bouncer died from his injuries and Simon went to jail. But a three- to five-year term for manslaughter became a life sentence without possibility of parole when Simon joined a prison gang and was involved in a riot where a guard lost his life. He'd been interviewed by the Puffs, who wondered if Simon had a grievance with his brother. They found nothing and Simon was crossed off the suspect list. Abby had checked to see where he was when she promoted to homicide. At that time he was housed in a prison in the high desert. She saw no point in contacting him. He'd been in prison for thirty-four years; there was no information he could give her except about the latest trends in prison tattoos.

Switching yearbooks, she flipped to *H,* where she located her mother and noticed how much Patricia Horn looked like Abby Hart. Her hair was fixed in the style of the year, and the smile was warm, not forced. Not liking the emotions the photos stirred up, Abby grabbed the Jordan yearbook again and turned to *R* and found Lowell Rollins. She frowned when she saw Louis Rollins right next to his brother. Louis was older by two years; why was he here?

Murphy reentered the office, carrying two mugs of what her nose told her was coffee.

"Sorry about that. I'd like to go for a little bit longer, if you're able. I even brought a bribe with me." He handed her a mug. "What's wrong? Did you find something?"

"Just a mystery." She sipped her coffee and pointed to Louis. "I thought he was older. I remember Rollins saying so the other day."

"He was, but he was also developmentally disabled. At that time kids like him were often held back a year or two."

"So that's why he's here. He worked at the Triple Seven washing dishes and was interviewed after the fire but was no help."

"But it bugs you."

"I guess. Not sure why."

"From what I learned, he didn't graduate high school. Dropped out about a year before he would have finished." Luke folded his arms and sat on the corner of his desk. "Your father was a party animal from everything I gleaned."

"Yeah?" Abby turned a few more pages, but she encouraged Luke to keep going while she looked.

"So was Rollins. And they were close. Buck and Lobo — they were the ringleaders for a lot of pranks and troublemaking, from what my mom and others say. There were four or five guys who ran with them, and their high jinks made high school interesting. Kent came on the scene later. Rollins met him at Berkeley."

"Gavin Kent?"

Luke nodded. "He's older; he was in college on the GI bill when he met Rollins. I got all this from an article that ran after he was first elected governor." He pulled the article out of a file and gave it to Abby.

"I know that my father enlisted right after

high school, but he never saw combat. Rollins was 4-F — I saw that somewhere." She glanced at the article. "My dad moved back to Long Beach and went to Long Beach State with his service money."

"Yes, I think that is when Buck reconnected with Rollins," Luke said. "Rollins was working on a master's degree. Everyone I talked to who knew them said they acted as if no time had passed — they were still great friends. And they were hot to start a big, successful business." He pointed to some names on the board, and Abby recognized the names of businesses her parents started that failed.

Luke continued and Abby enjoyed the narrative. "They finally hit pay dirt with the Triple Seven. Everyone who was around Long Beach then says the restaurant was a special place. It and the *Queen Mary* put us on the map. Buck Morgan and Lowell Rollins got some big names to patronize the place and perform there. By that time all their juvenile pranks were far behind them."

He sipped his coffee. "Kent was a war hero, very decorated. It's no wonder he's tough to get through."

"That's right; you've tried to talk to Rollins."

"*Tried.* The standard line is 'The governor

doesn't live in the past.' " His brow fur-rowed. "You didn't have any better luck. Do you think he'd talk to you if the case were officially reactivated?"

"You know I can't do that. You, on the other hand, are not subject to Cox's orders. You can keep asking questions."

"I still don't think Rollins is a killer."

"We don't have to agree at first. The facts will prove who is right."

He cocked his head. "I suppose." He leaned forward and pulled out a pen and a legal pad. "Let's get as much done as we can tonight."

Abby sat back in the chair and pulled it closer to the desk, nodding in agreement.

Time passed unnoticed for Abby. It wasn't until her phone began to play "Bang Bang" that she saw it was almost midnight. A dispatch extension brought a frown.

"Interesting ringtone," Murphy said.

"No message to it — I just like oldies," she said as she stood to answer the call. "But I'm not on call, so it's odd. Excuse me for a second." She walked to the doorway and answered the phone.

A familiar dispatcher greeted her. "Detective Hart, sorry to bother you, but I have Westside Woody requesting you. It's an at-tempted homicide and the victim had your card in her pocket, so he wonders if you wished to respond."

Abby's stomach took a queasy roll and she turned to face Murphy. He stood, alarm showing on his face.

"Can you have Woody call me?" Abby asked.

At the dispatcher's affirmative, Abby ended the call and waited, pacing toward the exercise equipment. Any number of people would have her card — she gave it out often, especially when she was trying to find witnesses. She'd handed out several that day when she and Roper had worked the Jenkins case. So why was her stomach a pit of dread?

"What's wrong?" Murphy came toward her, his eyes wary.

Voicing what could only be called intuition, Abby said, "It might be Nadine."

CHAPTER 34

"It might be Nadine."

Abby watched Luke pale at the words, but he said nothing as they waited for the next call.

The phone rang a few minutes later. Abby told him it was Woody before she answered.

"Sorry to get you up, but I got a call about a woman down at Hotel Pacific, and wouldn't you know it — it's that runaway we talked about last week, Nadine Hoover. She's been beat up good. This may be a homicide before morning; she's circling the drain. I went through dispatch because I want this to be official if you want to respond."

Abby took a deep breath and worked to keep her reaction calm with Murphy's steady gaze focused on her. "I'm not on call this week."

"I know. I had dispatch call Jacoby before they called you. He put the ball in your court. If you want to respond, it's your case."

"All right. Is the scene secure?"

"Yep. I thought she was dead when I got there, so I buttoned everything up tight. I'll let them know you're on the way." He gave her the address and the names of the officers on scene.

Abby's mind churned, and she began to pace again, ignoring Murphy for a minute. Evidence gathering in the first hours after a murder was crucial. Nothing would be different with a living victim. "I can be there in about twenty. Woody, was a weapon used?"

"No, it looks like fists."

"Sexual assault? Defensive wounds?"

"Not apparent on the first. She was fully clothed. . . . Uh, some wounds, though, yeah. She fought back."

"Do me a favor — if they haven't cleaned her up, bag her hands. I'll try to get the lab tech over there as soon as I can to scrape under her nails."

"You got it."

She faced Murphy. "They found Nadine severely beaten in a hotel room on the west side."

"But she's alive?"

"Right now." Abby picked up Bandit and

headed for the door.

Murphy grabbed her arm. "I want to go with you."

She hesitated for a million reasons, but not wanting him to come wasn't one of them. The warmth that spread through her whole body from his touch, the hazel eyes that missed nothing, and the realization that she wanted to keep the connection she'd felt during their discussion all conspired to cause her to fumble for words.

Murphy obviously thought she didn't want him along.

"Look." He released her arm and crossed his. "You'll call me anyway and you know it. Besides, I can get ahold of her mother—"

The words finally formed. "Yes, you can come."

"What?"

"Just hurry. I have to drop Bandit off on the way, so there's no time to lose."

"Great. I'll just be a second."

Luke hadn't felt so tense and off-balance since the day he arrived home from overseas to see his injured little girl in the hospital and to bury his wife.

He'd hopped into Abby's car after giving his mom the news. Abby had a police radio in her car, and she turned it on so they could listen for any traffic related to Nadine's call.

"She was found at a room in the Hotel Pacific," Abby told him.

"Will Bill be there?"

"We're not on call. I'll have to see what's going on and call our lieutenant to see if Bill is approved to respond."

The detective then clammed up. They stopped at her house, which Luke thought fit her, solid lines and no-nonsense. She jogged in with the dog and jogged out a few minutes later with a thick briefcase Luke guessed was her crime scene field kit. She had her cop face on, and Luke found that it inspired him with confidence; they'd catch whoever did this to Nadine.

Hotel Pacific was very near the house that had brought Abby into Luke's life, he thought as they exited the freeway on the west side of the city. He and Bill had walked by the tired hotel several times during their fruitless search for Nadine.

Flashing lights of several police cars lit up the night in front of and along the alley beside the Pacific.

Luke unhooked his seat belt as Abby parked behind a black-and-white.

"I have an extra Windbreaker in my trunk.

Wear it, and I hope I don't have to tell you not to touch anything." She faced him, hands together in front of her chest. "And you will not, under any circumstances, give any statement to the press, unless approved."

"Of course not." Luke wondered where that came from but didn't pause to debate the point. He reached across the car and grabbed her arm as she opened the car door. She turned and he saw something indefinable cross her face briefly and then the cop face was in place. "Thanks for bringing me along."

"Sure."

Luke released her arm, and both of them got out of the car, stopping at the trunk, where Abby handed Luke a Windbreaker with *Police* stenciled on the back. He put it on as they walked toward the hotel room with the open door and the obvious police presence.

The first thing that caught Luke's eye when he could see through the open door — and the thing that compressed his chest — was the pink-and-green backpack he'd seen Nadine carrying a thousand times. Her teen girl giggle resonated in his memory, and he prayed that despite the evidence to the contrary she'd be okay.

It looked as though the contents of the pack had been dumped out and strewn over the bed. A furious struggle had obviously taken place. There was blood spatter on the wall behind the bed with more blood pooled on the floor. Luke guessed that was where the girl ended up. The one nightstand in the room was knocked over and the cheap lamp broken.

"Who called?" Abby asked the uniform handling the scene.

"Hotel manager. Apparently there were complaints from several other hotel occupants." He rolled his eyes, and Luke got the hint that that was likely because the other rooms were rented by the hour.

"He didn't act on the first complaint, which was —" the officer checked his notes — "around eleven. It took two more complaints for him to check on the room and then call us. By the time Woody got here, the suspect was gone and the girl had been pounded. We interviewed as many people as we could. All we got was they heard noise but did nothing."

Another officer stepped forward. "Detective, there was one guy who got involved, a john. He apparently saw what was happening — the door was cracked open — and confronted the assailant. Got slugged for

292

his trouble; then he fled. His, uh, 'date' was still here when we arrived. Woody talked to her."

Luke watched Abby biting her lip as she considered this.

"A good lead?" he asked.

"It could be if we can ever talk to the Good Samaritan. Odds are it was a married man having a tryst with a hooker, and the last thing he'll want to do is be a witness. I'll bet Woody knew the working girl because this is his beat. I hope he has more for us when we get to the hospital."

She stepped inside the room and motioned for Luke to stay in the doorway. Even from there the smell hit him. Old pizza and sweat. He could see leftover pizza and old fries in Destination X wrappers on the bureau. From the trash strewn about, he bet Nadine had been holed up here for a while. Coins and one or two bills comingled with the trash on the floor. So this was no ordinary robbery.

He concentrated on watching Abby and started when someone tapped his shoulder. He stepped aside for the lab tech.

"Two weeks in a row on call?" she asked Abby.

"Long story." Abby turned an intense gaze to Luke. "Do you recognize anything here?

Step inside for a minute."

"The backpack is hers, and some of the clothes I recognize as probably hers." He did a slow sweep of the room. "I don't see her phone. She had a neon-green case for her phone."

Abby folded her arms and turned back to the lab tech. "When you finish with the pictures, I'd like all the stuff that looks like it belongs in the backpack in an evidence bag. I'll take it to the hospital on the off chance the victim can tell us if there is anything that doesn't belong to her. Process the backpack yourself. I'm hoping you'll get some evidence off of it. If the suspect was angry and if he's the one that emptied it, maybe we'll get lucky with saliva —"

"How'd you get a live one?" the lab tech asked.

Luke jerked back in her direction. *Live one.* Abby was homicide. Would that be how Nadine would eventually be classified?

CHAPTER 35

Hands on hips, Abby cocked her head and considered the tech's question and the wounded expression on Murphy's face.

"She's hanging on, at the hospital in critical."

"Part of the long story?"

"Yeah. I'll need you over there to check her fingernails for trace evidence. I'm off to talk to the hotel manager."

The manager was no help. He'd rented the room a week earlier to a blonde girl who said her name was Helen Smith. He saw nothing, he heard nothing, and he only called the police because other clients were complaining. As to the guy who got involved, since he hadn't checked in yet, the manager knew nothing about him. Twenty minutes later Abby and Luke were on their way to Memorial Medical Center.

Frustrated, Abby worked through the bits and pieces of the puzzle she had so far. The hotel was close to Destination X, and if Nadine had her card, Abby guessed it was the one she'd given Mr. Piggy. Did she run to hide because Abby had spooked her? Or was she already hiding from whoever it was who beat her?

"I need coffee," she said as she pulled into a 7-Eleven driveway. "Do you want anything?"

"No thanks." Luke regarded her with those eyes, and it made her tingle with warmth as she hurried into the store. She selected and poured coffee on autopilot as possible scenarios about what happened to Nadine ran through her mind. Had the girl run away with a dark purpose and had that caught up to her? What would bring about such a savage beating? Abby could only pray that Nadine would soon be able to tell her. She kept her scenarios to herself when she got back into the car to continue to the hospital.

When they walked into the emergency room, Abby got a confused smile from Woody when he saw Murphy. It changed to welcome when he saw the coffee she'd brought for him. Abby knew he hated hospital coffee.

"Bless you," he said as he took the cup.

"No problem. How is she doing?"

"Not as bad as I initially thought, but bad enough. Possible head injury, broken arm and nose, internal bleeding, and fractured ribs."

Abby heard Murphy mutter something as Woody listed the injuries. She didn't look his way.

"She needs surgery, but they're waiting on the mom for permission. I sent a unit to pick her up. Hands are bagged, but if she needs to go into surgery . . ." Woody's voice trailed off, and Abby knew that the hospital would need her sterile in surgery.

"Lab is on the way," she told Woody.

"How'd she get your card?" Woody pulled it out of his pocket. It was the one she'd left at Destination X, with a note to Nadine scribbled on the back.

"I talked to a manager at Destination X who said he'd seen her." She sipped her coffee. "I guess I hoped she'd contact me."

Woody regarded her for a moment, and Abby knew he was wondering what had gotten into her.

"I talked to Georgie on scene," he said after a minute.

Abby knew the name. Georgie was a working girl everyone on the west side had arrested for one thing or another.

"Her john confronted the suspect, got

popped in the mouth for his trouble. But that could be the reason the guy stopped punching our vic and fled, so maybe the interference saved the kid's life." He reached into his pocket for an interview card and handed it to her. "Here's what she had to say. And the john was a regular, so there's a small —" he held his hand up, pinching the index finger and thumb together — "chance we'll get a shot at him. Georgie says she'll call me if he shows up again."

Just then the lab tech trotted in.

"I'll take her back there," Woody said. "Why don't you wait for the mom and bring her up to speed."

"Sounds good," Abby said, and she and Murphy sat in the waiting room. She bent to study Woody's notes.

"You left your card for her?" Murphy's question jolted Abby from her thoughts.

"Um, yeah. I wanted the creep at Destination X to call me when she stopped by. Easier to give him a card than to trust him to look up my number. I give my card to a lot of people." Abby hiked one shoulder, not sure why the subject made her uncomfortable.

Murphy smiled. "Thanks. It was a decent thing for you to do." His phone rang, and he looked at the number and grimaced. "It's

Glynnis. The officers must be at her house."
He stepped aside to take the call.

Abby turned her attention back to the card Woody had given her.

Georgie described the beater as "big like a giant." When she was pressed, Woody got her to specify: the man was six-five to six-six, heavy but all muscle. Abby considered this, trying to place a name to such a description, but not having the same luck she'd had when Lil' Sporty's name came to mind. After a few minutes she drew a blank and let her gaze wander around the waiting room, resting on Murphy, who finished up his call. Pain etched his features, and Abby felt it in her own being.

"The uniformed officers freaked her out, but she's on her way."

Abby returned her attention to Woody's notes. It wasn't long before she was pacing the waiting area. It was empty — this wasn't a bustling weekend; it was an early Wednesday morning. She barely noticed when Murphy got up to use the restroom. But the whoosh of the emergency room door opening got her full attention.

Though she'd never seen the woman before, Abby knew Nadine's mother immediately. It was the frantic eyes.

"Mrs. Hoover?"

"Yes, yes, where's my daughter? What happened to my daughter?"

"I'm Detective Hart. I'll be handling her case. Let me see if I can find the doctor for you." Abby stepped toward the nurses' station.

But Mrs. Hoover grabbed her arm. "What's happened to Nadine?" Her eyes bored into Abby's, a swirling mixture of anguished emotions — pain, fear, and anger.

"She was beaten, Mrs. Hoover, pretty seriously. We found her at a hotel on the west side — Hotel Pacific. There isn't much more I can tell you."

She paled. "It's been over a week. I've been searching, praying for her to come home safe. I —"

Abby feared the woman would faint and shook off her grip only to exchange it for a grip of her own. Taking both of the woman's arms, she led her to a chair. "Deep breaths, Mrs. Hoover." She knelt in front of the woman. "Is there someone I can call for you? Someone you want to be here with you?"

"Where's Luke? I want Luke."

CHAPTER 36

Abby wondered at the flash of discomfort she felt while she watched Murphy soothe Glynnis Hoover. They were obviously close. *Which is a good thing,* she told herself. *I have Ethan. He has Glynnis.*

After a few minutes they parted and Murphy led Hoover to a chair. Nearby there was a box of Kleenex and she made use of it.

"Mrs. Hoover," Abby said quietly, "I need to know more about the circumstances surrounding Nadine's disappearance. Have you any idea why she ran away?"

Glynnis bounced up, spitting nails. "Oh, *now* the police are concerned. Now, after my baby's been broken to pieces." The sobs started. "You didn't care before," she squeezed in between racking, shuddering breaths. "You didn't care when you could have helped my baby, could have found her."

Abby stayed quiet, not minding the

301

woman's outburst. She was angry and in pain and needed to direct her emotion somewhere.

Murphy jumped in and grabbed her shoulders. "Glynnis, that's not fair. Detective Hart didn't do this to Nadine, but she'll work hard to find out who did."

Glynnis Hoover shook him off and stormed away toward the restroom.

Murphy turned to Abby. "I'm sorry about that. She's distraught."

"Don't worry about it. I understand. If she needs to punch me, I can take it."

"I'd hate to think of anyone punching you," he said.

Abby let the comment pass.

He looked at her for a moment and then continued. "I'll tell you as much as I know about her leaving, but you probably already know everything. One of the reasons Glynnis is so upset is that Nadine gave no indication she was unhappy at home and considering running away. On the contrary, the family is very close. Nadine's father was killed in a traffic accident two years ago, and because of that, Nadine, her mom, and her younger brother have grown extremely close. Nadine got a job after she turned sixteen to help Glynnis with finances."

He ran a hand over his hair. "When she

disappeared, it was so out of the blue. She had plans to be with us; she was looking forward to Saturday night."

"But she sent her mother a text message?"

"Yeah, they used to text all the time. Glynnis has practically worn her fingers to the bone texting Nadine this past week, but since that one message, there's been nothing else."

"You saw the hotel room. Nadine had clothes with her; she'd packed a bag. That wasn't an indication she wanted to run away?" Abby asked, remembering what had been strewn over the bed.

"No, that weekend we had an overnight trip planned."

"You and Nadine and her mother?"

"No, no." He gave a little chuckle. "I guess I'm more tired than I thought. I told you I'm a part-time youth pastor at our church. That's how I know Nadine and her mother. I took a group of kids from church to San Diego for a Saturday night crusade the weekend she disappeared. Nadine had packed her backpack that morning and was going to catch a ride with her friend Janey to the church. She'd planned to pick up her pay from work and they would meet. But Janey showed up at church saying she didn't know where Nadine was. She ended up staying to help Glynnis search that night. As soon as I got back, I jumped in to help as well."

Abby considered this. "Did she have any issues at work?"

"None that I was aware of at the time. But this Sunday I spoke to Janey and she said something happened at work that seemed to upset Nadine. Nadine and Janey both work for Janey's stepfather, George Sanders. He owns Crunchers."

"Crunchers?"

"What's wrong? Do you know Sanders?"

"Unfortunately, I do." The junkyard had come up all too often recently. "I arrested him once a long time ago for a minor charge. He paid a fine, did community service, and that was it. He always seems to escape the serious charges."

"He's a crook, isn't he?"

"Let's just say he's shady. And he keeps a very talented attorney on retainer." He was a man who sent all of her cop instincts into the red zone. And Gunther had mentioned Crunchers in relation to the Dan Jenkins murder. Too many coincidences.

"What did Nadine do there?"

"She, um, helped with inventory and was trying to learn basic bookkeeping."

"Now it's my turn. What's wrong?"

Murphy gave a little grimace. "Janey confided in me that a couple of weeks before Nadine disappeared, two men came to the yard, men who were mad at Sanders. They wanted something from him." He told Abby what Janey had told him on Sunday. "I haven't had a chance to ask Sanders about those two guys or the security video. What I wouldn't give to be able to look at that video. I'd especially like to now, since I think I saw the big guy following me on Saturday night."

"What?" The thought of viewing taped activity at Crunchers made Abby sit up straight, but the last sentence really had her attention.

Murphy told her about his search with Bill and being shadowed. She knew then all roads would lead to Crunchers. She wanted to get up and pace, but first she showed him Woody's card with Georgie's description. "Look at this."

His eyes widened. "It's got to be the same guy."

"Bill and I will talk to Sanders. Did he see this guy?"

"He did, called him a BUG."

Abby knew the reference. "The text message also bothers me," she said. "There was no cell phone at the hotel. And you said her mother has been texting her?"

"Yes." They turned at the same time as Glynnis Hoover came back into the waiting room. Her eyes were puffy and red but she was composed. "The first couple of days I sent her a text every few minutes."

"And never got a response?"

"I explained all of this to the juvenile detectives," she hissed, arms held tight against her chest.

Abby let that go and held the woman's angry, pained gaze. "I can't speak to that, Mrs. Hoover. All I can tell you is that Nadine's case is mine now, and I will find out what happened and arrest whoever is responsible."

A large group of people poured into the emergency room, including her new partner, Bill Roper, and a woman Abby guessed was his wife. The mass swarmed around Glynnis while Bill pulled Abby aside and asked to be brought up to speed. While Abby told him what was going on, she couldn't help but notice the group crowding together. Some held hands while others had their arms around the person next to them. She believed in prayer but knew that prayer was often not enough when it came to bringing criminals to justice.

CHAPTER 37

Nadine came through surgery and was in recovery before Luke felt he could leave the hospital. The doctor's report was encouraging. He'd stopped her bleeding, set the worst fractures, and there was no indication of debilitating brain injury. She had a lot of healing to do and would probably need some plastic surgery, but her youth and strength gave her very good odds of a full recovery. Her mother was encouraged and was at Nadine's bedside, waiting for her to wake up.

Bill's wife, Gail, was a nurse at Memorial, so she'd stayed with Glynnis while Bill went with Abby when she left to file her report. Luke had hung in until about eight but wanted to go home and get some sleep.

"Is there anything else I can do?" Luke asked Glynnis before he left.

"Please, bring Gage to the hospital later. He's going to a friend's house right after school, but he'll want to see his sister." Gage was Nadine's little brother.

"No problem. What time should I pick him up?"

"Around three." She gave him a piece of paper with the address and the phone number for Gage's friend. "Thank you for everything, Luke."

"Just glad she's back." He placed an arm around her shoulders. "And happy to help my friends." Luke left the hospital relieved he'd have time for a nap. He was beat. But Nadine was alive and the prognosis was good.

His mother was already in the loop because of the prayer team, and when he got home, she was making arrangements to take a shift at the hospital to spend time with Glynnis.

Once in his room, he kicked his shoes off and fell into bed. When he closed his eyes, he thought of Abby Hart. A sliver of guilt snaked through him as his thoughts left Glynnis and Nadine and focused on Hart. So cool, so strong. He knew she'd find the person responsible for Nadine's condition. But the more he saw her, the more he wanted to see her and learn more about Abigail Hart off duty. A pang twisted in his chest as he remembered her engagement and knew he'd never get closer, even though he hoped to keep a connection to her through the Triple Seven investigation. Between the two of them, they'd solve the murders, he was sure.

Luke was up and ready for a run after ninety minutes of sleep. He'd perfected power naps in the service and was glad they still worked for him. He called Grace for an update.

"How are things?"

"Nadine is showing signs of waking up, but she hasn't opened her eyes yet. Glynnis finally closed her eyes, so I hope she gets some rest."

"Do you need me to bring anything besides Gage?"

"No, we're well stocked with prayers, love, and food."

Luke smiled as he hung up. Glynnis and Nadine had an army praying for them, which had to help.

He changed into running clothes. Madison was with a homeschool group visiting a museum today. He saw a text from her, so he returned it before he left on his run. Love you too! Learn lots today. Dad.

He set the phone down, and it immediately buzzed with an incoming call. The screen showed the number as unavailable. Luke guessed it was the PD, but the familiar voice disarmed him.

"Bullet, is that you?"

Luke smiled at the sound of the old nickname. "Ice Age? The tanning booth hasn't melted you yet?" Todd Orson had gotten the nickname Ice Age because of his pale complexion. But since Orson had joined the bureau, Luke had heard a rumor that he'd developed an addiction to tanning booths and his new nickname there was Agent Orange.

"Ha. Sharp wit as ever."

"Great to hear from you. It's been too long."

"Didn't you get my e-mail?"

"I did, but life has been crazy lately. I confess I let it go to the back of the brain."

"I've been promoted in a way, and that's why I sent the e-mail and why I'm on the phone with you. I'll be in your neck of the woods soon. Can you squeeze me into your schedule sometime soon?"

Luke sighed and wondered when he'd fit his friend in. "Are you in town now?"

"I'll be there by the weekend. You too busy?"

"Not for an old friend, but a lot is going on right now. Call me when you get into town and we'll make arrangements."

"Roger that. Take care, Bullet."

"You too. Good to hear from you."

Luke shoved the curiosity down deep and left for his run. He lived close to a bike path that paralleled a concrete riverbed, or flood control channel, and eventually led to Serenity Park. At the park there was a challenging exercise course, but today he didn't think he had time for it. He'd just travel out and back.

The San Gabriel River stretched from the foothills to the beach, emptying into the ocean between Seal Beach and Long Beach. When Luke hit the trail, the water was a thin ribbon in the center of a concrete basin. The flow increased in size and strength as it neared the ocean. It reached peak depth and width about a mile and a half from the park. Huge, uneven rocks lined both sides of the channel, so this was not a river one slid down the bank and swam in. Boaters could chug upriver for a bit if they entered from the ocean, and often on his run Luke would see water-skiers. It was more common that he shared the asphalt path with other joggers and bike riders.

Within a few minutes he was running at a good pace and enjoying the opportunity to work off the stress from the night before.

He thought about the big guy spotted in Nadine's hotel room and knew it was the same guy he and Bill had seen following them.

How did Nadine cross paths with such a man except at Crunchers?

What does Sanders know that he's been keeping back?

How could he withhold information that would have helped Nadine, his daughter's friend?

Does the security video tell the whole story?

The more questions raised by the situation, the angrier Luke got. His pace picked up, and he had generated a healthy sweat by the time he reached the last underpass before the branch to the park. When Luke took the right branch to cross over the channel, he'd end up in Long Beach at Serenity Park.

He'd crossed under several bridges along the way, and every so often homeless people set up camps beneath them. Luke wasn't surprised to see a person moving around under the bridge near the branch that would take him to his destination.

But what did surprise him was that there were two men. They weren't homeless, and they both acted as if they were waiting for him.

Breathing hard, he shortened his stride and prepared to stop a safe distance from the pair. They could be brothers. Hard-looking men, ex-military, he guessed, but older and before his time.

"You Murphy?" the one on Luke's left asked. He wore a plaid shirt open over a gray T-shirt. The other had on a dark-blue hoodie.

Luke stopped short of the pair, just under the bridge, and swallowed, working to regulate his breathing. At this point the path dipped down nearly even with the water. When there was a lot of rain and the flood control ran high, water splashed across the path. But it was summer now and the path was dry while the water level licked just below.

"Who's asking?" Luke asked, hands on hips, breathing slowing.

Plaid Shirt stepped forward. There was a bulge on the man's right side barely concealed by the open shirt, and Luke knew the man was armed.

"Consider me a friend. A friend with a friendly warning." He raised a hand and pointed an index finger. "Back off the Triple Seven. You have too much to lose."

Luke felt his face flush with anger. "Friends don't threaten friends."

"It's a warning." He reached into his shirt pocket and pulled out a piece of paper. When he unfolded it, Luke saw that it was a computer printout of a picture of Maddie and Olivia playing basketball in the driveway of his home.

Luke saw red. He felt as though he'd been kicked in the stomach. His nickname, Bullet, came from his temper; when he lost it, he went off like a shot fired. He lunged for the man, hitting him hard with a roundhouse left punch. Plaid Shirt was surprised by the move and put up no defense. He stumbled back and tripped on the rocks. His arms windmilled as he fell backward into the water of the flood control.

From the corner of his eye Luke saw motion in the direction of the other man and knew he had to move. He dove into the water after the first man even as he heard the crack of a gunshot.

CHAPTER 38

"Why didn't you call me?" Bill asked as soon as he and Abby walked out of the hospital.

"We weren't on call. I don't have the authority to approve overtime. And this wasn't a homicide."

"I could've helped, overtime or no. We're partners now."

He stopped at her car while Abby bit off a caustic remark. This was why she didn't want a partner. People didn't think the way she thought, and they were always ready to take offense where none was meant. She didn't want to fight with Bill. She was too busy fighting with herself, fighting feelings raging within her over a guy she kept insisting she didn't like.

Luke Murphy had taken charge of the situation in the hospital. He knew the right things to say, organized all the people who came to support Glynnis Hoover, and handled the emotional situation with wisdom and compassion. The people there listened to him and respected him. Abby saw a lot in the man that made her want to know more than old facts surrounding a twenty-seven-year-old homicide. But now there was Glynnis.

"You okay?"

Abby looked up and saw concern where irritation had been. She struggled to get her focus off Murphy and back where it should be — finding Nadine's attacker.

"Yeah, I'm just tired. I need some more coffee and one more look at the hotel room."

"Good. I want to see the place as well."

"Once we get some coffee in us and I file my paper, Crunchers should be open. We need to visit Crunchers."

"Glad to hear you say *we*. You think this has something to do with her work there?"

"Something made her run." She started the car and pulled away from the hospital. "I get the impression it wasn't home life. By the way, did you ever get in touch with Gunther about his Crunchers info?"

"Left a message. Haven't heard back." Bill tapped a rhythm on his doorframe. "As far as Nadine and Glynnis go, they're close. I've never seen any teen rebellion there."

She pulled into a convenient drive-through and ordered coffee. The sky was brightening with morning sun, and Abby was amazed she wasn't exhausted. Aggravated and a little off-balance, but not exhausted.

She handed Bill his coffee and took a big gulp of her own.

Bill sipped his coffee. "How'd Nadine get your card anyway?"

"I guess I did your friend a favor. He helped me out on the Murray homicide." She shrugged. "I stopped at Destination X on my way home and told the day manager to give it to her if he saw her. That reminds me — we need to go there as well, find out when she picked the card up."

"That was nice of you. Luke's a good friend. He'd either be a general by now or a good cop if his wife hadn't died."

"Did you serve with him in Iraq?" Abby struggled to remember if Bill was one of the many reservists on the department.

"I did, proudly. He's a great guy."

"How did his wife die?"

He frowned and rubbed his forehead with one hand. "Car accident." He paused. "She drove into oncoming traffic."

Abby sat back for a moment. She dealt with violent death every day, but when it touched someone she knew, the shock felt like a palpable blow.

Roper held her gaze with a knowing one. "Yeah, it was a jolt. And a miracle Madison wasn't killed as well. The worst part is that Luke was the reason Sherri got distracted. They were on the phone arguing. Luke had just finished his last deployment and was in Germany planning to re-up, but Sherri wanted him home permanently. He heard the crash; then the phone disconnected. The next call he received was someone telling him she was dead. So he tossed away thoughts of reenlistment and came home to take care of his daughter."

"Wow," Abby said, cringing for Luke. She had enough sense of his personality to bet he blamed himself.

Bill went on. "About a year after he came home, he decided to become a cop and thought he could juggle being a single father and a career in law enforcement. But a couple of months in, he realized the time involved. He felt he'd be a better father if he started his own business. That's why he got his PI license."

Bill talked a bit about their service but was quiet when they reached the hotel and he saw the damage to the room.

Abby let him go through it on his own while she dealt with the hotel manager again, hoping he'd give her a little more. He gave her nothing but grief, wanting the room back.

"It's my business! Business!"

"Nothing here. You can have your room back," Bill said after he finished. He looked at Abby, and she knew from the tight set of his jaw the amount of violence directed at Nadine affected him.

The few minutes back to the station were quiet, and for that, Abby was thankful. She needed to think.

"I need to catch up on my voice mail and file the paper on Nadine. Would you mind checking with auto theft, see if they have anything going on at Crunchers right now?"

Bill arched an eyebrow. "Good idea. I'll go there now."

They parted and Abby drained her coffee as she sat at her desk. Voice mail told her Dan Jenkins's widow had called.

Looking at the time, she saw it was still early, so she worked on the report about Nadine first.

She refilled her coffee cup before she made the call back.

When she called Marilynn Jenkins, she was relieved to hear that the woman seemed to be getting her balance back. The last two times they'd spoken, Marilynn had dissolved into tears after hello.

"I remembered something. I don't know if it's important or if it can help."

"Anything might help."

"Well, we had been storing some boxes for George Sanders in our garage. When Dan decided to run for office, he needed the space and returned the boxes. But after he did, he seemed upset for some reason."

"George Sanders from Crunchers?" Abby's entire body tensed as a connection cinched tight. The junkyard again. "I didn't know they were friends."

"They weren't, exactly. I'm a friend of his wife. George is not the friendly type. Anyway, a couple of years ago Haley asked me to keep the boxes for George, saying they were in her way and he'd never miss them. Well, now they were in our way, so Dan took them back to George."

"Do you know what was in the boxes?"

"I have no idea. I just thought that Dan was upset when he got home. I tried to find out what happened but he wouldn't tell me. Said he wasn't upset and was surprised that I thought he was."

"When was this?"

"A couple of weeks before . . ." Marilynn cleared her throat before she continued. "Like I said, I'm not sure it means anything,

320

and I'm sorry I didn't remember earlier. It doesn't relate to our business, and frankly it makes no sense to me."

"That's okay. Thanks for telling me now. I'll stop by later and we'll touch base about the investigation."

"Thank you."

Roper returned from auto theft as Abby was hanging up. "They got nothing. Sanders has been keeping his nose clean in regards to auto theft and receiving stolen property, but something personal did pop up."

"Oh?" Abby regarded her partner with keen interest.

"Yeah, a black-and-white was out at his house a month ago on a domestic violence investigation. They filed an information report because there were no injuries." He handed Abby a copy of a crime report.

She quickly read the narrative and saw that neighbors had called because they heard loud yelling and crashing that sounded like furniture breaking. Officers found the garage pretty much destroyed and Haley Sanders in tears, but no evidence of physical contact and she didn't want to prosecute.

"Interesting," Abby said. She told Bill what Mrs. Jenkins had just told her, noting that the date on the police report would coincide with a couple of weeks before Jenkins was murdered.

"That's too eerie," Bill said.

"I agree. I'm almost finished here; then we'll head to Crunchers."

CHAPTER 39

Luke felt the first bullet whistle by him before he hit the water. The gun's report echoed so loud under the bridge it sounded like a cannon. A moving target was hardest to hit, so he knew he had to keep going. The shock of the cold water against his hot, sweaty body was numbing, but bullets hitting the water and a sharp pain on his shin as it scraped a rock sobered him. He expected the guy he'd punched to grab him and fight, but that didn't happen as he pushed to get away from the shooter and lost the sense of where the man in the plaid shirt was.

His lungs felt like they were going to explode, but he kept swimming with a strong underwater stroke, helped along by the river's current. His knee hit another rock, and Luke wanted to scream but he kept going. When he finally had no choice but to surface, he took a quick breath and submerged again, expecting more gunshots.

None sounded and he let the current carry him. When he surfaced again, he kept his head up long enough to get his bearings and saw that he was in the middle of the channel and that the current had carried him very nearly to the ocean. He was about even with the River's End Café, at the bike path's end. Something caught his eye: plaid. He pulled up. It was the man he'd punched, floating facedown, also carried by the current.

Changing tack, and ignoring the pain in his leg from where he'd scraped it, he reached out to grab the man, who was not moving, and swam hard for the shore. On the Seal Beach side just past River's End, the bank was shallow and sandy. During low tide there were sandbanks visible where fishermen could stand and cast. Luke hit the sandbar, fighting the current and not wanting to pick up any more bruises. He held the man in the plaid shirt under the arms, pulling him up onto the sand. Fishermen on the rocks watched him with curiosity but none offered to help.

I didn't hit him hard enough to knock him out, Luke thought. But as he got the man's deadweight out of the water and took a closer look, he saw that this was not a drowning. There was a wound in the man's chest.

Breathing hard, kneeling in wet sand, Luke looked back the way he'd come. *Why is this guy dead when they were both after me?*

Several people on the rocks seemed to realize what they were looking at and rushed down to offer Luke assistance.

"Hey, pal, you okay?" one of them asked.

He looked up to a face he recognized — Gus, the cook from River's End — and shook his head. "Could you call 911?"

Gus pulled a cell phone out of a pocket.

Luke stood and brushed off his bloody, sandy legs, glad his shoes had stayed on when he went into the water. He stepped back from the dead man and checked himself to take inventory of his injuries. His left shin and knee both had deep, bloody gashes that were starting to ache.

He heard sirens and looked toward the Seal Beach Boulevard undercrossing. He was a good mile south thanks to the rapid current. But everything had happened in Seal Beach; familiar Long Beach cops would not be handling this crime.

Luke felt no satisfaction that the attempt on his life might be the thing that granted his dearest wish. *Another body could just be the thing that reopens the case.*

Crunchers occupied a few acres of industrial property north of Anaheim Street and west of the 710 freeway. Abby knew from Woody that there had always been a junkyard on the property. When he was a kid, it was rows and rows of wrecked cars. On Saturdays people could come in and search for usable parts from the cars. An accident involving a car falling on a child during one of those Saturdays ended that and caused the owner of the yard to go bankrupt. For a while environmentalists wanted the whole area cleaned up and made into a park, and a fight raged for years.

The city didn't have the money for cleanup, and while the environmentalists tried to raise it, they were not successful before Sanders stepped in and bought the lot. That was nearly twenty years ago, Abby realized, because he'd owned the place longer than she'd been a cop.

The lot was still a repository for wrecked cars, but only on a small scale. The majority of the space was taken up by recyclable material: cardboard, plastic, and cans and bottles. As she pulled the plain car into the lot, they passed a lineup of street people and homeless with shopping carts and improvised wheelbarrows loaded with all types of recyclable material waiting their turn for it to be weighed and bought by Crunchers.

"Wonder how much stolen material is buried in among all that," Bill commented as Abby parked the car.

She said nothing, concentrating instead on the tack she wanted to take with Sanders. He was cagey and slippery, and she fully expected he'd scream for a lawyer right off the bat. It was a warm day, and when she stepped out of the car, her nostrils were assaulted by the smell of old motor oil and musty cardboard.

The office was housed in a single-wide trailer. She walked up the steps ahead of Roper and opened the door. There was no one sitting at what Abby guessed was the receptionist's desk. The area was packed with file cabinets, some looking older than Abby. Practically hidden between a couple of cabinets was a door with the words *The Boss* written across it.

Abby knocked and heard cursing, then the sound of footsteps as the trailer shook.

George Sanders threw the door open. "Chalky, what is — ?" Anger faded to surprise. "Sorry; I thought it was someone else." His guard went up like a shade. "What brings you here, Detective Hart?"

"I'd like to talk to you about Nadine Hoover."

He scowled. "I already spoke to Murphy and her mother. I don't know where the kid ran, never saw her that day. She left me in the lurch, that's for sure."

"We found her."

"Great." He threw his hands up. "Problem solved. So why bug me?"

"She was beaten half to death." Roper spoke before Abby could stop him. "Probably by someone who works for you."

Sanders cursed. "Nope, we ain't going there. This conversation is over. Stay away from my business, my family, and me. Unless you got a warrant, you talk to my lawyer." With that, the door was slammed in their faces.

Abby said nothing as they drove away from the junkyard. She wasn't certain whether she could have gotten more out of Sanders or not, but it stung having a door slammed in her face. And they had nowhere near enough to ask a judge to issue a warrant for anything, certainly not security tapes.

"Sorry."

"What?" Abby glanced across the car at Roper.

"I guess I jumped in his mug too quick."

Taken aback because she wasn't used to male partners admitting they'd jumped the gun, Abby collected her thoughts before she answered. "Maybe you did and maybe you didn't. Sanders didn't just set up shop. It's unlikely we would have gotten him to talk under the best of circumstances."

She'd taken the freeway from Crunchers, deciding to talk to the widow Jenkins in person about Sanders. She lived in East Long Beach. Now as Abby made the transition from the northbound 710 to the southbound 405, she sighed and relaxed. Maybe Roper wouldn't be a bad partner.

"Even if we have hard evidence against him, unless we have something to deal with, he'll never give us the straight scoop about anything."

"Thanks. I guess you're right —"

The car radio beeped with emergency traffic as the dispatcher aired a shots-fired call on the flood control bike path. Though they were on the other side of the city, Abby turned it up to listen. Any kind of crime or violence was rare in that part of the flood control.

"Shots fired on the bike path?" Roper whistled. "My wife and her friends like to walk down there. I sure hope this is a case of someone hearing vehicle backfires."

Abby found herself agreeing. She loved running and biking on the bike path as well, which was on the whole a safe place. The thought of violence down there was unsettling.

"It's on the border. Might be a Seal Beach call." Roper had leaned forward to listen and repeated what the dispatcher said.

Abby hiked a shoulder. "You want to head that way until it's code 4?"

Roper looked up. "You don't mind?"

"No." Abby passed the exit for the Jenkins house and continued on the freeway, taking the exit that led toward the beach and the shots call. A minute later one of the responding units spoke up.

"Boy 10, I'm on scene and this looks like it's a Seal Beach caper. They're on scene."

"10-4, Boy 10. Are you code 4?" An emergency code red beep sounded in the car as dispatchers waited for Boy 10 to tell them there was no immediate danger. The code red would keep the air clear of routine traffic. Was the threat still there or was it as Roper had postulated — a simple mistake?

"Boy 10, this is code 4. The shooter fled in an unknown direction. I have a male victim here. Seal Beach wants confirmation medics are rolling."

"Paramedics are rolling. Can you advise about injuries?"

"GSW to the chest. Aw, this might be a 187."

Abby had turned around once she'd heard that the crime was not in their city. Even though she felt a jolt when she heard 187, it wasn't their city or their case. She and Bill were a short distance from the Jenkins house when Boy 10 came back on the air.

"The Seal Beach units have a request." He stopped transmitting for a moment. "Officer Jensen is asking that Detectives Hart and Roper respond if they're available."

The dispatcher answered Boy 10 while Abby and Bill exchanged surprised looks. Was this shooting related to one of their current cases?

"David Henry 4, are you on the air?"

Roper grabbed the radio mike to answer the dispatcher. "10-4, we copied the request and are en route."

CHAPTER 40

Abby and Bill followed the dispatcher's directions to the parking lot of River's End Café. The lot sparkled with emergency lights — police, fire, and paramedics. After they parked behind a black-and-white, she and Roper walked down a short embankment to the bike path. They had to squeeze around a paramedic rig and through a growing crowd of spectators. The bike path was busy all day with bikers, joggers, and walkers. This close to the beach meant a lot of watchers.

Abby saw a Seal Beach officer involved in a radio conversation. She didn't see Officer Jensen right away, and her curiosity festered. Why were they specifically requested? Orange County sheriff's deputies handled Seal Beach homicides, and it would be a while before they got here.

She saw a familiar Long Beach patch, Boy 10, and asked, "Who requested us?"

"One of the victims."

"There's more than one?"

He pointed. "One dead, one alive, and a weird situation."

Abby started that way, but her cell phone buzzed and she saw it was the homicide office. As she slipped the phone off her belt to answer, dispatch called them to a clear channel.

"I'll take that," Roper said, and Abby stepped away to take the call while he answered the radio.

"Detective Hart, do you have such a light caseload that you can handle homicides for Seal Beach?" Deputy Chief Cox's voice assaulted her ears and rocked Abby back on her heels.

"We were in the field already and were requested on scene by a Seal Beach unit."

"It's not your case. Get back to the city you work for and handle your own caseload."

The call ended and Abby flushed as anger lit her up in a wave of heat. Why was Cox micromanaging her all of a sudden? The fact that she was right on top of this call meant she was paying close attention to the radio and stepping all over the watch commander. She had the rank to do that, but in Abby's entire career she'd never heard of a DC sticking fingers directly in the pie as Cox just had with this phone call. She stared at the river, stunned, clenching and unclenching her fists.

"Abby."

She jerked around at the sound of her name and saw Roper watching her.

Blowing out a breath, she worked to keep her voice steady. "We were just ordered back to handle our own caseload."

"What?" Roper frowned. "Did you mention we were requested?"

Still working hard to stay calm, Abby looked toward the channel. "And we need to find out exactly why we were requested." She stepped past Roper toward Officer Jensen, who was climbing up the rock embankment. Anger with Cox overrode better judgment.

"Detective Hart." Officer Jensen extended his hand. "Detective Roper, thanks for responding."

"What can we do for you?"

He waved his hand. "Come take a look at the dead victim; tell me if you know him. The second victim is with medics. He's the one who actually requested you."

Abby frowned but said nothing as Jensen led her and Bill back down the way he'd come to where a body lay on the sand. Were these Long Beach crooks shooting it out in Seal Beach?

"Was the second victim shot as well?" Roper asked.

"Scraped up. Medics didn't think they'd need to transport. They said they'd release him once they were sure."

With that, they came to a stop at the body. Abby saw a fit-looking older man wearing a plaid shirt open over a gray T-shirt. His close-cropped hair made her think military or law enforcement, but she didn't know him. His blanched complexion told her that he'd lost a lot of blood.

"I've never seen him before." She turned to Bill. "You?"

"Nope." He knelt down to inspect the wound. "He probably took a shot right to the heart."

"According to the other victim, the shooting happened under the Seal Beach Boulevard bridge." Jensen pointed. "The pair ended up in the water and he dragged himself and this guy out."

"Did he say what the shooting was about?"

"The Triple Seven."

Abby jerked around at the sound of Luke Murphy's voice. Coming down the rocks was a bedraggled, bloody figure.

"There were two guys — this one and the

335

shooter — and they warned me to stop any investigation into the Triple Seven."

"The Triple Seven?" Jensen asked. "Are you two looking into that old case?"

"No —" Bill said.

Luke kept his gaze on Abby. Her face briefly registered shock and concern before the cop face set in stone. He'd requested her and Bill, hoping that this development would reactivate the case.

"I've been making inquiries," Luke cut in, "and obviously made someone mad." He limped to where everyone stood.

Abby looked away, back to the dead man.

Bill spoke up. "If they warned you, then why is this guy dead?"

Hands on hips, Luke tilted his head. "I don't know." He told them everything that happened, including the picture the two men showed him of Madison.

"Your daughter?" Abby stared, and Luke knew it angered her as much as it angered him.

"Was there anyone else on the path?" Bill asked.

"Not that I saw. I was running, my mind wandering. Then all of a sudden there were two guys waving me to a stop." He pointed to Plaid Shirt. "He went into the water first;

the other guy started shooting . . ." Luke raised his hands. "They must have seen me start my run. They could have driven down here to meet me. Once I was on the path, there's no mystery where I was headed."

"Does this mean Long Beach will take over the investigation?" Jensen asked. "Freddy — uh, Detective Wright — should be here momentarily."

Luke saw Bill and Abby exchange a glance.

"It would make sense for you two to take it over," Luke said, hoping they'd agree.

Finally Abby spoke up. "I doubt that will be possible. We've already been ordered back to the city. You guys have everything buttoned up, so I doubt we can justify being here anymore." With that, she glanced at Luke and Jensen, then turned and strode back to the parking lot.

Luke shot Bill a questioning glance and got a look that said, "I'll explain later." He followed his partner, leaving Luke to wonder what was going on.

CHAPTER 41

Abby climbed into her car and gripped the wheel to keep her hands from shaking, thankful Roper was a few seconds behind her. She'd told Woody she was ready for the consequences of stirring the Triple Seven pot. And she was, when the consequences were directed her way, not at Luke Murphy.

They threatened his *daughter*.

Abby remembered the cute, bright, pony-tailed girl and cringed. *No, Lord, that was not what I expected. I couldn't forgive myself if something happened to someone else because of me.*

"You okay?" Bill asked as he took his seat.

Abby's answer was cut off by the buzz of an incoming text. It was a summons from Cox to be in her office ASAP. Anger surged and Abby wanted to scream. She slammed her hand on the steering wheel.

"What?" Roper shifted in his seat.

Regretting her loss of control, Abby

showed him the message. "It's Cox. She wants us in her office now."

"What is up with that? She has it in for you. Is there something I should know?"

Abby blew out a breath, frustration piling on frustration in her mind. "Not on my part. We've never really meshed. But why she's on the warpath now, I don't know."

If she were a betting person, she'd bet it was the Triple Seven. As she threaded her way out of the crowded lot, she felt like she did at the end of a really long run when the lactic acid building up made every step painful and heavy.

It seemed that no one wanted her parents' killers found. Was she wrong to even try?

Realizing she had bigger problems with Cox at the moment, she conjured up Woody and one of his favorite sayings: "Patience always pays off." She repeated the Woody-ism over and over, knowing she had to keep her tongue and emotions in check when she spoke to Cox. There had to be a reason she was riding her like this. Hopefully with patience Abby would discover what it was.

At the station, she and Roper rode the elevator up to the third floor in silence. When they got to the chief's office, which was still Cox's until the chief returned, the secretary indicated that they could go right in.

Cox stood with her back to them. Abby noted that she'd begun boxing up her personal belongings, presumably to take them back to her office.

"I read Boy 10's call history." She spoke without turning.

"Chief, we were requested at that scene." Bill spoke up and Abby held her breath.

Cox turned. "I realize that."

Abby tried to read her. Was she contrite?

"But the problem I have is that I want the two of you concentrating on the most pressing current cases on your plate. Traveling to Seal Beach, requested or not, is a waste of time. Do I make myself clear?" She was angry but obviously on a tight leash and Abby wondered who was holding it.

Bill looked toward Abby, and she cleared her throat.

"Yes, Chief, we both understand perfectly." She turned to leave but Cox stopped her.

"I'm not finished. From the call history I understand there was some reference made to the Triple Seven today. This PI, Murphy, was threatened to stay away?"

"Yes, that's what he said," Abby answered.

"Understand this: if we receive a request

from the investigators on this shooting for information on the Triple Seven, and should the case need to be activated, I've officially made Carney the contact person for the case. Let me repeat: if that happens, it will be handled by O'Reilly and Carney. As I told you before, you will not be allowed to investigate the murders of your parents." She stepped away from the window and sat down at the desk. "You two can get back to work." She looked down at paperwork on the desk; they were dismissed.

Abby called Marilynn Jenkins and apologized for not coming by as promised.

"That's okay. I don't have much else to tell you. I don't know what was in the boxes that were in the garage. I even called Haley Sanders and asked about it, but she didn't know either."

After the conversation, Abby felt stymied. But she was tired, and her thinking was muddled. She began to pack her things up to leave.

"Are you on your way out?" Bill asked.

"Yes, I'm tired."

"You've been up for what, more than twenty-four hours?"

"I lost count." Guilt tore through her when she realized Bandit hadn't been let out in hours.

"I think I'm going to go back over to the hospital and check on Nadine," Bill said. "If anything comes up, I'll call you."

"Great, thanks."

Her mind wrestled over the problem with Cox. What was going on there? Abby hated gossip, but she needed to tap into some department scuttlebutt and figure out what was happening. It felt like something personal. But Abby couldn't recall ever crossing Cox in any way.

She started her car and left the PD lot. *I've hit the wall in so many areas,* she thought as fatigue turned into self-pity. *I'll never find my parents' killers. I'm spinning my wheels, and I've put Murphy and his whole family in danger.*

Driving on autopilot, she dwelled on the bloody scene at the river. Who threatened Murphy? Was he targeted because of his interview on *Good Morning Long Beach*? That piece had been picked up by other networks and rebroadcast several times. He was the face of the Triple Seven investigation right now.

Had she awoken the killers by revealing who she was? Was Murphy in danger because of her? Emotions swirled through her thoughts of the man. At the hospital she'd watched him take control of the crowd of church people and marveled at his grace and compassion. Ethan was always warm and helpful, but Luke seemed to have something more, some quality —

She stopped herself as she pulled into her driveway.

Why am I comparing them?

Guilt assailed her. *I love Ethan; I do,* she repeated over and over. After a minute she climbed out of the car and started toward her front door.

Abby's foot froze at her bottom step, and her hand reached for her weapon. The door, lock, and doorjamb had been destroyed with some kind of pry tool. This was brazen; it was broad daylight. She drew her automatic and held it down by her thigh as she backed up to her car for the radio. Once behind the door, she crouched down and reached for the radio mike.

"David Henry 4," she whispered as she keyed the radio.

"David Henry 4, go."

"David Henry 4, I've got a possible burglary in progress at my residence." Her voice stayed calm and level. "Can you send me a backup unit?"

"David Henry 4, 10-4. Any available unit to assist David Henry 8 prepare to copy the call

343

on your computer."

Abby set the mike down, confident backup would be with her shortly. Was this related to the Triple Seven? Were killers here now for her like they were for Murphy?

I'm ready, she thought, anticipation breaking through the caution, the fear, and waking her up. If she took the suspects into custody, she might finally get the answers she wanted. She raised her weapon and trained it on the door.

A second later the door burst open and there stood the BUG Murphy and Georgie had described. He was bigger than Abby thought possible and he had a crowbar in his hand. He fixed a hostile glare on her.

"Where is it?" was all he said as he started her way, slapping one meaty palm with the crowbar.

"Police. Stay right where you are," Abby ordered. She stood, two-handed grip on her gun, sights trained on the large man.

"I don't have time for this," he snarled as he stepped toward her, swinging the crowbar. "She said she gave it to you, and I want it now."

Abby ordered him again to stop, but she could see in his eyes as he raised the crowbar with malicious intent and continued toward her that he had no plans to stop. Her duty weapon was a .45 automatic, a gun she'd picked for stopping power. She'd seen suspects shot with 9mms keep moving. A .45 had better odds of dropping a target, the range master had assured her. But Abby backpedaled. Pulling the trigger would mean this guy would not be alive to tell her what this was about.

"One more chance — stop or I will fire."

He didn't stop.

Someone grabbed her from behind, looping his arms around her in a bear hug. Her finger depressed the trigger and a wild shot hit the BUG in the leg. As he stumbled forward, he cursed her in a rage. Abby struggled with the man who had her in a tight grasp even as she saw the crowbar coming closer. With all the strength she could muster, she twisted her body, turning the man on her back toward the BUG as the bar came down.

A strangled *oof* came from the man who had her from behind as the blow struck him square across his back. She heard the sickening crack of bone, and he released his grip immediately. But the force of the blow still drove her to the ground, grinding her knees into the pavement as the other man slid off her and rolled away screaming in pain. She struggled to turn and bring her gun around, fearing the crowbar's next target was her head. Then she heard her backup.

"Police. Drop it!" several voices yelled in unison.

Abby brought her hands over her head and tried to disappear into the concrete of her driveway as she knew what would come next.

The big man cursed, and she guessed he wasn't dropping the crowbar. A split second later a deafening volley of shots rang out.

It was only seconds, but it seemed an eternity before the firing stopped, and the attacker dropped the crowbar and toppled like a felled redwood in front of her.

CHAPTER 42

Luke began to feel the pain after he'd gotten home, taken a shower, and had something to eat. He'd pulled James and Grace aside, told them about the men in the flood control, and asked them to be careful and vigilant. He'd also made a list of friends from aikido, wondering if he should ask them for a little help.

"We have a weekend trip to the mountains with the homeschool group. Should we cancel?" Grace asked.

"No," Luke said. "It might be good for all of you to get away."

"I'll tag along," James said, "and look after the girls."

Luke was satisfied with that. As he limped into the kitchen, Grace and James made plans.

"You really need to see a doctor," Grace said as she watched him swallow some Advil.

"Mom, I don't want to take up the doctor's time for scratches."

"When was the last time you had a tetanus shot? The flood control is filled with bacteria."

Luke leaned against the counter. "I guess you're right. The last thing I'd want is some flesh-eating scum in me."

"Yuck." Maddie made a face.

"And it was gross in that water." He threw his hands up. "You win; I'll go."

"That is what urgent care is for," Grace said.

Luke kissed Maddie good-bye and grabbed his car keys. He'd just started the engine when his phone buzzed with a call from Bill.

"Hey, I'm on my way to urgent care."

"Good," Bill said. "With all the gunk in the flood control I hope you don't come down with typhoid or something."

"Ha, you're as bad as my mother."

"Grace is a smart woman. I'm just leaving work, on my way to see Nadine. I'll drop by, make sure the nurse gives you a shot that hurts."

Luke laughed. He prayed that Bill coming meant Abby as well since it was not their EOW. At the very least he hoped he'd find out what was going on with the partners,

348

why they didn't stay and talk to Wright from OC Sheriff's.

Urgent care was quiet. He'd seen a doctor, had his wounds checked, and gotten a tetanus shot by the time Bill arrived.

"You are really milking this, aren't you?" Bill said with a smile as he gave the nurse a wink. "Maybe they should give you a Band-Aid with little teddy bears on it."

"Funny guy. The last thing I want to pick up right now is some lethal bacteria. So what — ?"

An emergency beep sounded from Bill's radio.

Bill pulled the radio from his pocket and turned up the volume.

Luke heard their homicide call sign and went rigid.

Bill met his eyes. "Problem at Abby's house. Follow me over there?"

Bill didn't have to ask twice as Luke raced out of urgent care after him.

They kept to speed laws just barely. Luke almost raced past Bill because he had heard the code for an officer-involved shooting, 998, blaring from his friend's radio just before they parted.

As it was, they had to pull over at one point for a paramedic rig and a black-and-white rolling code 3. When they reached Abby's street, they had to park down the block because of all the emergency vehicles.

Was someone after her like they came for him?

Luke caught up to Bill quickly.

"Was she hurt?" Luke asked, noting that his friend had the handheld radio up to his ear.

"No. No officer was hurt. But the burglars went down," Bill said as they reached the driveway. A crowd of neighbors had already massed on the sidewalk.

"She's my partner," Bill told the uniformed officer separating the crowd from the scene with yellow tape. "He's with me."

Luke slipped under the tape with Bill.

Walking up the drive through the busy police activity, Luke calmed as he saw Abby standing, fine, talking to a patrol sergeant. She had a scrape on one side of her face and her pants were torn at the knees, but she looked okay and Luke relaxed a bit.

Paramedics were working on someone while uniformed officers were spreading a yellow tarp over another figure.

What happened here?

Abby arched a brow and tilted her head his way when she saw the two of them approach, and it was then he saw Bandit in her arms. She was holding on to him like a lifeline.

"You okay, partner?" Bill asked, stepping ahead of Luke.

"A little scraped, but yeah, I'm fine."

"Was this another Triple Seven threat?" Luke asked.

Abby shook her head. "Neither of these guys said anything about the Triple Seven. I'm glad you're here, Mr. Murphy. Take a look." She pointed to the yellow tarp. "Tell me if that's the man you saw at Crunchers."

He let the formal greeting go for the moment and walked with Bill to the tarp. Bill peeled back a corner. It was, without a doubt, the big guy he'd seen at the junkyard and then later with Bill.

"That's him," he said, turning back to Abby, noting she was all cop, not a frightened civilian victim. Still, knowing what she'd just been through, he had to ask. "Are you sure you're okay?"

"I'm fine. A couple scratches from hitting the pavement is all. But they trashed my house."

He looked over her shoulder to the front door and saw the damage there. "If this wasn't about the Triple Seven, what did he want?"

She gave a heavy sigh. "He just asked me where *it* was."

"Where what was?"

"I don't know. He also said that *she* gave it to me."

Luke frowned. "She? Nadine?"

"I don't know. His partner is hurt bad." She pointed toward the medics, who were loading the injured man into the ambulance rig. "Hopefully he'll talk later."

"If he's able," the patrol sergeant said. "He took quite a shot to the back." He looked at Abby. "Lieutenant Jacoby is on the way. Are you up to going over what happened with me while we wait?"

"I'm fine. Let's do it."

Luke saw another homicide team and someone he bet was from the DA's shooting team coming up the drive. They joined Abby and the patrol sergeant. He was dying to know exactly what happened and wanted to follow Abby and listen to what she had to say. He decided to ask another uniformed officer and saw that Bill had beaten him to it.

He heard the officer tell Bill what he knew. Luke's hands went cold, and he clenched and unclenched his fists after he heard what Abby had gone through.

"What would that guy want with Abby?"

Luke asked.

"I don't know, bro. I don't know."

What was going on?

The ambulance pulled out with the injured man, sirens screaming, so Luke knew it was serious. He prayed the guy would survive and shed some light on the situation. Lieutenant Jacoby arrived, and Bill walked with him to the group around Abby. There were also three uniformed officers in the group. Luke had heard a total of four officers, including Abby, fired their weapons, and knew that this would be a long, drawn-out investigation.

He took a seat on her front porch steps and waited for her to finish. While he waited, a lab tech left Abby's house as the public service crew arrived. They walked past him to repair her door. He stood and saw for the first time how much damage had been done there. Inside the house was also a mess.

It was about half an hour before the walk-through ended and Abby joined Luke.

She peered around him at the public service crew.

"How are you holding up?" Luke asked.

"I'm fine, really. Okay." She held the little dog close and stroked his head.

"Is there anything I can do to help? Maybe

help make sure the house is secured so you can sleep safe tonight?"

"Public service is here to do that. I appreciate your concern, but there's nothing you can help with right now."

She was so removed from the warm, vibrant person he'd shared information with the night before that Luke was taken aback. His phone buzzed with a call from his mom.

"I have to take this," he said, and she moved away to speak to the public service crew. Luke stepped off the porch to answer the call.

"Nadine is awake. Groggy, but awake," his mother told him. "It looks like the worst is over."

"That's great to hear."

She asked about the tetanus shot and he told her. He also told her what happened at Abby's and asked that she pray.

"Is this related to the Triple Seven?" Grace asked.

"I wish I knew" was all Luke could say.

CHAPTER 43

Running through Abby's mind in those few moments after the shooting stopped and she picked herself up off the ground was *Bandit*. Her ruined door and the violent nature of the men who'd violated her house made her fear the worst.

"You okay?" one of the officers asked as she started for the door.

"My dog," she said as she ran for the door, the officer on her heels.

"Ma'am, we have to clear the house!"

Abby didn't care. The only thing she wanted at that moment was the little furry body. If they'd hurt him . . . She couldn't think of it.

"Bandit! Bandit!"

Nothing. Then she heard a muffled squeal coming from the kitchen and rushed in there. When she didn't see him, fear began to cascade through her.

The cabinet! He was in the cabinet; she

could hear him scratching. A chair had been thrown against the door. Abby pulled it aside, and relief flooded her as Bandit jumped into her arms.

"Thank you, Lord," she whispered into his fur.

Her composure returned quickly. She was certain she'd done everything she could do regarding her assailant. He wouldn't stop. She knew he'd meant to kill her with the crowbar and that knowledge kept her from second-guessing her actions. She figured that the second man was a lookout for the first, and she chastised herself for not being more aware, more attuned to her surroundings.

She blamed that on Luke. *If I hadn't been thinking about him, I would have noticed trouble sooner.*

The walk-through went smoothly, and as a matter of routine, her gun was surrendered to the range officer. The same was true for the three uniformed officers who'd fired as well. All in all, a total of fifteen shots had been fired, but it would take an autopsy to determine how many hit the big guy. The rounds that had missed impacted her garage door. There was nothing in the garage to be damaged, so she'd deal with that problem later.

As the DA shooting investigator left, Jacoby approached her, concern in his features. "I want you to take the rest of the week off."

She started to protest. "I'm fine, really."

"Right now, maybe. But take the time off just in case." He gave her a look that brooked no disagreement, and she was too tired to argue.

Since it was Wednesday, that meant she would not have to be at work until the following Monday. The state of her house helped her decide she was thankful for Jacoby's order. It would take at least three days to clean up the damage. If she wanted to head into the station on her own time over the weekend, she would.

"You okay?" Bill asked.

"I'm fine, just tired and hungry. It's been a long day."

"I second that. I meant to ask you earlier: are you keeping your friend?"

"What?" Abby frowned and then realized he was talking about Bandit. "Oh, I guess so. The governor didn't want him." Her adrenaline high crashed all at once, and she nearly sagged against Bill, as fatigue slammed down like the crowbar.

Jacoby saved her telling Bill that Abby was officially off duty. She let them talk shop while she sat on the porch steps. It looked as if public service would finish soon. But she wouldn't be alone until the coroner came to remove the body.

Luke finished his phone call and flashed her a smile. Her heart fluttered in spite of the anger she was trying to feel toward him. He was easy on the eyes, and having him this close and this helpful strained all of Abby's hard-layered self-control.

"I just got a call from my mom at the hospital. Nadine is awake." He knelt next to her.

"I'm glad to hear that," Abby said. Was Nadine the key to what happened here at her house? Was she the *she* the big guy mentioned? "I hope we can talk to her soon."

"Maybe in the morning."

"Good." She noticed his gaze travel to the door repair going on behind her. "They work fast. Glad I'll be able to stay in my own room tonight."

"You sure you want to sleep here tonight? Maybe you should stay at a friend's or something."

"This is my home. I —" She almost explained that she had bounced around too many times to strange beds and homes when she was in foster care. It would take an army to pry her out of this place she'd called home for the last five years. *I really am tired,* she thought, *to almost share stuff with him I've only shared with Ethan.*

"Yes? You were saying?" Luke asked.

"Nothing — just that I want to stay in my own home."

"Well, will you at least let us help you clean up?"

"Yeah." Bill joined them as Jacoby left the scene. Most of the black-and-whites had left as well. The chaos was winding down. "We have the time to help."

Abby looked from one man to the other, on the verge of being rude. Mess or no mess, she just wanted the peace and quiet of her own house and her own thoughts. The sound of a car squealing to a stop on the street kept her from answering and turned everyone's attention toward the noise.

Woody pushed past the tape and rushed toward her at a jog, concern creasing his face.

Cool relief flooded Abby like honey and chased away the rude. She needed Woody and his calm strength to center her.

"Don't tell me this was because of the Triple Seven." He stopped in front of Abby, eyes roaming from public service working on the front door, to the tarp covering the dead guy, to Luke and Bill, then coming to rest on her.

"No, it wasn't. I don't know what exactly it was about." Abby paused, realizing Woody wasn't alone. Slowly walking up her drive in his wake was Asa. "I think it was about that runaway girl."

Asa had never returned her phone call, and now here he was. *Funny,* she thought. *So much has happened, I forgot what I was going to ask him.*

"The girl?" Woody was thoroughly confused. He looked at Bill. "That straight up? This isn't related to the new ripple in the Triple Seven invest?"

"I don't think so."

Asa reached them, and Abby worked to keep shock from her face. He looked worse than the dead guy under the tarp. His nose had been red and bulbous from drinking when he retired, but now it looked twice as bad. And his skin was an unhealthy, waxy color. He'd moved to Idaho to enjoy a quiet retirement. Obviously he hadn't been outside much. As she looked from Woody to Asa, a sick feeling slapped her: Woody had called Asa and told him about Abby breaking her silence.

"Asa," she said, "I didn't know you were

coming for a visit. Don't tell me you came back because of me?"

Woody spoke up. "I just picked him up at the airport. Got a call you were in trouble when we pulled out of the lot."

Both ignoring a direct response. They had been partners for years and could finish each other's sentences. Abby knew there was more going on between them than she would ever be privy to.

"Nearly killed us getting here," Asa said in his booze-roughened voice before he popped a breath mint into his mouth. "Glad you're okay."

Abby felt an uncomfortable twinge, realizing he was probably drunk. She'd seen him drink enough liquor to put most people under the table without even developing a slur or a hitch in his step. But the faraway gaze in his eyes gave away his physical state.

"Let's take a look at this guy," Woody said to Asa. The coroner had arrived and knelt beside the body to inventory the man's property. Bill walked with them to the body.

Abby turned to see Luke watching her, and suddenly exhaustion and hunger socked her like a one-two punch.

Luke followed. "Everything hitting you about now?"

He always reads me. But she was too tired

to be angry. She said nothing. She held Bandit close, loving the feel of his rough tongue as he licked her hand.

Woody, Asa, and Bill were arguing about something while the coroner loaded up the dead man on the gurney.

"I just want to help," Luke said softly.

Abby didn't trust herself to look at him. She realized at that moment that she'd rather face ten men armed with crowbars than this one man she felt an attraction to. She needed to call Ethan.

When Woody and the others finished arguing and walked to the porch, and when they'd all decided they were going to order pizza and help her clean up, she had no strength to protest.

Everything in her life was spinning out of her hard-fought universe of control. Did she really want to fix it all herself? Could she?

"I guess I can use the help," she said and let Woody pull her to her feet.

CHAPTER 44

Abby's phone rang with her normal ringtone, one that sounded like an old-fashioned telephone bell, and a glance down told her it was Aunt Dede. Before answering, she surveyed the group of men helping her put her house back together. Asa was the only one not doing something. He sat in the corner, looking as though he'd nod off any second. Woody and Luke were working in her kitchen, and Bill was on the phone ordering pizza.

"Woody," she called out, "this is my aunt. I have to take it."

"Go right ahead. We'll head to your office after we get this room cleaned up."

Abby stepped into her bedroom and closed the door. There was no mess in this room. The intruders had trashed everything else, and Abby was grateful they hadn't come in here and done the same. *Maybe I interrupted them.*

"Hey, Dede." She sat on the bed and set Bandit next to her.

"Abby, how are you?"

"I've been better."

"Oh, you don't sound good."

"I'll survive." Abby did her best to sound brighter. "What's up?"

"I talked to Ethan. He mentioned a video going around. Something about a train. He's pretty upset about it."

Abby sighed and pinched the bridge of her nose, trying to stop the flood of tears that threatened. *Not this, not now.*

"I talked to him about that." She explained about the train video.

Dede sighed. "I can't force you to be careful. I can and do pray that you will use good judgment."

"I always try."

"I also saw a report on the Triple Seven, a news story about the cold case and the connection to Governor Rollins. Everyone says he'll be the next senator from California, so it's big news even here. Are you investigating that case?"

Abby leaned back in her bed and thought about the attempt on Luke's life. Her head felt as if a ton of bricks had descended on it. She made a decision.

"I'm not . . . uh, I won't. If it is reactivated,

two other detectives will take it on."

"That's for the best. Does Woody think you're still in jeopardy?"

Abby swallowed and looked up at her ceiling. "He was worried, but, well, it's been twenty-seven years, after all, and like I said, I'm out of it." She didn't think her voice would hold if she told Dede about Luke.

Her aunt was quiet for a few seconds. "I know how hard that is for you. You've invested a lot over the years in unraveling that case."

Abby closed her eyes, a thick lump in her throat. At that moment she believed she'd never find the answers she'd been looking for practically her whole life.

"I hope you don't get mad at Ethan for telling me about the video," Dede was saying. "It scared him, and when he spoke to you, he felt you were distant. He's concerned that sometimes your job is too much of an obsession. Something I've told you for years."

Abby bit her bottom lip. She felt like her world was quicksand and she was sinking. "I'm zonked right now. I don't want to go into this with you. I'm good at what I do. I help people. Ethan used to be proud of me."

"He still is. But what about when you get married? Where will Ethan fit in then?"

Now Abby was silent. She didn't want to admit she wondered how Ethan would handle her leaving for 2 a.m. callouts.

"I accept his trips. Isn't marriage a partnership?" She thought the question lame as soon as the words were out of her mouth.

"And when you have children?"

Abby sighed, deflated. "I really don't want to have this conversation right now."

"You sound beat. Please pray about all of this — your job, Ethan. And remember that I firmly believe your parents' killers will never escape God's judgment. No one does."

"I will; I do. Now I have to go."

"All right. I'm praying for you and I love you."

"I love you too." She tossed the phone to the end of the bed and sagged back, everything smashing in at once. She needed to have a face-to-face talk with Ethan.

Tears threatened with the force of terrorists, and she fought them. Not with a house full of friends and colleagues. She buried her face in a pillow and struggled for composure.

After Abby closed the door to her room to take her phone call, Luke surveyed the room across the hall that was obviously her office. The bad guys had really done a number here, emptying the bookshelves and throwing papers around. But nothing looked permanently damaged. He began putting books on the shelves and neatly stacking scattered papers back on her desk.

He smiled to himself when he noticed the authors of some of her novels. Mickey Spillane, Raymond Chandler, Rex Stout, Dashiell Hammett, and Agatha Christie were all authors Luke loved to read. The old-time sleuths and PIs were heroes to him, hence the term *shamus* on his business card. The music he saw was a little different. Mixed in with praise music, there was some old jazz — Ella Fitzgerald, Frank Sinatra, Louis Armstrong. *Fits the time period of the books,* he thought. They'd talked about the cold case they had in common but nothing about everyday interests they shared.

He picked up a picture frame and turned it over to see a photo of Abby and Ethan, and his smile faded. There was really no use for him and Abby to discuss common interests, was there? He set the picture on Abby's desk and continued putting books on the shelves. He was almost done when he heard Bill holler that the pizza had arrived.

Abby came out of her bedroom. She looked surprised to see him in her office. And her expression was so profoundly sad, he felt his chest tighten.

"Oh, hey, thanks for doing that."

Was there a catch in her voice?

"Sure, no problem. Doesn't look like he broke anything, just tossed everything around."

"I wish I knew what they were looking for." She stepped into the office.

"I couldn't help but notice your taste in reading material. The old sleuths, huh?"

She faced him, a slight smile on her face, and Luke felt warmed to see it.

"Yeah, Chandler is probably my favorite. You, as a shamus, should appreciate that."

Luke laughed. "I can, and that's where I got the term. My all-time favorite shamus, Philip Marlowe."

"Sometimes I wish I could channel Spillane's Mike Hammer," she said, blinking. "It's not a Christian attitude, I confess."

Luke smiled broadly, understanding the reference. "Ah, you'd meet force with force and pound out the truth if you found someone to pound?"

"Let's just say when the bad guys trash

my house, my sanctuary, a part of me wishes I could respond in kind." All humor faded from her eyes, and Luke saw the pain cross her face, if only for a second.

He couldn't stop himself. He stepped close and put a hand on her shoulder. "Hey, we'll figure this out," he whispered. Before he knew it, she was in his arms, crying softly on his shoulder. Wrapping his arms around her more tightly, he rested his cheek on her soft hair. "Let it out. You'll feel better," he whispered, all the while praying for her, for him, and for these feelings he knew he had no right to have.

After what seemed like too short a minute, she pushed away.

"I'm sorry," she said, turning away and grabbing for some Kleenex on her desk.

"Don't. It's not your fault," he said to her back as she blew her nose and wiped her face. He shoved his hands in his pockets, at a loss for what to do now. "You've been through so much. I'm amazed that you're still standing."

"I'm fine. I'll be okay."

"I know." He stepped to the door. "Take your time. I think the pizza is here. You come out when you're ready."

He left her there and felt hollow and lost

with every step that took him farther from her.

Mortified she'd so completely lost control, and doubly so that she'd felt so safe and warm in Luke's arms, Abby shut herself in her bathroom. Her shoulders seemed to burn with the memory of his strong embrace.

Get a grip, she scolded herself.

She rinsed her face off, not wanting everyone to know she'd been crying. Their voices wafted in, along with the smell of pizza. Grabbing a towel, she dried her face and checked it in the mirror. Her eyes were bloodshot, but that could be from lack of sleep. She felt reasonably certain no one would rush to the conclusion that she'd been crying. She was about to join the crowd when Woody called out.

"Abby, someone at the door to see you."

"Be right out." She wondered if it was the coroner or the last units clearing the scene. Taking a deep breath, she walked into the living room, and there in the doorway stood Jessica Brennan. Abby almost said, "Thank you, Lord," out loud. If she needed a shoulder to cry on, it should be someone neutral like Jessica.

"Wow, last thing I expected was to see

your house full of men," she said with a laugh.

"It's been a long day," Abby said. She sighed as she accepted her friend's hug.

"I guess." Jessica looked at her with an odd expression. "I just wanted to come by and say that now I know why you're so good."

"What?"

"So good at being a cop. You've been a victim and you really do understand."

Abby lost her voice for a moment. *Victim? No. On a mission, yes. But no victimhood for me.* But she realized Jessica spoke of her parents.

"It was so long ago . . ." She held her hands up, not really sure what to say.

Jessica wiped her eyes. "Yeah, but still, how horrible!"

"Do you want to come in? We're having pizza and trying to clean up a mess."

Jessica peered into the house. "What happened?"

"Come in and I'll explain."

Jessica joined the group and Bill told her what had happened. Abby stayed close to Woody and Jessica, fearing even a look at Luke.

Between pizza and talking, they were eventually able to put the entire house back together, though some things had been destroyed. She was out a television set, a DVD player, and a coffee machine. The food helped; she was hungrier than she thought and figured that was why she'd lost control so easily. She vowed that it would not happen again.

Her laptop was unscathed, so she and Jessica went online to pick out replacement items while Luke talked at length with Woody about the threat to him and his family by the mysterious pair under the bridge. Abby caught snippets.

"They must have been watching me, my house, for a while," he said. "I never realized."

"You'll be more vigilant now," Woody said.

"You bet," he said with steel in his voice. He could take care of himself, of that Abby had no doubt.

Asa didn't contribute much to anything, but he did speak to Abby for a few minutes.

"I don't think you should have ever told Rollins who you were," he said. "This Triple Seven can of worms should have stayed closed."

"Why?" Abby asked.

"After all this time, do you really think you'll solve it?"

Regret pinched her heart. "No, I'm out of

372

it. Carney and O'Reilly will get it and I'll stay out."

For the first time all night, Asa smiled. "That's for the best. I'm sure you'll see that someday."

When everyone left and Abby had the house to herself again, a tight knot formed in her stomach, not over the incident with Luke, but over Asa. He knew something he wasn't saying. A disturbing question rose in her thoughts and would have kept her awake if she weren't dead on her feet.

What if he's known all these years who the killers are and he's been hiding them?

CHAPTER 45

"It had nothing to do with the Triple Seven?" Ethan asked, his face scrunched with concern on the screen of Abby's computer. It was Sunday night. He'd heard about the attack in her driveway because he had set up a Google alert for her on his phone.

"No, we're not sure why it happened. The injured man won't talk."

"I'm glad you thought so quickly and that you're okay."

This was a pleasant talk over Skype, and they had mended a few things.

"But I'm not happy to see the Triple Seven in the news."

"I'm out of it, Ethan. Another team has been assigned the case. And you might hear a lot more about it. There's a PI here — he's related to the cook who saved me." She told him about Luke and that he was investigating the Triple Seven case privately.

She didn't mention the embrace and flushed as she recognized how difficult it was to forget that.

"I've decided that I need to let it go," she said. "You and Dede have been right all these years."

"Good." He paused and Abby knew he had something significant to say. "Abby, you are such a smart, gifted woman. I know that your gifts would be so much more valued and valuable out on the mission field."

"We've been through this. I'm not called to the mission field like you are."

"Just pray about it. That's all I ask."

Abby did her best to keep smiling and promised that she would, but after they ended the call, she knew that even without the Triple Seven, her heart and her mission were in helping people devastated by crime.

By Monday morning, Abby was glad her days off were finished and she could bury herself in work. The better part of her weekend she'd spent explaining to friends and people at church why she'd been hiding her true identity. Everyone understood, but a few were hurt because they felt she didn't trust them. She really had no idea how to respond to that and prayed she'd have the opportunity to show them they were wrong.

She was first in the office purposely because she wanted to catch up without interruptions. At some point in the day she'd also have to go to the range and retrieve her duty weapon. Happy though she was to be back, she was thankful Jacoby had forced her to take the time off. The horror of the attack had faded, but the memory of Luke's embrace lingered and Abby wasn't sure how to deal with that.

She also still pondered her conversation with Ethan. It wasn't the first time he'd said he thought Abby would be an asset to him and his team. They ended the call praying together, but it continued to nag her how Ethan seemed to think it would be an easy thing to walk away from a career she loved, a career she was good at.

First things first, she started a strong pot of coffee. She needed something to get her mind off disturbing thoughts about loyalty and Luke Murphy. She hated how she kept winding back to the feel of his strong arms around her. True, she could cut herself some slack for the weak moment, but she couldn't forgive herself for still thinking about it days later.

The trouble was, she and Luke would always have strong interests in the Triple

Seven. She'd come to realize his sharp mind and instincts could be a huge help. Yet the more she was around him, the more she wanted to be, and that was not helpful. She'd solve the case and their connection would end. Period. She did not want any further entanglement.

When Abby forced her thoughts off Murphy, they veered onto disturbing questions about just what Asa knew. If he did know something, she hoped and prayed that it was his secret alone. Her mind could never fathom that sort of betrayal from Woody as well.

Sighing, she tried to clear her mind of all but getting caught up on mail and e-mail. There were still numerous e-mails from journalists and news outlets. She responded to all of them by referring them to press relations.

An e-mail came in as she hit Send on one of them. The new one was from Fred Wright, the OC detective.

She picked up the phone and called him.

"That was quick."

"You got me early. What's up?"

"Just thought you'd like to know about the autopsy on that guy from the shooting on the bike trail. A ricochet killed him."

"Ricochet?"

"Yep, best we can figure, the bullet fragmented on the bridge pylon and a big piece hit the guy in the sweet spot. He died instantly. So Murphy was probably the target and the other guy a poor marksman."

"Lucky for Murphy. Did you get an ID?"

"Not yet. Prints aren't in the system. And the gun he had on him, the serial number had been filed off."

"Thanks for the information." Abby hung up, wishing that case were hers but glad in the end that it was Wright's because he would share what he could.

A few more e-mails caught her eye. The big man and his partner who'd been at her house were identified as Dac Malloy and Trevor Taylor, residents of Las Vegas, Nevada. Bill had cc'd her on e-mails he sent to LVPD, requesting information, if they had any, on the pair. Since the big guy had been seen at Crunchers, he also made inquiries about George Sanders.

Good thinking, Roper.

There were return e-mails from the Las Vegas cops waiting, and she saw the direction the answers to his inquiries were taking their investigation. Malloy was well known to the LVPD as Las Vegas muscle, had many arrests for assault on file. George Sanders was also well known to the PD as a wannabe high roller and a mean drunk.

Did Malloy and Taylor come here to lean on Sanders for something, or did they work for him? Abby drummed the desk with her pen and frowned. *If that is the connection, it was possible Nadine saw or heard something she shouldn't have. But if that's what happened, why did Nadine run away? And why try to kill her? If Sanders was the problem, why not go after him?*

Every question spawned another.

The last e-mail she opened was a note from Bill. Sanders had retained counsel after their visit. He'd called in his big-name attorney: Ira Green. That sounded familiar, and when she scrolled though an earlier e-mail, she saw that Trevor Taylor had invoked his rights in the hospital and wielded the same attorney. *Hmm.*

The coffee finished brewing, and she poured a cup. She stepped to her mail slot to retrieve her snail mail and intra-office mail. As she hadn't been in since Wednesday, there was quite a stack. She grabbed it, bunching it together as best she could so it would fit under her arm, and returned to her desk and dumped the pile. A generic gray-and-white media envelope caught her eye immediately, and she pulled it from the stack.

Leaning back, she looked at the neatly printed handwritten address, as if it had been copied directly from her business card. She opened it, and out came a DVD and a note written on notebook paper.

Detective Hart, I don't know where to turn. Please help me. I'm hiding because I saw something I shouldn't, and now I'm in trouble. If they find me, they will kill me, and if they know I sent you this DVD, they'll kill my whole family. They have my phone; they know all my contacts. Please watch it and put them in jail so I can go home.

Nadine

The security video Murphy mentioned.
Shock brought a burning sensation to Abby's throat, and she stood, pressing one hand to her mouth and the other to her stomach. She was glad beyond measure that she had the office to herself. It was several minutes before she could pick the disc up and put it in the DVD player. She powered on the TV and hit Play. As the black-and-white picture came into focus, she could see that it was a static surveillance video with a view of the front and side of a small building. There was a time stamp on it. What she

was watching had taken place a month ago. It was couple of minutes before she realized she was looking at the office at Crunchers — the porch and the front door, and the door farther down the side of the trailer.

She watched and after five minutes was about to hit Fast-Forward when the side door opened and a man stepped out, followed by another man she instantly recognized as George Sanders. A third figure emerged who could only be Dac Malloy, and behind him was Trevor Taylor.

Sanders shoved the first man in front of him so hard that the man stumbled and fell to one knee at the bottom of the stairs. Taylor lashed out with a vicious kick to the head that sent the downed man sprawling.

Abby hit Pause and stepped close to the screen. She couldn't identify the man who'd been kicked, though there was something familiar about him.

Stepping back, she hit Play again and watched as a horrific tandem beating took place. The man in the middle had no chance as Taylor and then Malloy took turns pummeling him. At one point Taylor picked the guy up and held him so Malloy could smack him in the face with something. Abby guessed it was a sap, a sand-filled leather weapon often used by enforcers, and that this was standard operating procedure for the pair.

As she watched the beating progress, recognition slowly dawned. Shock pulsed through Abby and she felt numb. There on the screen, in a time frame covering five minutes and a few seconds, she was witnessing Malloy and Taylor beat Dan Jenkins to death while George Sanders watched.

CHAPTER 46

"Hey, good to see you, Bullet."

Ice Age Orson walked up to the table where Luke sat and extended his hand. Luke stood and gripped it with a smile. Orson was grayer at the temples than Luke remembered, but he hadn't gone to fat like some of those they'd served with. They were even in height, but Orson was more thickly muscled than Luke. He'd always looked formidable, and time hadn't changed that.

"Likewise, Ice Age. Have a seat." Luke motioned to the other side of the booth. He'd gotten them a semiprivate table at a local restaurant called Hof's Hut.

They both ordered coffee and made small talk for a few minutes.

"Even though she's beautiful, you didn't come all the way to Long Beach to see the latest pictures of my daughter," Luke said finally. "What's up?"

"Perceptive as always. Actually, I've

wanted to catch up for a while. Hear you have quite a colorful career going as a PI. You're a YouTube star."

Luke smiled. "Go ahead, get your digs in. But the creep is in jail and three girls are safe at home."

Orson laughed. "No digs here — you got good moves. I also saw a bit about your cold case, the Triple Seven, and I thought it was interesting. You make any headway on it?"

"Yes and no." Luke told him about his investigation to date.

"Really? Hart's parents were murdered in that restaurant?"

"Yeah." Luke felt his heart race a bit at the thought of Abby and worked to stay frosty and professional.

"Her name has come up in my sphere of influence. I know colleagues who've worked with her; they say she's sharp."

"I agree." He sipped his coffee. "The thing is, after that interview about the cold case, someone almost killed me trying to warn me away."

"What?"

"Happened on the bike path where I jog." Luke filled his friend in on the attempt on his life. "Last I heard, they still haven't identified the dead guy."

"That story hadn't reached me. Glad

you're okay. But not surprised you came out on top. They don't know who they're messing with."

"I'm hoping you might be able to help with an ID. His prints aren't in the system." He slid Detective Wright's card across the table. On the back he'd written the coroner's case number for the unidentified attacker. "The guys looked ex-military. If there's anything you can do, I'd appreciate it."

Orson took the card. "I'll see what I can find out."

"Is the FBI interested in helping with the Triple Seven?" Luke asked, curiosity growing exponentially.

"Well, that's partly why I wanted to see you. I've just been assigned a new gig. It's a federal grant, so it may only last until the money runs out, but there's a lot of money right now. You've heard of Senator Harriet Shore?"

"I've heard the name. She's from Virginia, correct?"

"She is, and like you, she lost someone years ago and the crime has never been solved. Thirty years ago her older sister and the sister's boyfriend were shot and killed while they were parked at a lovers' lane. So cold cases are near and dear to her heart.

She appropriated the money for this Cold Case Task Force, CCTF, and pretty much gave us carte blanche as to how to staff it and work it."

"And you're going to work the Triple Seven?"

Orson shook his head slowly. "Nope, I'm hoping you will, under the federal banner."

"Huh?" Luke was certain his face was a question mark.

"I'm hiring for the CCTF, putting together teams. I can hire retired cops or agents; I can hire PIs; I can hire pretty much anyone I want if I can justify the hire. I have an East Coast team already up and running. It's made up of retreads from a couple of sheriffs' offices, a cop, and a DA investigator, headed up by an agent. I want you on my West Coast team."

"I don't know what to say." Luke's mind jumbled with too many thoughts. "Would I have to move to Washington?"

"No, you'd be based here. You would have to travel occasionally, but only in the western states, and probably the longest trip would be a week."

"Wow" was all he could say. While Luke loved the freedom of working for himself as a PI, there were times when the license didn't give him complete access. Sometimes police agencies were downright hostile. Here he was being offered federal access.

"Think about it. I'll e-mail you the full monty on the gig. And the West Coast case we're considering looking into. I'll even take a look at anyone you think might also be interested in joining the team. I'll be around for a few days and will touch base before I fly back. It is a big deal, so give it some thought."

CHAPTER 47

Abby wasted no time letting her lieutenant view the video.

"Sanders will speed-dial Green." Jacoby rubbed his chin as he watched the DVD for the third time.

Abby, Bill, and Jacoby were in a conference room awaiting the DA. The chief was back in town and in a meeting with Cox, so for the time being, the deputy chief was out of Abby's hair. The chief himself was not a micromanager and he told Jacoby to "Handle it. Call me only if you're stuck."

"And Ira Green will assail the chain of evidence and the source of the DVD," Bill said.

"I know, but we can authenticate the DVD. I can't see a judge throwing out something like that."

"How is the girl?" Jacoby asked.

"She should recover fully, from what I hear," Bill said.

"Good."

The door opened and DA Drew wheeled herself inside. Injured years ago in a street robbery, Marlene Drew was paralyzed from the waist down. She was such a tiger and so passionately committed to her job, people often said the wheelchair seemed to disappear when Drew got going in court.

After making eye contact with everyone present, Drew said, "Let me see this bombshell."

It didn't take Drew long to decide what she wanted to do.

"Bring him in. I'll deal with any and all motions Ira Green throws at me."

Bill and Abby were followed to Crunchers by two black-and-whites. One covered a rear exit while the other two officers followed Bill and Abby up the steps to the trailer.

There was a man sitting at the desk just outside the door that said Boss. Abby knew him as Chalky; he'd been a sort of bouncer for Sanders for years. He stood, a big gut straining at a grease-stained T-shirt.

"What do you want?"

Abby ignored him and reached for the Boss's door.

"You can't go in there!"

The uniformed officers restrained the man

as Abby and Bill entered Sanders's office.

Unlike the outer area, Sanders's office was clean and uncluttered. He sat behind an ornate oak desk. His face twisted in anger when he saw Abby, and he slapped the desktop.

"I told you to talk to my lawyer. You're violating my rights."

Abby said nothing. She slid a still photo taken from the DVD showing Sanders standing by while Dac Malloy slugged Dan Jenkins.

All the bluster faded along with the color from Sanders's face. Abby waited a beat.

"George Sanders, you're under arrest for the murder of Daniel Jenkins." She went on to advise him of his rights while Bill handcuffed him.

Sanders stayed quiet as he was led out of the office and put in Abby and Bill's plain car. The fat man in the outer office was yelling about police brutality and promising to call Ira Green.

Bill drove while Abby sat in the backseat with the prisoner. They'd just driven out of the lot when Sanders spoke up, surprising Abby.

"I liked Dan Jenkins. You have to understand — if I'd have tried to stop them, they would have turned on me."

Abby cleared her throat before speaking. "Are you waiving your right to representation?"

Sanders let out a bone-weary sigh. "I'm dead like Jenkins if I do. But I do know something that would be of interest to you if you want to make a deal."

Abby's eyes narrowed and her defenses activated. She wasn't going to be played for a fool by someone like George Sanders.

"What kind of deal?"

"I have information you want. But if I tell you, you can't let Green know I talked. You'll have to say you developed the information on your own."

"What's in it for you?"

Sanders finally faced her. "Maybe a clear conscience. Maybe I'm just tired of hiding what I know and I don't want to see anyone else get hurt, most of all me. I'll let Green mount a vigorous defense for me regarding Jenkins and take my chances. But if the reason Dan Jenkins was killed stays hidden, someone else could die, maybe even you. I don't want another death on my head."

"Me? I don't trust you as far as I can throw you. What information do you think you have that's so important we'd keep quiet for you?"

"I can give you the Triple Seven murderers."

Chapter 48

"Relax." Bill grabbed Abby's arm. "You look as if you just mainlined a triple shot of espresso."

Espresso? She felt like a million ants were crawling under her skin. "How can you say relax? This guy says he knows what I've been looking for practically my whole life."

They'd put Sanders in an interview room while they waited for DA Drew, and Abby had been pacing like a caged tiger.

"Consider the source."

That stopped her. She held her partner's gaze. "You're right. He's trying to save his own skin." Some of her jitter faded but not all of it. It galled her to realize that she would so easily trust a professional liar to solve the biggest mystery of her life. It took all her strength to stand still until they heard Drew's wheelchair coming down the hall.

"Thanks for coming," Abby said, working to tamp down raging emotions.

"That's what I'm here for. I want to hear what he has to say, but you know that we'll need solid proof to back up any allegation."

Abby nodded.

Everyone filed into the conference room and took their places across from Sanders. Drew clicked on a digital recorder.

"It starts back years ago." Sanders sipped his coffee.

Abby wanted to scream. It had already been a good fifty minutes since he first made his statement. *Get on with it.*

"We were in high school. I was a year behind your dad." Sanders tilted his head toward Abby. She kept her face blank and empty, struggling to keep the emotions swirling inside her from showing. She'd seen Sanders's picture in the yearbook the other night at Murphy's. For twenty-seven years she'd dreamed about discovering the identity of her parents' killers. Was that really going to happen today because of him?

"Buck Morgan and Lowell Rollins — they were tight."

"The governor?" Drew interrupted.

"Back then it was Buck and Lobo — that was his nickname — joined at the hip. They were always up to something, usually something no good. But one night Buck and

Lobo got in over their heads. It was a night they stole a car —"

"You saw this?" Drew again, and Abby knew it was because this was complete hearsay and would never be admissible in court even if Sanders wanted to testify. Not to mention statute of limitations on auto theft.

"No, but I heard the story from Lowell's brother. He was a simpleton, and he hung around with kids my age, not kids his own age. The bottom line, Lowell was driving a stolen car and he hit and killed a man out for a walk."

"Who?" Drew and Abby spoke in unison.

"Don't know. Just know they killed him. They ditched the car and ran, and that hit-and-run was never solved. According to Louis, Buck and Lobo made a blood oath to never tell what happened that night. And that oath held for years." He paused and drained his coffee.

"What does this have to do with the Triple Seven?" Drew asked.

Thank you, Abby thought. *Get to the point, Sanders.*

"I'm getting there," Sanders answered Drew but kept his eyes on Abby. "Fast-forward several years to the Triple Seven. Buck and Lobo weren't so close anymore.

Lowell wanted to throw his hat into the political ring. He'd helped start the Triple Seven, but the day-to-day operation was completely in your parents' laps. Buck was a loose cannon at the time. Your mom handled everything; that woman was a saint. She was the reason that restaurant was so big, so successful, but your dad was snorting and gambling away all the profits."

"There's no mention of that in any report," Abby said.

"Because Rollins buried it. Or I should say his wife-to-be did. She was his publicist at the time. She believed Lowell was destined for big things and felt that even if Rollins had never done drugs, if it was discovered that his partner was an addict, it would torpedo his political career. Alyssa didn't even want Buck in rehab. Too many tongues would wag."

Abby stood and leaned against the wall, biting her tongue. True, she'd never heard that her father was a saint, but a drug addict and out-of-control gambler?

"Your mom, on the other hand, wanted out of the partnership. She hated Alyssa and felt if she bought Lowell out, she could then force Buck into rehab. She was ready to hock everything to buy Lowell out. But the restaurant was too big a stage for Lowell's political aspirations for Alyssa to let him walk out of it."

"There was never evidence of any buyout offer in the investigation twenty-seven years ago." Abby could see the pages of the investigation in her mind. If there had been such evidence, Lowell Rollins would have been the prime suspect.

"It was hidden and the books cooked. Why do you think everything burned? Your house and the restaurant? Patricia had squirreled some money away from Buck and who knows what else. She had the money to buy Lowell out, but Lowell flat-out refused. So Patricia brought up the joyride. Buck had told her about it, and she held that over Lowell's head, threatening to spill unless Lowell walked away from the Triple Seven. And that was the straw that broke the camel's back."

"Are you saying that Lowell Rollins killed my mother and father to keep a decades-old secret?" Abby cut Drew off.

But the DA raised her hand before Sanders could answer. "If you're going to tell me that the governor is my suspect in this murder, you are going to need cold, hard proof."

"Let me finish. Patricia was the only uncontrollable asset as far as Alyssa was

397

concerned. Buck was controllable. I'm saying that Alyssa told Gavin Kent to handle it. Gavin pretty much did the same thing back then that he does now — he handled things."

"So now it's the First Lady of the state of California who ordered the killing?" Drew's tone was acid with skepticism.

"I'm not saying that was what was meant, but that's what happened. Louis Rollins, Gavin Kent, and Buck's drug supplier, a guy known as Coke Pipe, visited the restaurant that day. And what went down is not what any of you think."

"Then what did go down?" Abby asked.

"Kent told your mom to back off and stop threatening Lobo. There was a fight. Shooting started. Louis wasn't clear on what exactly happened. But Patricia got hit, Gavin took a bullet in the leg, and your dad killed Coke Pipe."

"There were only two bodies."

"Yep, I know that. It wasn't your dad who was buried with your mom. It was Piper Shea. Your dad is still alive."

CHAPTER 49

"Hey, Nadine, how do you feel?" Luke bent down over the girl. She looked so frail, bruised, and battered. But even with two black eyes and a puffy face, she could still focus, and she was awake. He'd spoken to Bill after coffee with Ice Age and knew about the video Nadine sent Abby. He hoped Nadine would be able to answer a few questions while her mom stepped out for coffee.

"I'm sore, Pastor Luke." Nadine sounded as if her mouth were full of marbles.

"Then take it easy. Don't talk if it's hard."

"It's okay. My mom said you never stopped looking for me."

"Of course not. I am the number one shamus, aren't I?"

That brought a crooked smile to her face.

"Do you remember anything about what happened to you?"

The smile faded. "No. I remember running away from Crunchers. There were two men; they threatened me, took my phone . . ." Her brows scrunched together and she seemed to be in pain.

"No rush, Nadine. No rush." He patted her shoulder.

"I want to remember, but that's about it. I know I was scared. But . . ."

"Do you remember mailing something to Detective Hart?"

Her concentration looked pained.

"It's okay, Nadine. You rest. Things will sort themselves out, I'm sure."

Glynnis came back into the room with two coffees, and Luke groaned inside. She was trying to move close and he didn't want to hurt her. And he had too much work to do to stay for coffee.

"Oh, baby, it's so good to see your eyes open." Glynnis handed Luke his coffee and bent down to give Nadine a kiss. "I hope you feel better."

"I do, Mom. I do."

Luke cleared his throat. "I better be going."

Glynnis turned toward him. "Luke, I thought you'd stay for lunch!"

"I'm up to my neck in work. I'll have to take a rain check."

Glynnis argued for a bit, but Luke won

out. He needed to look into the threat on his life. He'd worked all weekend, talking to neighbors, asking if anyone had seen anything out of the ordinary. He'd gotten the description of a car, and he hoped that lead would take him somewhere.

His parents were with Madison; they'd opted to spend the whole week in the mountains after the homeschool weekend. Luke had asked them to be vigilant, to notice people around them. The best he could guess was that the two men who accosted him had taken the picture of Maddie and her friend in the driveway just after the meeting with Governor Rollins. It bothered him that he'd not noticed anything out of place, but then he hadn't expected any issues.

He left the hospital for the Seal Beach PD and a meeting with Detective Wright about the two men who jumped him on the bike path. Seal Beach gave Wright a place to work so he didn't have to travel back and forth to Santa Ana, where the OCSD offices were. Luke was anxious for the meeting; he'd been praying that the men who jumped him would finally be identified.

Fred Wright met him in the lobby. "Hey, Murphy, you don't look so bedraggled today." He extended his hand.

Luke shook it. "Or as waterlogged, I'll bet. Thanks for talking to me."

"No problem. Let's go to my makeshift office."

Luke followed Wright back to a conference room and took a seat near the head of the table while Wright sat at the head.

"Thanks for enlisting the help of your fed friend. We got a name on the dead man now, from the military data bank."

"So soon? I gave Orson that info this morning."

"He punched the right buttons. Name was Gordon West. His DD-214 indicates a dishonorable discharge twenty years ago."

"Gordon West, huh?"

"Yep. I found a brief trail for him after he left the military. He worked for a multinational private security force for a while. I don't know if he still works for them. They won't give me any information, citing privacy issues."

"Did Orson have anything to add?"

"He mentioned the guy seemed to be living off the grid. It's possible he was fired and then found someone shady to work for."

"That would jibe with the dishonorable discharge."

"Yep, but doesn't really help us find who sent him to threaten you. Ballistics won't help because the fragment that killed him can't tell us much."

"The only answers will come when we find out who did the Triple Seven murders. It seems like that killer would be the only person with motive to try to scare me off."

"I agree. I asked my captain to see if we can get together with LB and reactivate the cold case."

Luke's spirits soared. "That's awesome, something I've wanted to have happen for such a long time. Detective Hart knows the case inside and out."

Wright shook his head. "I don't think I'll work with her. I think Carney and O'Reilly would be the ones assigned if it's reactivated."

Luke remembered Abby had told him that. Both those men went to his church, and he knew they would do a great job. But this should be Abby's gig.

CHAPTER 50

"What do you mean my father's alive? His body was next to my mother's." Abby could see the crime scene photo in her mind's eye as she stared at Sanders and felt the room shift. She fought for balance, feeling like a child in the schoolyard after spinning round and round while staring at the sky.

"*A* body was next to your mother's."

"Wait, wait." Drew frowned and gave an impatient wave of her hand. "What is your proof?"

"A drug dealer named Piper Shea was there, not Buck Morgan." He faced Abby, who was having a difficult time finding her voice. "You can verify that much. Piper went missing back then; I'm sure there's a record."

"Again, how do you know all of this?" Drew repeated her question while everything faded into the background for Abby. She could hear Sanders tell Drew that he knew these things because Louis Rollins told him. He wove a tale of childhood friendships and trust while she tried to remember every bit of the investigation so she could hurl back at him without a shadow of a doubt that he was a liar.

"You okay?"

"What?" She jerked toward Bill and saw concern in his eyes. Glancing down at her hands, she saw that her knuckles were white from her grip on the back of a chair.

All she could do was shake her head and tune back in to what Sanders was saying.

"Louis, Kent, and Coke Pipe went to the restaurant that day to scare Patricia out of any thought of buying out Lowell. No one was supposed to get hurt. But Buck was high and a fight started — shots were fired."

Evidence of multiple gunshots. No weapons recovered.

"Patricia got hit and died instantly."

Female subject cause of death: single gunshot wound to the head.

"Buck killed Piper with a shotgun; the last round he had went to Piper's face."

Male subject suffered multiple gunshot wounds — shotgun pellets recovered from face and body.

"That was when Kent had the upper hand. He was the only one with bullets still in his gun, but he was wounded. There was a standoff between him and your father. He told Buck to run and never look back or he'd kill you."

Abby stared and motioned for Sanders to keep talking, not trusting herself to speak. Her ears roared with the sound of her life crashing into an iceberg.

"Buck ran. He took off through the front door with Kent screaming after him that if he ever surfaced, you were dead. Kent was furious. He looked at the two bodies on the floor of the restaurant and knew it would destroy Rollins's political aspirations if he were implicated in anything. He told Louis to torch the place, destroy all the evidence.

"Louis told me he asked about you, and Kent just screamed, 'Burn it all!' They poured lighter fluid over the bodies and set the place on fire, locking the doors and beating feet away from the inferno."

He looked again at Abby. "Kent knew you were there; he wanted you dead. Why you didn't hear anything, I don't know."

"My parents' office was soundproof. They did that so I could sleep there when they both had to work." The roar in Abby's ears made her voice sound far away.

"Kent wanted to be sure all evidence was destroyed, so he went to your house, and he torched that as well. Buck disappeared, and Alyssa and Gavin cleaned everything up so nothing would impede Rollins's run for office."

"This is all very interesting and it might make a good Lifetime movie," DA Drew spoke up. "But it's impossible to prove. And what does it have to do with Nadine Hoover and Dan Jenkins?"

Sanders ignored Drew. "There was so much chaos after the fire. Louis came to me to get rid of the gun."

"You have the murder weapon?"

"I did. But it was in a box my wife gave to Dan Jenkins to store in his garage. After so many years, I'd gotten careless and lost track of the box. Also in that box was paperwork proving Patricia Morgan offered to buy Lowell out. Louis thought it would be insurance for himself." Sanders made a rude noise. "He thought wrong obviously. There was nothing in it for me to go public, so I just hung on to it." He held Abby's gaze as his last words gave her a jolt, cutting through the roar and the fog.

He then turned to Drew. "Jenkins was just an unfortunate accident."

"You're saying he was killed because he poked his nose in the box?" Drew asked.

"He was cleaning out his garage. Not

much made sense to him, but he saw the names Patricia Morgan and Lowell Rollins, and he made a phone call."

"He called Rollins?"

"Yeah, but of course he got Kent. Before Kent called him back, his wife told him the box was mine. He brought the box back to me but asked questions he shouldn't have asked. Kent dispatched his janitors to clean up and . . . well, you saw what happened."

"Malloy and Taylor are employed by Gavin Kent?"

Sanders smirked. "Not in any way you'll be able to trace."

The roar in Abby's head subsided, leaving her feeling numb. There was police work to do. "Where is the box now?" she asked.

"Hidden in the yard. If we can make a deal, I'll tell you where."

"How does the girl, Nadine, fit?" Bill asked.

"Nadine was there when Kent's boys came to see about the box. I sent her home because I knew Jenkins was on his way. I didn't realize that she was so curious about what they wanted she'd replay the security video. Why she burned a DVD and ran, I don't know."

"I hope we get the chance to ask her." Abby thought about the broken girl she'd seen in the hospital. "Malloy and Taylor didn't get the box?"

"No. I told Kent I'd only give it to him to avoid any other mess-ups. He never made it to the yard."

"There is so much here that can't be corroborated," Drew said. "I can't talk any kind of deal without that box."

"Tell us where it is." Abby got in Sanders's face.

"It's in a cubbyhole under the office."

"Does anyone else know where this box is?"

"Kent does."

CHAPTER 51

Abby and Bill grabbed a car and headed for the junkyard. It had been a long day and it was now starting to get dark. She wished they could have taken a black-and-white and rolled code 3, lights and sirens. They were almost to the exit for Crunchers when she heard sirens and looked over her shoulder. Fire trucks were roaring up the freeway behind them.

"What is this?" Bill asked as he pulled over.

Abby turned back, and it was then she saw the smoke. She clicked on the plain car's flashers as Bill stepped on it to follow the trucks. There was a sick feeling in the pit of her stomach as Abby realized where the smoke was coming from.

A few minutes later they came to a stop behind the pumper. She couldn't bring herself to open the car door and follow her partner. The office and a good portion of the yard at Crunchers was on fire.

"I wish you had called me sooner." Luke shoved his hands in his pockets. He wanted to punch something, so until he could, the safest place for his fists was in his pockets.

"Buddy —" Bill rubbed his face with both hands — "everything went down so fast."

It was after midnight. Bill was soot-covered and looked exhausted, but he'd stopped by on his way home to tell Luke about Sanders and the fire at Crunchers. Luke could smell the smoke lingering on his friend's clothes from the junkyard fire.

"How did Abby take the news?"

"She didn't say much. Bottom line: Sanders's story is just a fairy tale without any evidence."

Luke leaned against Bill's car. They'd stepped outside so as not to wake anybody up. "I'm having trouble processing everything you've told me. I can't imagine what she's going through." He rubbed his chin. "Her father still alive? If that's true, where has he been all this time?"

"Consider the source, as far as that goes. I told her the same thing. Sanders is out for Sanders, period."

"But why lie about something like that?"

"I don't know. But he's dead on for the

murder of Dan Jenkins. No fanciful tale will change that."

"And the other guy? The one who attacked Abby?"

"Not talking, but not going anywhere either. His back was broken. He's likely to be in a wheelchair for the rest of his life." Bill paused and rubbed his eyes. "By the way, how's Nadine? Gail says you talked to her."

Luke didn't want to change the subject. "She doesn't remember much, but she may as time goes on. She might be released in a couple of days. What will you and Abby do now?"

"Build our case against Sanders in the Jenkins case."

"Abby should be on the Triple Seven."

"For the first time, I agree with Cox: she's too close." He clapped a hand on Luke's shoulder. "I gotta go home and get to bed. Take care."

Luke stepped onto the sidewalk and watched as Bill climbed into his car and drove away. He could only imagine what Abby Hart was going through after this emotional day.

He turned to go back into the house and then stopped. He had his car keys in his pocket. He pulled them out and looked at them for a moment.

Sighing, knowing that he couldn't leave this alone and go to sleep, he hopped into his truck and directed it to Abby's house.

My father still alive.

Abby paced the confines of her small house. She'd come home and jumped into the shower, feeling numb and lost. The fire at Crunchers was still a dangerous smoldering pile when she and Bill left. Woody and just about every uniformed officer available had been called in to assist when it was at its worst.

But for the first time she could remember, she didn't feel like talking to her friend. The nagging pinprick that had started after her brief talk with Asa had grown like cancer. In the back of her mind she feared Woody knew her father was alive.

Was that why they wanted me to stay away from the Triple Seven investigation?

The first thing she'd done when she got out of the shower was pull out her copies of the autopsy reports.

Female subject suffered a single gunshot wound to the head.

Male subject suffered multiple gunshot wounds to the head, face, and neck area.

413

Both subjects deceased before the fire started.

And the fire had done further damage. Dental records had identified her mother's body. But not only had her father not seen a dentist, his body had been too damaged. Even his fingerprints were gone.

Yet, a positive identification was made. She flipped through the paperwork and discovered something she had never noticed before. They simply identified the corpse next to her mother as her father; they did not even do DNA. Granted, at the time DNA was just becoming standard . . . Still, it left a door open that led to *Sanders was telling the truth.*

Abby had never even considered the possibility that one of her parents had survived. *Why would I?*

She groaned and stomped into the kitchen for some comfort food. She poured a big glass of milk and grabbed a package of Oreo cookies. She was about to deposit herself at the kitchen table, where she'd set her book, when a knock sounded at the door. Instantly on edge, she put the milk and cookies down and grabbed her weapon. Keeping it by her side, she stepped toward the door, noting that it was after midnight.

"Who is it?"

"Luke Murphy."

She sagged against the doorjamb and very nearly dropped her weapon. He was the one person who would understand what she was going through but the last person she wanted at her door right now.

"It's late," she called out.

"I know, but I saw your light on. I need to talk; I was hoping you did as well. Abby, I just want to help."

Abby straightened up and put her gun away before answering the door.

"Bill must have talked to you," she said, motioning him inside.

"Yeah, he did. And I'm having trouble digesting everything he said. I was hoping to get a copy of the transcript of your interview with Sanders. That might not be okay —"

"I'll e-mail you a copy. You're the only person besides me with a personal connection to this case, so . . ."

"You can trust me."

She held his gaze for a minute, then walked to the kitchen, and he followed her.

"I'm drinking milk. Can I get you anything?"

He shook his head and smiled. "Milk and cookies? I noticed all the Oreo packages the other day. I guess you like them."

"I do." She sat at the table and he took the chair across from her.

She played with a cookie, suddenly feeling the need to talk. "They've always been my favorite. The last foster home I was in, the mother kept all the food under lock and key. I saw Oreos in the cupboard once, but she never let us have any. One night I snuck out of my room and tried to get to the cookies. She heard me and was furious. She grabbed my arm so hard she broke it."

"Whoa." Luke cringed.

"In the emergency room they called the police. The officer who came out took my statement. After he wrote everything down, he left. They set my arm, and I was waiting for social services to come take me to a new place when the officer came back. He gave me a whole bag of Oreos and told me they were all mine and that I didn't have to share with anyone if I didn't want to." She sipped her milk.

"Good for him."

"Ever since then, they've been my comfort food of choice."

"I get it. I lost my uncle, but you lost everything." He met her eyes, and Abby saw such warmth in his clear, calm gaze that she almost sighed. She had to keep talking.

"I was so angry for a long time. But when

Dede came into my life and took me to church, I heard the message of the gospel and I thought I'd found a measure of peace." Abby brought both hands to her face, but the roar returned and her balance teetered.

"If my father is alive, and has been all this time, how am I supposed to have peace with that?"

"There must be something I can do," he said in a whisper, leaning closer.

Abby opened her eyes and feared he might come around the table and take her in his arms again. But her phone rang. She grabbed for it and saw that it was Ethan.

She stood. "I need to take this."

"Sure. I just wanted to let you know if you ever need to talk . . ." With that, he headed out, leaving her to her phone conversation.

CHAPTER 52

"Ethan, I'm so glad you called."

"I was afraid I'd wake you. But I have some news."

"First, I have so much to tell you." Forcing her voice to remain steady, Abby poured out everything Sanders had said. He let her go on without interruption, and when she finished, he was silent for a long moment.

"Are you still there?" she asked, grabbing Kleenex and blowing her nose.

"Yeah. I'm just . . . Well, Abby, you know how I feel about your position in homicide. And as far as the Triple Seven goes . . ."

"But this goes beyond homicide, Ethan. Did you hear everything I said? What do I do if my father really is alive?"

"It's not like you to so readily believe someone like this Sanders character. Surely he has some angle, some reason for making an off-the-wall statement like that."

"I don't know. I need to go back over the

report, and I can't do that officially because they don't want me investigating my parents' murders."

"Abby, you need to let this go. Give it to God. If you can't do that, it will swallow you. We've had this conversation before."

Abby bristled, not wanting to be lectured but not sure what Ethan could really do or say to help her. "This changes things. I don't think it's possible, my father being alive, but I have to find out the truth."

"Part of the reason I wanted to talk is to tell you that I'm coming home early. I'll be back in three days. Please pray about this and don't do anything we'll both regret."

"We'll both regret? What is that supposed to mean?"

"I just don't want you doing anything that could jeopardize our future together. Surely you don't want that either."

"Of course not."

"I can hear the *but* in your voice. *But* you have to solve this crime."

"Ethan, you have to understand —"

"I'm trying. All I ask is that you pray before you do anything."

Pray.

Abby said good-bye and paced, knowing she should try to get some sleep but more unsettled than ever. *I have prayed,* she thought, *and my prayer has not been answered.*

After a bit, she lay down on her bed. Bandit jumped up to lie next to her. No matter what, she knew she had to prepare the Jenkins case in the morning. She couldn't concern herself with what was happening in the Triple Seven investigation.

Chapter 53

By early Tuesday, Luke had read the transcript of the interview with George Sanders over and over. There was no mention of his uncle, which didn't surprise him; it fit with the theory that Uncle Luke was in the freezer and heard nothing. At the time, the big thing was a Sony Walkman to play music, and his mother had told him that his uncle had it on all the time, like people and their iPods today.

And it was well documented that Buck Morgan kept a shotgun in the restaurant for protection. The story Sanders told was plausible. But if Buck Morgan was still alive, how could he stay hidden for so long, and how could he leave his daughter that day to be murdered?

Luke drove down to Serenity Park. He had with him the picture of the restaurant in the background and the interview printed out, and he tried to see that day in his mind, filling in blanks with his imagination. He got out of his truck and walked to where he envisioned the front of the restaurant was.

Gavin Kent, Louis Rollins, and the drug dealer come in — did they threaten Patricia? The idea was to get her to back off, according to Sanders. His wife being threatened couldn't have sat well with Buck. *The Morgans both know Abby is in the office asleep; did they try to mollify the men?* Patricia was trying to buy Rollins out; was money there? Did the drug dealer want Patricia's money to settle Buck's debts?

Were both Kent and Louis armed? Somewhere in the mix, a fight started and guns went off and Patricia and the drug dealer were killed, according to Sanders. Kent was wounded and Buck Morgan fled.

Luke frowned. He could not wrap his mind around a father leaving his daughter to be murdered. *If that's what happened, then what kind of man is Buck Morgan?*

If it were me, I'd do anything and everything to try to protect my daughter with the last breath in my body.

He turned when he heard a car door shut. It was Ice Age Orson. He'd called and Luke asked him to meet at the park.

"Hey, great place for a meeting. Brought you a cup of joe."

"Thanks, I could use it." Luke accepted the coffee as he and Orson took a seat on one of the benches. It was very near the memorial plaque.

Orson noted the photo. "What's that?"

"Oh, it's a picture of this area before the park." He handed his friend the picture.

Orson held the photo up and compared the areas before and after.

"Hate to say it, but I like it better with the park. This was the restaurant that burned?"

"Yep. Taking my uncle and two other people with it."

"You making any headway?"

"Some new information has surfaced — not sure how much it will help."

"Okay, then let's move back to the future. Have you decided to take the job?" Agent Orson sipped his coffee and regarded Luke with anticipation.

"It's tempting, I'll admit, but I'm still thinking. And I need to sit down with my family. I got your e-mail but I haven't read through it. I wanted to thank you for helping Detective Wright out with that ID. I have another favor to ask."

Orson tilted his head. "Ask."

"Some of what has surfaced concerns a person on the governor's staff."

"I hope this isn't headed where I think it's

headed."

"I guess it is. Can you find out any information on Gavin Kent?"

Orson studied his coffee. "You cast a wide net. Anything specific?"

"Is there any connection between him and the dead guy who accosted me on the bike path?"

Orson gave him a look that said he was thinking. For a minute they sipped their coffees in silence. Finally Orson spoke up. "Since the case has my interest, I'll see what I can do. But I'll be beyond discreet. Clear?"

"Clear."

CHAPTER 54

Tuesday morning for Abby began busy, borderline frantic. She was the first in the office. She quickly filed all the paperwork from the day before that she'd not had a chance to file. She made arrangements to visit Trevor Taylor, who was in County/ USC's jail ward recovering from being hit with a crowbar. She noted he'd been deemed stable enough for transport. He had also retained Ira Green for his defense. She doubted she'd get anywhere but wanted to try anyway.

"Abby."

She looked up and saw Ben Carney walking her way. She liked Ben and his partner, Jack. They both had great reputations at work and from time to time showed up for volleyball on the beach. She knew them on and off duty, and they were honest, hardworking guys.

"Hi, Ben, what's up?"

"I know that you probably heard Jack and I were assigned to the Triple Seven case." Abby said nothing and he continued. "I was hoping to get the file from you. For some reason I can't pull up anything online."

"I don't have the file." Abby sat back in her chair. "I have my own unofficial file, but I don't have the department file."

"Huh. It's not here."

"What?" Abby got up and strode to the file room, Carney on her heels.

Sure enough, the thick accordion file was gone, a large empty space in the drawer where it should be. Hands on hips, she said, "I'll admit I've been through it several times, but I always put it back."

Ben picked up the sign-out board. "The last person to sign it out was your partner, Bill, but he signed it back in."

Abby frowned. The homicide file room was not a secure room, but it was only to be accessed by authorized personnel. It was an office full of cops on their honor to sign out a file and sign it back in when finished.

"When I try to open what was scanned into the computer, all I get is an error message." Carney led her back to his desk and showed her what was happening.

Three attempts at opening CR#88-0065 all resulted in the same message: *Error. File not found.*

"I don't understand," Abby said, truly perplexed. The rest of the homicide detail began to file in. "What about the evidence?"

Carney answered, "I haven't been up to check the evidence yet."

There wasn't much physical evidence, but a box of odds and ends, including shell casing and bullet fragments removed from the bodies, was stored in an evidence locker on the fifth floor. Abby started for the elevator as Bill caught her eye.

"Back in a minute." With a feeling of dread she stepped off the elevator and asked the clerk for the box relating to CR#88-0065. Five minutes later she was walking back into the homicide office where Bill, Ben, and Jack were sipping coffee and discussing the problem.

They looked at her as she approached her desk.

"That evidence is missing as well." She sat down heavily, wondering what had happened to the reports and the evidence. Granted, there wasn't much, and she had her own personal file, but what she had was not official. Where would it get her if they ever did arrest a suspect?

"We need to talk to Jacoby."

As if on cue, the LT stepped into the office. His face was a study in cop blank. "If this is about the Triple Seven, it's not me you need to speak to. DC Cox is waiting for you in her office."

Shortly after that, the four investigators stood in front of DC Cox's desk.

"There's been no break-in, no breach of security," she said. "I removed the files and the evidence."

Abby couldn't stifle the gasp. "Why?"

"To save you from yourself. Governor Rollins requested all the items be transferred to the California Highway Patrol Protective Services Division. From now on, they will handle any ongoing investigation."

"I've never heard of such a thing." Abby couldn't contain herself, in spite of Ben's cautioning hand on her arm. "That case is ours to investigate and close, not CHP's."

"You're out of line. I told you that you would not be able to investigate your parents' murders. Governor Rollins did this as much to protect you as to solve the crime —"

"Solve or cover up?"

Cox was up from her chair. "Enough! Ever since you decided to tell the world you were Abby Morgan, the governor and I have been trying to protect you, to keep you from jeopardizing your career. He wants the truth as much as you do. But you are so blinded by obsession, you'll believe a lie told by a scumbag like George Sanders."

She held her hand up to keep Abby from speaking. "No more about the Triple Seven; it is no longer our investigation. You have the Dan Jenkins case to prepare. If it comes to my attention you are in any way stepping on the CHP investigation, there will be consequences."

Reluctantly Abby bit her tongue and returned to homicide with the others.

"You know, I'm not big on gossip," Ben said. "But there is a rumor going around about Cox."

"What?" Abby asked.

"That she's been offered a job on the governor's team — you know, when he officially starts his run for the senate."

"What are you saying?" Bill asked.

Carney shook his head. "Nothing, just repeating gossip."

"Ever since you decided to tell the world you were Abby Morgan, the governor and I have been trying to protect you, to keep you from jeopardizing your career."

Abby fumed and chewed on Cox's statement — *no wonder she'd been micromanaging* — while she filed the gossip tidbit away, wondering whether it was true and, if so, what it meant for the Triple Seven. She prayed she could keep it together as fury rose inside like a wave.

Abby turned off her computer and gathered her things as soon as they returned to the office.

"Where are you going?" Bill asked.

"I'm angry. I need to think. I'll be back."

She headed straight for Woody's. All doubts she'd had about Woody and Asa took a backseat to her frustration. Rollins's move convinced her that Kent was her killer and that at least in part, Sanders was telling the truth. Her parents' murders had probably been ordered by Rollins.

And there was nothing she could do about it.

Woody rented a house from another cop. It was in north Long Beach off Del Amo Boulevard, very close to the border of the city of Lakewood. He should be home after working so many hours helping fire with the Crunchers inferno. She was not disappointed when she saw both of his cars in the drive. Woody alternated between a beat-up pickup truck and an old Saturn sedan.

She grabbed the six-pack of tea she'd brought for him and the package of Oreos she'd brought for herself and walked to the front door. Woody answered after a couple of knocks, but he was unshaven and appeared to have just gotten up.

"Abby, what a surprise."

"Sorry to wake you but something's happened." She held out the tea. "This is for you."

"Come on in." He took the tea and stepped aside to motion her in. "You didn't wake me. I haven't slept. Been dealing with Asa all night. He was drunker than a skunk and wanted to get in the car and drive. I've been a strong-arm babysitter since I got home."

Ralph and Ed attacked her with wagging tails, and she wished she'd brought Bandit. After she paid the dogs the proper amount of attention, Woody led her through his sparsely furnished living room. His house was decorated in early American dorm room: used couch, big-screen TV in the living room, and nothing else. He'd lost about everything in his last divorce and seemed to have no motivation to buy furniture. The place was clean because Woody was a neat freak, but it would never win a decorator's award.

Asa snored on the sofa, and even though she didn't get close, Abby could smell the alcohol. In the kitchen Woody did have a semi-new table and chairs, and that was where they stopped. He put the bottles of tea down, took one, and opened it.

"Have a seat. Did something come up after the fire?"

Abby sighed. Few people, not even Woody, knew the entire scope of Sanders's statements concerning the Triple Seven. She settled into a chair, pack of Oreos in front of her, and told him everything.

Woody made a fist and tapped his chin, contemplative after she finished.

"Is it possible my dad is still alive?" she asked after he said nothing for what seemed an eternity.

"I don't see how. But that day . . . Man, I hate to say it. I was hungover. I was focused on the fire." His forehead scrunched as if he were trying to remember.

"All the cars in the lot were accounted for, and arson did think that the fire was started with lighter fluid because it spread so fast." He smacked the table with both palms, then asked the question Abby had been asking herself. "If he is alive, where has he been all this time?"

He continued. "Do I believe Gavin Kent and Louis Rollins could do something like kill your parents? Yes. Kent has a Napoleon complex and was a bully until Mrs. Rollins cleaned him up."

"Mrs. Rollins?"

Woody nodded and took a long swallow of tea. Abby absentmindedly stroked Ralph's head.

"She was the push behind Lowell. A year after the Triple Seven burned, she got him elected to the city council, and suddenly Kent the bully was a glorified secretary. Louis was dead by then. Alyssa and Lowell were married shortly thereafter, and the Triple Seven invest was on the road to freezing. I remember the Puffs digging everywhere and getting nothing but frustrated."

"Do you remember the drug dealer, Coke Pipe?"

"I do. I arrested him a couple of times, outstanding warrants and such. I remember hearing that he fled to Mexico to escape some woman's angry husband. I don't know how long ago that was."

"What did he look like? Could he be mistaken for my dad?"

"You've seen the photos; he wouldn't have to. Those bodies were burnt. And the man . . . well, his face had been destroyed with a shotgun blast at close range . . ." His voice trailed off.

Abby stood to pace the kitchen. "Sanders

is such a slime that I should hesitate to believe him, according to Cox. But now Kent wouldn't look so guilty if Rollins hadn't taken the case away." Even as she said the words, her anger flared again.

"And then Cox all but admitted she's been hounding me because she and the governor are worried about me."

"Cox is up for a job in the governor's entourage."

"You've heard that too?"

Woody nodded. "She and Kent are tight, or at least they were."

"What?" Abby had never heard this. In fact, at the press conference, Kent was downright rude to Cox.

"Oh, back in the day, they dated, almost got married."

"How come I never heard this?"

"It was a long time ago. Anyway, they broke up after the Triple Seven fire. And you never liked to take part in gossip anyway. It's just something I know about through Asa."

"Do you think that's why she so willingly gave the investigation to the CHP?"

"That's odd; I agree with you there. I've never heard of the Chippies taking on a murder invest like the Triple Seven." Woody rose and put out a hand to stop her pacing.

"But she had to have the chief's approval to do it. Maybe she is looking out for you. Whatever the case, it's not worth losing your job over."

"What makes you think my job is in jeopardy?"

"You're angry. It's all over your face. And bingeing on Oreos is a dead giveaway. If you've been ordered to leave it alone, leave it alone. The truth will come out; it always does."

Luke's phone buzzed after he and Orson parted ways, and he saw that the call was from Arvli and the *Good Morning Long Beach* crew. He answered, actually happy for the interruption since he wasn't getting anywhere trying to reconstruct a twenty-seven-year-old murder scene in his head.

"What's up, Arvli?"

"Hey, I know you have the inside track on the Triple Seven story, you being connected and all. Is there any way you can get me an interview with Detective Hart? Everyone is trying to get her, and since this is a local story, do you think she might talk to us?"

"That's a good question. There have been a few developments that I can't talk about right now. Can you give me a little time? I'll talk to her and get back to you."

"Sure. You know that we're ready to go at the drop of a hat. Call me. This will be great."

Luke promised and ended the call. He juggled his phone, wondering if he should call Bill first or if he dared call Abby. Before he could decide, the phone rang again and it was Bill. He was going to chide Bill for mind reading when the tone of his friend's voice gave him pause.

"Where are you? Have you seen or heard from Abby?"

"Serenity Park, and no, I haven't seen her. What's happened?"

"She stormed out of here, all upset. I'm afraid she'll do something rash." As Bill explained what had happened, Luke felt his own anger rise. Abby must be right when she thought that Rollins was the guilty party. Why else would he hijack the investigation right when it seemed it was being blown wide-open?

"Can he do that?"

"Rollins is the governor. He's given the case to the section of the CHP assigned as his protective detail. They're not investigators, per se."

"What about what Sanders had to say?"

"All hearsay, no way to substantiate. But it's off our plate. All we can do is move

forward on our case against Sanders for killing Dan Jenkins. What happens to the Triple
Seven case now is anyone's guess."

CHAPTER 55

"The truth will come out; it always does."
What is that truth? Is my dad still alive?

Abby didn't go straight back to the station. She stopped at El Dorado Park and got out of the car to walk and try to clear her head.

Woody had helped somewhat. He helped her regain balance. He knew what she knew; he wasn't hiding anything, and that left her with a healthy skepticism for what Sanders said about her father. The junk man had to have an angle, and she was determined to find out what it was. But how?

She thought of Murphy and his whiteboard. When he started his investigation, he went back to high school years. Did what happened at the Triple Seven really start there? Her mind raced with possibilities and questions, and she stopped, staring out over the duck pond.

One case defines you.

Ethan's words haunted her. Abby knew then and there, no matter what she said to Dede and to Ethan, that she didn't trust God's justice. She couldn't wait patiently anymore for an arrest; she *needed* to know now.

What could she do to force the issue? Something unethical? Illegal?

Unable to answer the question, she got back in her car and drove for the station.

When her phone rang with a call from Luke, she let it go to voice mail, not ready to talk to him.

Back at the station she went straight to Jacoby and submitted a request for two weeks' vacation.

He looked at the slip and then up at Abby. "This wouldn't have anything to do with the Triple Seven, would it?"

"Of course it does. I can't concentrate right now. I need some time off to get my mind right." She told the truth without telling all of it. And she prayed Ethan would understand. She'd been saving her vacation time so they could take a month-long honeymoon. "Bill can handle the Jenkins case."

Jacoby studied her for a moment before nodding and signing the request. "Finish out the day. Have a great vacation."

CHAPTER 56

It was six in the evening before Asa came out of it. Woody had slept some, but worry for Abby kept him awake. If Rollins was the impetus behind the Triple Seven killing, he had money and resources now to go to any lengths to keep it quiet, buried, and forever cold. And motive to stop anyone from trying to prove it.

But Buck Morgan being alive?

I can't get my old gray head around that.

As Asa stirred, Woody turned on the coffeemaker. If his friend did know something, Woody planned to get it out of him if it was the last thing he did.

When Asa could walk, Woody threw him into the shower screaming and cursing. He left him a towel and a robe and told him to come into the kitchen when he was ready.

About twenty minutes later, red-faced and angry, Asa entered the kitchen, and Woody shoved a cup of coffee at him.

Asa sniffed it and cursed. "I need a drink, not coffee."

"Coffee only, until you tell me what you know." He pushed his friend into a chair, ignoring the spilled coffee. After Asa stopped protesting and had half a cup of coffee in him, Woody told him what Abby had shared. It didn't surprise him that Asa was not surprised.

"You know more than you've ever said. Tell me what's going on."

Asa drained the coffee cup and Woody refilled it.

"What goes around comes around — wasn't that what we always used to say?" Asa said after minutes of silence. "Some puke would do a crime and get off, and we'd say, 'What goes around comes around; he'll get his.' Ha! Doesn't always happen that way. Some pukes turn their crimes into solid gold."

"What are you saying? Is Sanders telling the truth?" Woody felt anger that his partner could have held such a piece of information all this time and shame that he'd never guessed or pried.

Asa looked at him with bleary, bloodshot eyes. "It was a couple months after the place burned. You were away on one of your honeymoons. I was working solo and drinking with Rollins and his crowd from time to time."

This surprised Woody, but he said nothing. Back in the day, Rollins didn't hang with the common folk, at least not when Alyssa was around.

"One night Louis comes to the party later than the rest of us and he's scared. I didn't understand what he was babbling about. I caught snatches of 'Buck Morgan and kid,' but Kent grabbed ahold of him and beat the snot out of him. I tried to break it up, but Kent got in my mug and told me to mind my own business or I'd be sorry." He paused and sipped the coffee, grimacing.

"You knew me back then. I told him he'd be the sorry one; I'd put his butt in jail. Later, I pieced together what Louis had rambled about. He said that Buck came to him and told him he needed to go to the police and tell the truth about the Triple Seven. I rolled it over and over, wondering what it could mean. Buck was dead as far as I knew. I planned on asking Louis, but two nights later he was dead in a hit-and-run."

"Did Kent have something to do with that?"

"I don't know. But I planned on going to the Puffs with what I'd heard and see if they could make sense of it. Tell them maybe they should look Kent's way."

Woody whistled. "That would have been a whole new avenue of investigation."

"Don't I know it. Twenty-five years ago a little pressure on two-bit Kent would have broken the case wide-open." He cursed and held his head in his hands. For a brief minute Woody feared he would begin sobbing.

But Asa shuddered and looked up. "Then I got something in the mail. You know what went on at those parties before you straightened up."

Woody nodded. He knew all too well. Besides the drinking, there were women and a lot of juvenile high jinks. More than one officer had been fired during the course of his career because of something directly related to an after-shift party at a cop bar.

"Someone took pictures of me with a woman." He inhaled deeply. "At least I thought she was a woman. Turned out she was underage. With the picture of us was a copy of her high school ID. The note said that if I said or did anything related to the Triple Seven, the pictures would go straight to the girl's parents and to IA."

Woody felt like he was going to be sick. He'd stopped partying with Asa after the

fire. Buck and Patricia were people he liked
and respected, and seeing them burnt up
like that made him throw everything up.
Ever since that night, he couldn't stand the
smell of alcohol or even think about taking
a drink. Staying sober for twenty-seven
years hadn't helped him save three mar-
riages, but it had kept him from the type of
trouble Asa just described.

"So you stayed quiet."

"I did. Did what I'd heard even make
sense? Buck was dead, memorialized, and
everyone moved on. I wanted my career,
my name. You know I even managed to
sober up for a time."

Woody nodded. "You started in again after
Miriam died. But it got worse after you
began working with Abby."

Asa gave a mirthless chuckle. "Yeah, it did.
That girl brought back so many memories.
Maybe I should have retired as soon as she
came back. Life is made up of maybes, isn't
it? She is such a good cop, better than I ever
was. When I saw how smart she was, I
thought she deserved to know the truth. But
what truth? After all this time, I just don't
know what it is anymore."

Now Asa did cry, not a sob, but tears running down his face. For something to do,
Woody poured him some more coffee.

"There's no evidence now," Woody said, half to himself. "Even if you'd recorded what Louis said, there's no evidence to convict anyone of anything."

CHAPTER 57

Don't do anything to jeopardize our future.

Abby could hear Ethan's words in her head when she filed for vacation time. With all the turmoil in her heart right now, she could hear him telling her to pray. Abby didn't want to pray. She wanted to break down doors and get the truth.

The first door she wanted to kick was the one to Trevor Taylor. Even though she was on vacation, she hadn't canceled her appointment to talk to him. But halfway to LA, Ira Green called and said she wasn't getting anywhere near his client. Abby had no choice but to head home with her tail between her legs.

First thing through the door, she hugged Bandit. He began to lick her face, and it was then she realized she was crying. Collapsing in her big chair with the little dog, Abby let the tears fall until her ribs hurt. As a child in foster care, she used to kick dirt clods and imagine she was smashing her parents' killers to dust. They were faceless dirt clods then. Now the faces were in front of her . . . or were they?

When she was done crying, she picked herself up and grabbed her investigation book. The only other avenue she had to work with was Kelsey Cox. If Kent were the killer, and he and Cox were a couple back then, she would know. Especially if Kent had been shot. And a question nagged — if they were engaged, why didn't they get married? Why break up after the fire?

She opened her book on the kitchen table and began reviewing what she had memorized. She'd never read the name Kelsey Cox anywhere.

Abby went through the scribe list of all the officers who checked on scene for the Triple Seven fire. Cox was in patrol back then and it had been a big fire, but she was not listed as having been on scene for any reason. Next Abby moved to the fire at her house. Her parents' home was just off Second Street near an elementary school and not far from the restaurant. There was Cox. She was an eastside day patrol unit and one of the first responders.

Did that mean anything at all? she wondered in exasperation. If Kent set the fire, was Cox there to cover up for him? Hide evidence?

"Arggh." Abby closed her eyes and patted both sides of her head, wanting to scream in frustration. She could hear Asa's voice: *"Straws, you're grasping at straws"* — something he'd said a few times during her training when she tried to make things fit that didn't.

Her phone rang again and she recognized Luke's number. She almost didn't answer because she wanted — too much — to hear his voice, talk this out with him. He would understand her frustration. Finally, before it went to voice mail, she answered.

"Abby, where are you?"

"Home. I took two weeks' vacation time."

"Are you okay?"

The genuine concern in his voice gave her pause. Was she?

"I am."

"Something tells me you're not taking a vacation."

"I don't need a lecture."

"I'm not a lecturer. Just wanted to ask you a question. Do you mind if I stop by?"

Drumming her fingers for a second before she answered, she said okay and wondered if she really should have.

■ ■ ■ ■

It broke his heart that Abby met him at the door looking for all the world like she was defeated. There was no fire in her eyes. Luke bent down to pick Bandit up when the little guy rushed over to say hello.

"Thanks for letting me come over. Bill told me you were upset."

"I'll admit I'm frustrated." She flung herself onto the couch, grabbing a pillow and hugging it to her chest. "I wanted to break down doors, scream, kick, but that won't get me anywhere. I've tried to connect Cox to some shadow conspiracy, and that's not happening, so how about I leak Sanders's unsubstantiated ravings to Walter Gunther?"

"That would be unethical."

"Yes, it would be." She looked at him, anger and pain in her eyes. "But if my parents were killed to protect Rollins, to ignite his political career, who is unethical?"

Luke sighed. He understood her frustration too well. "You believe Sanders, then?"

"Maybe I wouldn't if Cox hadn't been so quick to make sure I wouldn't be able to investigate anything. And even quicker to give the case to the very man who might be covering things up."

"She thinks you're too close; that's legitimate."

"Is it? She's close to this as well. She dated Gavin Kent years ago."

"Where did you hear that?"

"Woody."

"I guess that explains some things and raises more questions."

"Yeah, it does. I wonder if they're still close."

"If they are, isn't Cox behaving a little un-ethically?"

"Carney had a bit of gossip about that."

"Is gossip ever reliable?"

"This might be. Cox is up for a job with Rollins when he runs for senate."

Luke whistled. He wanted to say something, anything, that might brighten Abby's outlook. "Listen, I had a thought on my way over. Sometimes when old cases come up, make news, don't people call in tips, even kooks?"

"Uh-huh." She frowned. "I've been so busy, I haven't heard if any have come in on the Triple Seven."

"Maybe if you give an extensive cable interview, on your own time, you might generate some tips."

"And do what? Give them to the CHP to

be buried?"

"You don't know that will happen. If people are talking about a topic, politicians usually have to be aboveboard with said topic."

He could tell she was considering it.

"My friends at *Good Morning Long Beach* would like to do an interview. It's local, it's low-key, and you're on your own time."

"A private citizen?" She looked skeptical. "I don't think I want to be that provocative."

Luke raised an eyebrow and cocked his head, trying to think of something else.

Her phone rang with her homicide ringtone.

"It's Bill," Abby said, brows furrowed. "I wonder what's up."

She answered, and Luke watched as her features hardened. When she ended the call, she looked at Luke.

"George Sanders hung himself in county lockup."

"No way."

"So much for not being provocative. Call up your friends at *Good Morning Long Beach*. I'll give them an interview."

CHAPTER 58

Don't do anything to jeopardize our future.

While she stood in the studio watching the college kids set up for the talk show, Abby fidgeted nervously and prayed. *Lord, please, you know my heart in this. I just want the truth.* She prayed for the right words, and for forgiveness, though technically she was not doing anything out of policy — unless she released confidential or unsubstantiated information.

Abby and Luke sat down on the black-and-gold couch across from the grad student who hosted the show, Jay Casey.

The crew who ran the show did their best to put her at ease, but nervousness rippled through her like waves on the beach. Next to her, Luke was the picture of calm, and she hoped that would help her when the questions started.

"Good morning, Long Beach! I'm Jay Casey and today we have two special guests, both local heroes: one you know — Luke Murphy, our favorite private investigator — and the other hero is also someone who knows great personal tragedy.

"Thank you for being with us today, Luke and Detective Abigail Hart."

"My pleasure." She and Luke spoke at the same time, but then Casey directed his questions to Abby.

The interview started and Abby's butterflies disappeared. First Jay asked her about her background, and she shared the story of the Triple Seven and her own odyssey.

"I can't imagine having your parents murdered and never finding out why or by whom. So where does the investigation stand now?"

Abby swallowed. "Well, I'm not sure. Governor Rollins has decided the California Highway Patrol will do a better job at the investigation. The LBPD doesn't have it anymore."

"So you're saying that Governor Rollins has taken the investigation away from the LBPD?"

"Yes. While I have great respect for the highway patrol, the Triple Seven investigation is not their jurisdiction."

"Do you think the governor is hiding

something?"

"I don't know what to think. All I know is that for the first time in twenty-seven years we had some new information — information I can't comment on — and the governor snatches the investigation away. Maybe you can ask him, Jay. Maybe he'll come on *GMLB* and tell everyone why he did that."

"Wow, that's quite a story," Jay said. "It almost sounds as though the governor is trying to cover something up, doesn't it?"

"I wouldn't go that far," Abby said, "at least this early. Who knows? Maybe the CHP will solve the case once and for all."

"I wouldn't be as charitable as Detective Hart," Luke chimed in. "To me this definitely looks like a cover-up."

"Heavy charges to make. Maybe after twenty-seven years it just can't be solved."

"I don't believe that for a second," Abby said. "Good luck for bad people can't last forever. I look forward to a perp walk with my parents' killers center stage."

CHAPTER 59

Abby met her friend Jessica in the parking lot of River's End early Thursday morning. They were both on their bikes, and the plan was to ride from River's End to Newport Beach and back and then have breakfast. Abby wanted to be out of the house for the fallout from the interview. Cable news channels had picked it up in the afternoon, and people were asking Rollins for a statement about the case all day Wednesday. She hadn't seen an official response from the governor but was sure one would eventually come.

For Abby the early morning ride was therapeutic as well as being escapist. She'd been so busy lately her workouts had suffered; she needed a hard ride.

"You should do interviews more often," Jessica said as they started their ride down Ocean Avenue toward PCH.

"I don't think so."

"Why? It was great. You got the Triple Seven investigation going again, I'm sure of it."

"Yeah, but I didn't have permission to give an interview. I may be in trouble."

"I think Rollins should be in trouble for taking the investigation away."

Abby grunted in agreement as they finished their warm-up and began to ride harder.

When they reached Newport Beach, they stopped for a water break and she checked her phone. There was a message from DC Cox.

She returned the call and braced herself for the sky to fall on her head.

"Detective Hart, I realize you are on vacation, but in light of your recent off-duty activity, your presence is required at the station."

The formal niceness of the DC's tone took Abby by surprise. "When? I'm not at home right now. I'm out on my bike."

"Can you be here by 2 p.m.?"

Abby checked the time. "Yes. I'll be there."

She told Jessica as the two decided to head back to Long Beach.

"Are you in trouble?" Jessica asked.

"I have no idea."

■ ■ ■ ■

Cox was nowhere to be seen when Abby arrived at the DC's office. Her secretary directed Abby to a conference room. She walked into the room, and there, at the head of the large, oval table, sat Governor Lowell Rollins.

Her breath caught in her throat, and for a second she felt as if she'd forgotten how to breathe. She expected a dressing-down, a letter of reprimand, at the least, or suspension at the most. But she didn't expect this.

"Hello, Abby."

She swallowed. "Governor." She noticed that it was just the two of them. Neither Cox nor Kent was anywhere to be seen. She hadn't even noticed an entourage on her way up from the lobby.

"Please, have a seat. I came here to see you and hopefully to clear up a few things."

Abby didn't immediately comply.

"Please. Abby, your parents were my best friends in the world, and I realize I owe them — I owe you — some answers."

She took a chair two down from Rollins and wiped sweaty palms off on her jeans. "Why did you take the Triple Seven investigation away?"

He leaned forward. "I'll get to that. First, I wanted to give you some background. I've read the statement Sanders gave and I think that you owe me a chance to respond to his ravings."

His gray eyes bored into Abby and she waited for him to continue.

"Your parents and I grew up together. In fact, your father and his brother, Simon, were guests at my house for dinner more times than I can count. I was best man at your parents' wedding. Do you know where the name Triple Seven came from?"

"You were all born in July."

He nodded. "Yes, your mother's birthday was 7/5, mine is 7/6, and your dad's was 7/7. We felt we were lucky sevens and that the number would be lucky for business." He sat back, and a faraway look came over him. "It was, too, for a time — very lucky. The restaurant did phenomenally well. Your mother had no plans to buy me out, and no, your dad was not a crazed drug addict." He smiled and Abby looked away.

"I want you to forgive me. I lost so much that day, and it hurt me so much, I forgot how much you lost. I confess I forgot you all these years and I'm sorry. I owed it to your parents to make certain you were well taken care of, not shoved away like you were."

"I'm fine. My aunt did her best, and I have no animosity over how I was raised. The only animosity I feel is toward the people who killed my parents. I want them brought to justice. Sanders had the idea that Kent and your brother killed my parents."

Rollins huffed and shook his head. "For what purpose? What motive? My brother was . . . well, today they say developmentally disabled. True, he could be easily coerced, but he had a job as a busboy at the restaurant and was proud of it. He loved your parents as much as I did. Why would he hurt them? As for Gavin, at the time of the fire he was engaged and planning his wedding. What reason would he have to murder anyone?"

"Why would Sanders make up the story he told?"

A sad smile tugged at the corners of his mouth as Rollins said, "Jealousy? I don't know. He was underwater financially at the junkyard. George had a gambling problem. And from what I understand, you arrested him on a strong murder charge. Perhaps the man he killed held some markers; maybe Sanders owed him money. He certainly wasn't holding a box of evidence relating to the Triple Seven."

And I can't ask him now, Abby thought. "It's a strange coincidence that Crunchers burned to the ground after Sanders told me where he had proof hidden."

"Not so strange. I asked for an early copy of the arson investigator's report. Seems the fire was accidental — bad wiring in the office is what the investigator found. George was never meticulous about things."

Abby fought hard to keep her expression neutral. She'd forgotten to check on the cause of the fire at Crunchers, she'd been so preoccupied.

"Still, he made some serious allegations against Gavin Kent. Can I speak to Mr. Kent?"

Rollins gave an exasperated sigh. "I will ask him. But you have to see how insulting this is. He was a decorated soldier, wounded in battle. And he has been invaluable to me for many years."

"Why take the investigation away from the PD?"

"That was Gavin and Alyssa, overreacting to protect me, I think. I've had everything returned. Check with Kelsey Cox. I wanted to clear things up and depart to the capitol on good terms. And I wanted to offer you a job."

"A job?" Abby nearly fell out of her chair. This time there was no hiding her shock.

"Yes. You have a stellar work record, a spotless reputation. I could use you on my personal security detail. You'd be an asset. It's really no secret that I have all but officially declared I plan on running for the senate. On the national level I will need people I can trust around me. You'd make considerably more money working for me."

"I, uh . . ."

"No need to answer right now. Think about it. I'll be in town for a few more days. Kelsey Cox can get ahold of me when you have your answer. It's the least I can do to honor the memory of your parents, take good care of their daughter." He stood, and Abby realized the audience was over. He'd so flummoxed her with the job offer, she couldn't organize her thoughts quick enough.

"Why would Sanders say that my father was still alive?"

"Ah, that was the cruelest cut of all." He stepped close to her, and again the essence of his cologne hit her. "My dear, he was trying to get under your skin, to cloud your judgment. Buck Morgan was my best friend, and I'm certain he died that day." He patted her shoulder and headed for the door.

"My office will issue a statement with most of what I've just told you, so I'm hoping this puts the story to rest. Please give my offer some thought." And with that, he was gone.

CHAPTER 60

Abby climbed into her car, head spinning. Rollins had turned her attempt to blindside him with her interview on its ear. If she had known this meeting would take place, she would have been more prepared. And the job offer — wow. It was as if she were in an episode of *The X-Files*. Her phone began to ring and she saw that it was Detective Wright.

"Hello, Fred, what's up?"

"Some information I need to share with you and Murphy. Can we meet somewhere? Maybe for coffee or lunch?"

"Right now?" Abby was not up to seeing Luke or Wright at the moment.

"It's important."

"Then why not the Seal Beach PD?" At least that would be business.

"I have sensitive stuff to show you. I'd rather we were at a coffee shop or restaurant. I'm in Seal Beach; is there a place here you prefer?"

Abby sighed, feeling a hundred years old. "How about River's End?"

"Great. I'll call Murphy and meet you there."

"I'm just leaving the station, so I won't be long." Abby disconnected and tried to generate some interest or enthusiasm.

"I'm hoping this puts the story to rest."

Not hardly, Abby thought as Rollins's voice rang in her ears. Sanders told a story that was too plausible to be dismissed so easily. *How do you put the genie back in the bottle? How do you find the truth in a maze of lies, liars, and dead men?*

When she arrived at River's End, Luke was just getting out of his truck. He waited for her.

"Are you okay? You don't look happy," he said.

She'd gotten over the irritation she felt because he read her so easily. "I just had a one-on-one meeting with Governor Rollins."

"What?"

"Yep." She pointed to Wright, waiting by the entrance. "I'll explain to both of you."

When they reached the detective, he gestured across the flood control channel to

Serenity Park. "That's where the Triple Seven used to be," he said to Abby. "Funny you picked this place."

Abby cocked her head. "This is my favorite restaurant. I like to look across the way and imagine my folks and their business before the park."

"It's a great park," Luke said. "I take my daughter there often. What do you think of the plaque?" he asked Abby.

"I've never been to the park."

"What?" Luke stared at her as they were shown to a table.

"I like to imagine, but I've never been able to go there and see the reality."

Once they were seated, Abby changed the subject and told them about the meeting with the governor.

"I wish I'd known that he was going to give me the opportunity," she said as she finished. "I would have been better prepared."

"I'm sure he surprised you for just that reason," Luke observed.

"This makes what I have to show you all the more important," Wright said, holding up a manila envelope. He fanned his palm with the envelope. "I got some interesting information from a friend of Luke's —" he gave Luke a look — "who wishes to remain nameless until we get some hard evidence." He pulled a photo out of the envelope and handed it to Luke. "Does this guy look familiar?"

"That's him — that's the second man from the flood control. He was wearing the hoodie." His face was bright with excitement.

"Wait, catch me up. You've identified Luke's attackers?" Abby asked Detective Wright.

"With Luke's friend's help. The dead man was Gordon West. And now this guy."

"How'd you find him? Who is he?" Luke asked.

"I know him," Wright said. "He's an ex-OC deputy. Alonzo Ruiz. He was fired about ten years ago for beating a homeless man to death. It was the first homicide case I handled and one I'll never forget."

"But how'd you find him?" Luke asked again, handing the photo to Abby.

"Your friend was able to send me a list of known associates for West. I picked Ruiz out right away. The kind of intimidation you experienced was right up his alley. He was acquitted at trial but still lost his job because of his overall bad record."

"Has he been causing problems since then?"

"No, we thought he moved out of state. But there's more. When I retrieved his files to review, I found something interesting. Gavin Kent was listed on Ruiz's deputy application as a reference."

"Oh, you're kidding me. What a connection." Abby smiled.

"Have you contacted Kent about this?" Luke asked.

Wright shook his head. "I'm hoping to find a more recent connection. Ruiz graduated from the academy fifteen years ago."

Sandy appeared to take their orders. Luke asked for coffee. Abby did the same, and Wright ordered iced tea.

"So Kent could say he lost contact." Abby rubbed her temples after Sandy left. "I don't believe in coincidences. Maybe Sanders was a liar and a cheat, but I'll bet a paycheck that there was a grain of truth in what he said. I asked Rollins if I could talk to Kent."

"That was a good question," Luke said. "What did he say?"

"That it would be an insult to the man."

"Hmmm," Wright said. "Then I'd better dig to find a more recent connection. And we're looking for Ruiz. Every deputy in OC knows him."

"Thanks, Fred. I really owe you. I'm not on this case; you don't need to keep me in the loop."

"Hey, if my parents had been in the ground for twenty-seven years and their killers out free, I'd be working just as hard as you to get to the truth."

CHAPTER 61

After Wright left to return to work, Abby lingered with Luke in the River's End parking lot.

"So who is this friend, the one that helped Fred identify the two men who attacked you?" Excited by the identification but guarded, Abby couldn't shake the feeling that she was Charlie Brown preparing to kick the football only to have it pulled away.

"He's a buddy who works for the FBI. He came to town to offer me a job."

"A job? With the FBI?" Abby stepped back. "I did not see that coming. Don't you like being your own boss?"

"Yes, I do, but he made me an interesting offer. I'd be on a federal task force, working on cold cases."

Abby folded her arms and held his gaze. "Helping people like us?"

He nodded and smiled, and Abby's heart raced a bit. "Yep," he said. "Helping them find closure."

At that she laughed mirthlessly and kicked at some sand in the lot. "I've always believed that finding killers helps people affected by murder move on, heal."

"You don't believe that anymore?"

"I don't know what to believe anymore. I thought I could solve my parents' murders, but the closer I get, the further away the solution seems."

She looked back into his eyes, and for a moment she feared he was going to reach out and touch her hand. He understood. He knew what she was going through, and none of it was a mystery to him.

She looked away. "I'd like to hear more about —" Her phone rang. "It's Woody," she said as she answered. "Hi, I was —"

Woody cut her off, sounding rushed and panicked. "Where are you?"

Abby frowned. "River's End."

"Thank God you're close. Get over to the governor's house, now."

Abby leaned forward, tense. "What is it?"

"It's Asa. He's gone and he's planning something stupid."

"Like what? Should I call 911?"

"No! I think I can handle it. But you're closer than I am. I'm in the car now. Meet me there." The tone of his voice sent a shiver up Abby's spine. He ended the call.

"What is it?" Luke asked.

"I have to go. Sorry to leave —"

"No way you're leaving me, not with that look on your face."

"Fine, I don't want to argue." She turned. "Just get in my car. I'll explain on the way."

CHAPTER 62

"If the governor is here, I'm sure he has security," Luke said after Abby told him what Woody said. "How can Asa expect to get anywhere near him?"

"If he's drunk, he's likely to go over there and make a fool of himself. And in the past, Rollins has kept his security detail light when home. He only ramps things up during election times or if there's a protest going on about something." Abby darted through traffic, traveling as fast as she dared.

She turned on Second Street, headed for the Naples area of Long Beach. She knew where the governor lived because once or twice there had been alerts to watch for protesters for one issue or another. He had a big house on Sixty-Fourth Place, right near the water. It was a nice place, and in spite of being on the peninsula where the houses were crowded together, it was sort of private because people had to know how to get there. There was one confusing way in and one way out.

When Abby turned from Bay Shore to Ocean Boulevard, she stepped on it. She didn't think Asa had a rental car, so he had to be in one of Woody's cars. She looked for his truck or his Saturn sedan as she got closer. Sixty-Fourth Place, where the governor lived, was little more than a block long, and this part of Long Beach was on the peninsula, so the street ended at the sand.

She arrived at Sixty-Fourth Place and slowed. When she turned, there was Woody's beat-up Saturn right in front of the governor's house parked at the red curb. Next to the Saturn in the middle of the street, emergency lights flashing, was a dark sedan with a state license plate indicating it probably belonged to the governor's security detail. It was empty and the driver's door stood open.

"What is going on?" Abby said, half to herself. She parked behind the Saturn and turned to Luke as she pulled her off-duty 9mm from her purse.

He spoke before she could. "Don't say it. I'm coming in with you."

"I don't know what's happening. I think you should stay here and give me a chance to find out."

Luke shook his head and Abby saw a steadfast resolve in his eyes. Worry about what Asa had planned lessened as she soaked in the knowledge that she could count on Luke no matter what.

She opened her car door.

They both started for the front entrance. The entryway was right on the street. In this neighborhood the houses had no yards. What made it exclusive was the proximity of the ocean and the fact it was on the peninsula.

Abby saw quickly that the door was ajar. She turned to Luke. "I don't know. I have a bad feeling about this."

"Me too." He peered over her shoulder, and she turned in time to see Woody's battered pickup come careening around the corner and screech to a stop behind her car.

He jumped out and ran toward them. "Where's Asa?"

"I don't know. Inside, I guess. The security car is empty."

"We have to stop him," he yelled as he pushed past Luke into the house.

Abby followed with Luke on her heels.

CHAPTER 63

Luke hurried to keep up with Abby. She'd flown past him after Woody. The fact that they were both armed did not escape his notice. But he'd always been quicker with his wits than with a gun, so he just prayed to the Lord for protection and wisdom.

The inside of the house looked like a museum. There were glass cases everywhere — books, collectibles, and assorted photos in them. Woody seemed to know just where he was going, and Abby stayed close to him while Luke followed her. They'd gotten through the entryway and entered what looked like a den when they heard voices.

"I won't keep your secret any longer."

"You're a crazy drunk. No one will believe anything you say."

"They will if you shoot that gun," Woody said. He'd stepped into a double doorway and moved to the right. Abby followed and Luke heard her gasp.

The scene before him made Luke hold his breath. Kent and another man both had their guns trained on Asa. The shock was that Asa had a woman in front of him, holding her like a human shield, with a gun to her head. He recognized the woman as Kelsey Cox. Asa also had what looked like a vest of road flares around his chest. He was sweating bullets, and Cox's eyes bugged out in terror.

"Asa, what are you doing? Stop this!" Abby pleaded as she knelt partially behind a couch. Luke slid in behind her.

"See what you stirred up?" Kent screamed at Abby. "The psycho nutbags crawled out of the woodwork because of the interview you gave the other day."

Asa shifted. "Tell her! You killed her mother and then tried to kill her! I don't care what you do to me; just tell the truth!"

"This isn't the way to get to the truth," Woody pleaded with his friend from behind the cover of a high-back chair. "Let Cox go."

"You just wouldn't stop," Kent fumed, his rage directed toward Abby, not Asa. "You wouldn't stop opening doors that should have stayed closed."

"It's my job to close homicides with an arrest."

The atmosphere in the room shifted as a frost settled over the space between Kent and Abby, and for a minute it seemed everyone forgot Asa, except the security guy. Luke saw the man steady his aim at Asa while Woody and Abby concentrated on Kent.

"Your job is to do as you're told. But like your father, you just don't listen." Kent grated the words out through clenched teeth. Luke could almost see steam coming out of the man's ears. Luke crawled along the back of the couch to get closer to Asa, hoping to remove Cox and defuse the situation. He prayed that the security man didn't shoot.

"Is that what happened that day? He didn't listen?"

Luke stopped at the decisive tone in Abby's voice. Something was going to happen.

"No, he didn't." Kent stepped from the doorway he was using as cover. "Is that what you want to hear? He was a bloody hothead and he just wouldn't listen!"

Luke pulled his legs up under himself, preparing to jump into action, when suddenly Cox elbowed Asa and lurched forward. The room exploded in gunfire — from the security man and Asa, he thought — and shattering glass.

Luke ducked, covering his head with his hands, and all he could think was *Abby.* Was she out of the line of fire?

It seemed an eternity before he felt it was safe to raise his head. When he did, Kent was gone, and Luke caught a glimpse of Abby, disappearing through the doorway where Kent had been.

"Oh, Lord." He breathed a prayer and leaped to his feet, preparing to go after her.

Asa was moaning, and the security man was tending to Cox. Luke took a step toward the door and froze.

Woody was down.

CHAPTER 64

Abby never ducked. She zeroed in on Kent, aware of glass flying and ignoring her own personal safety. All she could see was Kent's fleeing back. He disappeared through the door and she charged after him. Down a long hallway, he went through another door, heading toward the back of the house, the beach side, Abby guessed. She couldn't imagine where he thought he was going to go; they were on a peninsula, for heaven's sake. She accelerated as Kent led her through a maze of rooms, and suddenly she was in the kitchen.

A stunned woman leaned against the sink as if she'd just been shoved there.

"Where?" Abby yelled and the woman pointed.

Out the back door Abby ran, squinting when she stepped into the sunlight. She looked left and saw Kent jump over a retaining wall and hit the wooden boardwalk that ran along the beach, between the houses and the sand. He landed wrong, stumbled, and cursed before he got up and limped away toward the street, circling back to where the cars were. Abby hurried after him, adrenaline taking her over the wall easily. She hit the wooden boardwalk at a run.

"Stop, Kent! You're not getting away!"

He came to a curb where the street and the boardwalk met and looked over his shoulder, a mocking grin on his face. As he turned back, he tripped over the curb, sprawling into the street and cursing as he slid.

Breath coming hard, fury her fuel, Abby reached the man and pointed her weapon. "Stay right there. You're under arrest."

He writhed on the asphalt and rolled over to face her, gun still in his hand. "Or what? You'll put me out of my misery? Go ahead, I dare you."

"Drop it!" she warned as her breathing slowed but her anger intensified. "I don't want you dead. I have too many questions." Abby heard sirens in the distance and tightened her sweaty grip on the gun. It felt like it was a hundred degrees outside.

"About your daddy? Or maybe your mom? I killed her, shot her right in the head. Is that what you wanted to know?"

Abby flinched, her finger tight on the trigger. A loud voice in her head screamed *"Shoot!"*

Kent sneered and pulled himself up to a sitting position. He held the gun across his lap while supporting himself on one elbow.

He looked behind her but Abby didn't turn.

"Why did you kill them?"

"Shoot me. You want to. All you'll get from me is that Sanders had it just about right."

His hand moved and Abby tensed, almost squeezing the trigger.

But in a quick, fluid movement, Kent pointed the gun at his chin and fired. Abby lurched forward, but there was nothing she could do to stop him.

"Noooo!" A bloodcurdling scream came from behind her. Abby turned as Kelsey Cox shoved past her.

"No, no, no," she wailed as she fell to her knees next to the man.

Abby knelt beside her, but she could already tell there would be no pulse. She put a hand on Cox's shoulder to move her away from the body, and the woman shook it off.

"You killed him; you killed him," she

wailed. Sobbing, she cradled Kent's head in her lap.

Abby stood and stepped back. Shocked at how close she had come to pulling the trigger.

Another set of footsteps ran up behind her. It was Luke.

"What happened?" His face said he feared the worst.

"He shot himself," Abby said. It was then she saw the blood on Luke's pants and hands.

"Not mine," he said before Abby even had the strength to ask. "Asa didn't make it."

Abby felt punched in the stomach, and that was a punch too many as far as she was concerned.

She leaned into Luke, ignoring the blood and letting him place a supporting arm around her as a fleet of emergency vehicles began filling the street in front of them.

CHAPTER 65

ONE WEEK LATER

"For real? You're going to retire?" Abby looked across the table at Woody and a lump formed in her throat.

"Yep," he said, his head still sporting a bandage. He'd been grazed by a stray bullet that day in the governor's house and suffered a slight concussion and received ten stitches.

"I'm tired. I've been in harness a long time. It's about time I stepped aside for some youngster."

The waitress set down their lunches and gave Woody a gentle pat as she went back to work.

Woody and Abby had just come from a private and hushed memorial for Asa, and she knew losing Asa in the way that he did weighed heavily. Asa had been thoroughly disgraced as a psychotic drunk who went postal. He'd stormed into the governor's house with flares wrapped around himself, apparently hoping it looked enough like a bomb to give him a brief advantage. It had. Rollins, his wife, and one security man had fled to a panic room, where they stayed until the entire incident was over. The second security man — the one who shot Asa — was being hailed as a hero. Luke and Woody received some kudos as well. In spite of Woody's head injury, with Luke's help he'd gotten up and together they tried hard to save Asa's life. But Asa had bled to death in the governor's living room.

"Will you leave the state?" She worked hard to keep her voice from breaking. *I hurt over Asa as well,* she thought.

"Haven't thought that far. I do have to make arrangements for Asa's affairs. Luke and I are planning a trip up to Idaho to clean out his house and tie up some loose ends."

"Murphy?" She knew Luke and Woody had become chummy since that day, but this surprised her. All of them had been interviewed and reinterviewed by LA County officials about what happened. The LA DA had taken over the investigation at the request of the Long Beach police chief.

Woody took a bite of his sandwich. For her part Abby had lost her appetite.

With Kent's death, some things became clearer for Abby, while others were a lot more muddled. The man confessed to being a killer and then killed himself, seeing to it that the Triple Seven case would never be wrapped up and closed with a neat bow. It was closed, however. The chief read everyone's reports on the incident that day and decided that the case was, for all intents and purposes, solved.

Kent was not buried with the stigma of being a convicted murderer; the governor eulogized him as a loyal but troubled employee.

Kelsey Cox officially filed retirement papers, and the rumor was that she would take the job left open by Kent's death. But Abby had not seen anything from the governor confirming that news.

Abby felt numb and cheated. She'd always had the Triple Seven investigation and she'd always had Woody. Now she would lose him as well.

With no clear resolution.

"There's still so much to clear up," she said. "I was hoping you'd help me look for Alonzo Ruiz, the man who jumped Murphy —"

"Abby, the case has been closed. Kent told you he did it."

"But the threads, Woody — I need to tie up the threads. Did Kent do it for Rollins, and if he did, do we really want Rollins to be a senator?"

Woody sighed and pain creased his features. "Don't." He leaned forward. "Don't be like Asa."

"What do you mean?"

"That case ate him up and spit him out a psycho. He wouldn't listen to me and let it go, and look what happened."

"Woody, I —"

"Let it go. If Rollins is guilty, it will come out eventually. He can run, but he can't hide."

Something snapped in Abby as Woody quoted her motto. He was right — she knew it in her head, but in her heart? She told everyone that she trusted God, but did she?

She looked away, then turned back to reply. "Letting go feels like giving up." She barely kept her composure.

He hiked one shoulder. "Sometimes giving up and stepping back gives you a clearer perspective."

"Okay." She picked up her Diet Coke and gave a mock toast before drinking.

Woody smiled. "How's Ethan?" he asked, changing the subject and cutting through Abby's rising wave of self-pity.

"He's doing a lot of speaking, sharing about his successful mission trip. His Power-Point presentation is really inspiring."

"Doesn't sound like you're too excited about that." He took a drink of his iced tea.

Abby waited a moment before responding. "It's not that. It's just that after all that's happened, he's asked me to take a leave of absence and travel with him on his next mission trip. He thinks I need to put some distance between me and the shoot-out before I go back to work." She picked up a fry and put it in her mouth.

"Maybe that would be a good thing."

Abby swallowed. "You sound like Dede."

Woody reached across the table and gripped her forearm. "Abby, you've been invested in finding your parents' killers for your whole life. Why can't you just believe you did find him and that now he's dead?"

"Do you?"

He sighed, and it broke her heart how tired and old he looked. "There's just nowhere left to go."

"My dad?"

"I knew your dad. There is no way he would have stayed away from you unless he were dead. You have to believe that."

Abby picked up her Diet Coke again to

help swallow the sob that threatened, and wondered why she couldn't believe it.

CHAPTER 66

Luke placed a bouquet of flowers at the base of the Triple Seven memorial plaque. It was a beautiful June day, perfect for kite flying with Maddie, but she wasn't with him, and his thoughts were on everything that had happened over the past couple weeks.

He'd decided to take Orson up on his offer. He'd talked it over with his family, and they told him they'd be behind him, whatever he decided. While he loved being a private investigator, he knew intimately and painfully how important it was to know the whys and the hows associated with crimes, especially crimes that devastated a life. *Maybe by helping other people get closure, I'll eventually feel the same for myself.*

That day in the governor's house replayed in his mind. What happened would never be crystal clear, but he'd pieced it together as best he could after reading the reports filed by the officers who responded and talking to everyone he could. When Cox elbowed Asa, the security man fired, hitting Asa in the right hip. Asa fell right and pulled the trigger on his gun, which he'd rigged to be fully automatic. That led to a spray of bullets around the room that shattered all the glass. One bullet actually struck Woody, leaving a crease across his head that bled a lot and eventually took stitches. Luke discovered several small cuts across his own back from glass when he finally got home that night. It was a miracle no one else was killed.

He'd wanted to charge after Abby but couldn't until he made certain Woody was all right. After that, there was Asa. The security man's bullet had traversed Asa's upper thigh and cut the femoral artery. He and Woody tried, but there was nothing they could do.

When he did bolt out of the house after Abby and came upon the scene with Kent, it took his breath away. He feared Abby had shot the man. She talked little about exactly what had happened. Luke had never seen her look so lost, so dazed, and he understood. There would be no neat end to the Triple Seven, only a partially built puzzle with key pieces missing. They'd only spoken briefly since that day, and since she was still on vacation, even Bill had not seen her. He wanted to call her but knew that Ethan was home and it wasn't his place.

He turned at the sound of a car parking, and his eyes widened in surprise. And then a flash of attraction and anticipation flared that he worked to douse.

It was Abby.

She climbed out of the car, turning to the right as Bandit trotted across the driver's seat and jumped out. She walked with the little dog on a leash to where he stood.

"I didn't expect to see you here," Luke said.

"First time for everything," she said. "Besides, I know the date." She turned away from him to read the plaque.

He understood. Today was the twenty-seventh anniversary.

She read the inscription out loud and faltered as if something was wrong. " 'No farewell words were spoken; there was no time to say good-bye. You were gone before we knew it, and only God knows why. We take comfort in this: "Nothing in all creation is hidden from God's sight. Everything is uncovered and laid bare before the eyes of him to whom we must give account." Hebrews 4:13.' "

She turned toward Luke, face flushed. "Who picked the saying?"

"My mom. Why? What's wrong?" He watched as she fought for composure.

"It's just, uh . . . Well, that verse, it's my verse . . . my verse for homicide. I guess it surprises me to find it here." She leaned down and picked up Bandit, holding him close.

"It's a great verse, definitely wisdom for people like us."

"People like us?" She faced him, eyes liquid.

"People who may never know what really happened in an incident that has defined us."

"Are you defined by the Triple Seven?"

"I am. All my life I've been chasing my uncle, trying to live up to the memory of my first hero. I haven't always believed that, or understood it, but now I think I do."

She rested her cheek on the dog's head, and Luke saw a tear fall.

Luke felt an overwhelming urge to wipe it away, but he kept his distance.

Abby sniffed, raised her head, and swiped at the tear. "Does that mean you can put it behind you, move on, and trust without doubt that the guilty will get what they deserve?"

"Abby, I move on one day at a time, and I trust moment by moment, believing that one day it won't be a struggle." He sighed and held her gaze. "I can't let it consume me. I believe the verse with all my heart. And I move forward knowing it applies to the guilty in the Triple Seven, all of them, and that God's justice is more perfect than mine or the LBPD's."

She turned away and didn't say anything for a few minutes, just stared out at the park, resting her head on the dog. He was about to say something else when she put the dog down and faced him. Her eyes were clear and she looked steady, he thought.

"It was finally coming to that conclusion myself that brought me here today."

"God's justice?"

"Yeah. I can't ignore that truth and have any peace. I can't chase shadows anymore. Woody is afraid I'll become as consumed by it as Asa was that day and do something crazy."

"I could never see you doing anything that crazy." He smiled, and his heart leaped in his chest when she returned it in kind.

"I hope you're right. Maybe I can't put everything behind me at once, but I do believe in God's justice. Maybe I'll never have all the answers — maybe I will — but

I can't be stuck in neutral for the rest of my life."

"I'm glad. You have a wedding to plan." Saying the words was like plunging knives through his heart.

"Ethan and I have postponed that. It's complicated." She looked away from him and at her watch. "I have to meet him for a counseling appointment."

She stepped close, and Luke held his breath. When she put a hand on his arm, it took all his strength not to reach out to her.

"Thanks. For everything. I hope at some point, when all the smoke has cleared, we can sit down and talk about what happened. I think you're the only person who truly understands how I feel about things."

She rose to her tiptoes and lightly kissed his cheek, then turned and left him standing there. Luke watched her car for a long time, until it was long out of sight.

DISCUSSION QUESTIONS

1. Because of a childhood experience, Detective Abby Hart is driven to solve homicides in Long Beach. Can you point to a similarly defining event — positive or negative — in your own life? How might your life have turned out differently if that event hadn't happened?
2. Abby's fiancé, Ethan, considers her work as a homicide detective dark and dangerous, but Abby believes she brings hope and justice to people. Why is Ethan really concerned about Abby? What prevents her from being totally objective about her job?
3. Luke Murphy and his friend Bill coined the term "hard blessings" when they served in the military together. What does this mean to you? What hard blessings have you experienced in life?
4. Abby takes a victim's dog to the animal shelter, but why doesn't she leave Bandit there? In what ways can you relate to her

feelings in that moment?

5. Officer Robert Woods has had a special connection to Abby for twenty-seven years. Yet he discourages her from pursuing her parents' murders. Is he acting in her best interest? Why or why not?

6. Why is Deputy Chief Kelsey Cox so antagonistic toward Abby? Have you ever had a boss who was hard on you? How did you handle the criticism or attitude?

7. Throughout the story, Abby wrestles with forgiveness and concludes that it's easier to say she forgives someone than to feel it. She wonders, *How do you forgive a monster?* What answer do you have for that question? When have you struggled to not only offer forgiveness but really feel it as well? What keeps you from feeling it?

8. Luke searches day after day for missing teens like Nadine. Compare his determination to go after runaways with the parable of the lost sheep told in Luke 15. Have you had personal experience with a "lost sheep" or a determined "shepherd"? How did your story turn out?

9. In chapter 33, Abby wonders if her obsession with her parents' cold case means she doesn't trust God. What do you think of the response Luke gives? How would you answer her question?

10. Even without knowing her well, Luke notes that Abby isn't one to seek vengeance. What does he base his opinion on? Why does Abby's aunt Dede warn her about wanting revenge? Are Dede's concerns justified?

11. Abby's motto — *You can run, but you can't hide* — is based on Hebrews 4:13. How does she acknowledge the truth of the verse? Where does she fall short? What does this verse say to you?

12. Near the end of the story, Abby says, "Letting go feels like giving up." Do you feel the same way? Describe a time when you had to let go of something. Did you feel peace about your decision or despair? How do you know when you've made the right choice?

ABOUT THE AUTHOR

A former Long Beach, California, police officer of twenty-two years, **Janice Cantore** worked a variety of assignments, including patrol, administration, juvenile investigations, and training. She's always enjoyed writing and published two short articles on faith at work for *Cop and Christ* and *Today's Christian Woman* before tackling novels. She now lives in a small town in southern Oregon, where she enjoys exploring the forests, rivers, and lakes with her two Labrador retrievers — Maggie and Abbie.

Janice writes suspense novels designed to keep readers engrossed and leave them inspired. *Drawing Fire* is the first book in her new series, Cold Case Justice. Janice also authored *Critical Pursuit, Visible Threat,* and the Pacific Coast Justice series, which includes *Accused, Abducted,* and *Avenged.*

Visit Janice's website at www.janicecantore

.com and connect with her on Facebook at www.facebook.com/JaniceCantore.